Long Reach

by

Nancy Stevenson

Copyright Notice
This is a work of fiction. Names, characters, places, and incidents are either the product of the author's imagination or are used fictitiously, and any resemblance to actual persons living or dead, business establishments, events, or locales, is entirely coincidental.

Long Reach

COPYRIGHT © 2023 by Nancy Stevenson

All rights reserved. No part of this book may be used or reproduced in any manner whatsoever without written permission of the author or The Wild Rose Press, Inc. except in the case of brief quotations embodied in critical articles or reviews.
Contact Information: info@thewildrosepress.com

Cover Art by *Lisa Dawn MacDonald*

The Wild Rose Press, Inc.
PO Box 708
Adams Basin, NY 14410-0708
Visit us at www.thewildrosepress.com

Publishing History
First Edition, 2024
Trade Paperback ISBN 978-1-5092-5535-1
Digital ISBN 978-1-5092-5536-8

Published in the United States of America

Dedication

To the beloved friends who introduced our family to many wonders of the Georgia Strait.

The river is within us, the sea is all around us;
The sea is the land's edge also, the granite
Into which it reaches, the beaches where it tosses
Its hints of earlier and earlier creation:
The starfish, the hermit crab, the whale's backbone;
The pools where it offers to our curiosity
The more delicate algae and the sea anemone.
It tosses up our losses, the torn seine,
The shattered lobster pot, the broken oar
And the gear of foreign dead men. The sea has many voices,
Many gods and many voices.

—T.S. Eliot

Chapter One

August 2, 1998

Albert knew he should be grateful. Here he was, a newly trained Mountie, in the famed Inside Passage of the Georgia Strait, British Columbia, a plum placement for his first assignment. On good days, Grant's Mill, the lifeblood of the town of Grant's Landing, puffed feathery white clouds of steam over breeze-tossed water into blue skies. White seagulls darted like ballet dancers into waves, each crest tipped with flecks of light. But today, he stared at the heavy smog, a smothering, orange blanket that prevented even a riffle on the water. The ever-swirling seagulls sat immobilized on the rocks. He covered his nose to avoid the smell, worse than rotting potatoes after a blighted harvest in the Alberta home he had escaped. The clouds of steam had become toxic paint-peeling fumes, a cancer in the town's lifeblood. He rued the day he'd been assigned to this alien world.

Tempers raged under the weight of the weather inversion. The harbormaster had roared at him driving his rubber boat through the harbor: "Slow down, or I'll have you barred from water duty." That would mean returning to traffic management or late-night street cop in this town filled with burly loggers, tough shrimpers, and gangs who sucked clams from the deep with vacuum hoses. He worried when tourists called him "Sergeant."

He had only earned the title of constable, and a provisional constable at that.

Albert tied down his boat and headed up the ramp to the Sea Breeze for a long overdue lunch. Being out on the water all morning made him hungry, but then he'd been hungry all his life.

His radio screeched. "Emergency, emergency. Fishing accident at Seymour Narrows. Cormorant en route."

He pressed the respond button. "Mackey here, 2:08 P.M. On my way."

He raced back down the ramp, unhitched his boat, and jumped in. One pull and the motor charged right up. He ran the outboard motor too fast when throwing it into gear, and the boat lurched forward, pushing him half off the seat. Its wake reverberated off the harbor breakwater. Halyards on the rigging of docked sailboats jangled. Smaller boats bounced in their slips. Like many who lived alone, Albert lectured himself out loud on a regular basis. "Damn, Mackey. Will you never learn?"

He eased the pace down through the giant pilings of the breakwater, then revved the motor until the boat planed. Even with the small craft's 15 horsepower, it was a good forty minutes out past Grant's Landing and around the bell buoy beyond the foot of Joshua Island.

In the shrinking distance to the Narrows, he could see a jumble of fishing boats, aluminum fourteen-footers, giant yachts, and everything in between, all with lines out. *Probably tangled, too,* he thought. *How do these guys, well, mostly guys, call that fishing?* More like bumper cars at the Fair. Grown men in small outboards raced giant luxury boats for an open space, complete with *fuck you* and flashing the finger. Males, males,

males. Most looked like locals, with one or two wearing signs like billboards saying *tourist*: the crisp new waterproof, the unstained fish box. *I have signs all over me too, perhaps, signs that say rookie.*

He was drawing closer fast. *Fishing should be wading a quiet stream with an occasional skirl from an eagle, and the soft whistle of my fly line playing out over my head.* Mackey slowed and angled toward a cluster of skiffs. One man was waving his volunteer flag. He deepened his voice to add a note of authority. "What happened here?"

"Hell if we rightly know," the nearest fisherman responded. "We saw this skiff running in circles, with a woman in the bow." He waved at a blood-spattered woman in another small aluminum boat, bobbing dead in the water nearby. "That's her there. She acted like she didn't know what to do. Didn't want help, either, when we went over."

A man from another boat joined in. "She yelled at us, 'Stay away. Don't come near.' She even picked up an oar and threatened us. I saw a guy hanging on to the rim of her boat, but when the skiff came round again, he was gone."

"We spotted him a minute later." The first man gestured toward a third skiff with the flag-waver, as the familiar *whop, whop* of a helicopter rose in the distance. "Pulled him into Jacob's boat. Jacob called the Rescue Center to send the copter. Guy's hurt pretty bad. I don't think she is. She was flailing her arms like a crazy person, screaming, 'Watch out' and then, 'My husband, my husband,' like she was trying to convince herself." He shook his head. "What was she trying to do, murder the guy and us too?"

The helicopter drew closer, the noise growing to a roar as it hovered overhead. The water churned. Mackey's rubber boat bounced like a cork in the waves. Jacob pointed to the wounded man. A line dropped from the helicopter, carrying a helmeted rescuer in a harness with a kit strapped to his chest. He waved at the other boats to move back and hovered in midair while the fishing boats bumped in haste to clear space.

The rescuer landed on the struts of Jacob's boat, one leg on each side for balance. He examined the bleeding victim on the bottom, pulled bandages from the kit, wrapped tourniquets around the injured man's head and badly gashed leg. He ignored the drumbeat of the rotors, the boat bouncing in the water as he unfolded a stretcher from his kit. With Jacob's help, he lifted the body onto the stretcher, adjusted the harness, and signaled the copter.

The bundle of rescuer and stretcher jerked forward as the line went taut. The pair swung out over the circle of boats. Then the bundle moved straight up. Mackey could see only the bottom of the rescuer's boots until the package neared the Cormorant's door. Somebody pulled the bundle flat to slide it into the open space, and a hand reached out and closed the door. The helicopter turned toward Grant's Landing and flew away.

The circle of boatmen, dazed by the action and the dimming *whop, whop, whop* of the disappearing Cormorant, sat speechless. Mackey glanced at the blood-spattered woman in the aluminum skiff. *Walking wounded*, he thought, noting bruises and a few cuts, but nothing that looked serious. She sat with her hands over her ears, her eyes following the helicopter.

Mackey had to take control. He ran through a

checklist in his head. Take names. Contacts. Assume authority. Protect evidence. Get the facts.

"Thanks, guys. Thank you for your fast action and fast thinking." He rolled his shoulders back and took a breath. "Give me your names. I'll take the lady into town. Would anyone be willing to tow the boat to the RCMP dock?"

Jacob raised his hand. "I live in Grant's. Day's shot now anyway. Tide's run."

"Great." He nudged his boat closer to the woman's skiff and spoke to her for the first time. "My name is Albert Mackey. I'm a constable with the RCMP. I can take you to the hospital to check up on your companion. These men will tow in your skiff."

The woman didn't look up.

"My name is Albert Mackey. I'm with the Royal Canadian Mounted Police." The woman lifted her head. "These men will help you into my boat. It's faster than yours. We'll get to the hospital as quick as we can."

The woman glanced around for her things and grabbed for her backpack.

Albert kept his craft steady. "Hand her over carefully, guys. Does she have anything with her besides that pack?"

The woman's body shook. She couldn't stand. The men leaned over the rim of her skiff, lifted her like a log and slid her onto the seat next to Mackey. After she was settled, Mackey ran over his list. "And guys, let's assume everything is okay, but for the sake of my report, could you leave everything in the vic…the wounded man's boat, just as you found it. No getting in to start the motor or hook up the tow line. Routine, you know. We have to check for fingerprints and all. The fewer we find, the better."

The men nodded, and one saluted. Mackey signaled in return. He took out his emergency kit and wrapped gauze around the woman's bleeding hands and forehead. His radio crackled, and he took a moment to listen.

"The man in the water has been delivered to the hospital. They have him in treatment now," he told her. "We'll get there as fast as we can." The woman stared at him, her mouth open. "Do you want to tell me what happened?"

The woman continued to stare blankly. He tried to soften the moment. He had spent his childhood listening to his dad's endless talk. He'd learned about consoling silence from his mom. Clearly, this woman needed gentle handling and as much comfort as he could give.

He started his motor, a little embarrassed to do it in front of these accomplished watermen. His outboard responded on one pull and Albert, relieved, eased into gear like an old pro. He patted the top of the outboard in gratitude. With a wave to the fishermen, he headed back to the mainland at a steady clip.

He reported in by radio. "Mackey here. 4:45 P.M. Have rescued man's companion. She needs some treatment, but her condition is stable. I'll deliver her to the hospital in my squad. Over and out."

He guided his craft through a series of wakes from cruisers and fishing boats returning to port. Was her condition really stable, he wondered. *Only time will tell.*

Chapter Two

Nora sat in the hospital waiting room, staring at a crack in the wall and through the crack to water surging over the gunnels. She half believed the crack could act like a camera lens, focusing down onto the action. She couldn't make the frame fast forward or reverse, it just kept revealing the blurry edges, the gray water with streaks of blood. She had raised her club over the dogfish, gritting her teeth. She closed her eyes before the club reached its head, which made her hit her own hand. A scream rang in her ears, mixed with the sound of metal bashing flesh. Waves white with foam broke over the boat rim. The fierce mouth of the dogfish slashed at her hand, its strong body writhing and jerking.

Nora watched in disbelief as a fat red drop landed on the soggy towel she held. She patted her own mouth in confusion. It was the dogfish that should have been bleeding.

Nora hated fishing. At least, she hated fishing when they were out for long hours. This day had been interminable. She hated catching these sharks that seemed destined to find her line. True, no one of them could swallow her whole, but they traveled in packs, threatening to mangle and devour all creatures, living or dead. Predators of the deep, they searched out filthy carrion and live creatures to rip, tear, and demolish, leaving only skeletons behind. She knew they searched for her.

Cold and wet, Nora desperately wanted to quit, but she had persuaded herself years ago that if she asked to go fishing with Joe, she would never suggest turning for home. Miserable with cold, she'd muttered under her breath, "I hate this, I hate you." He drove the outboard and trolled while she caught her dogfish. The boat lurched and turned in tight circles. Nora lost her balance and fell toward the flailing dogfish. She registered a scream, his or hers, she wasn't sure.

She caught herself and looked where Joe had been, but he was gone. She saw a body in the water, a face so distorted with pain, she wasn't certain if it could be Joe. The motor. She had to turn off the motor.

That was the story she had told the gentle but persistent ranger as they drove from the harbor to the hospital. She hadn't been able to relate much beyond blood, waves, and Joe's pained face.

As she stared into the crack, rerunning the film in her head, she caught a glimpse of another scene. Her husband standing up with a salmon on his line, while he yelled for her to turn off the motor. Still holding the dogfish with her pliers on the hook in its thrashing body, she moved to follow his orders. A scream. Blood everywhere. Dimly, she also saw a tin boat pulling away with three big yellow-slickered men in it. She turned her lens onto this boat, red-rimmed, scuffed like their own and dozens of others on the water that day and every day.

A nurse appeared beside her, and her vision of the boat and water vanished. The nurse spoke in a voice both gentle and firm. "You can come into your husband's room now."

Nora followed her out of the waiting area. Joe's

room was a short way down the hall. She walked in slowly, her eyes riveted to the floor. Her head felt heavy, too heavy to lift to see Joe's face. Glancing from side to side, she caught glimpses of tubes and machines lining his bed. A steady *bleep-bleep* permeated the room, as if she had walked into a hospital docu-drama. The penetrating smell of bleach made her eyes water. Her hands shook so badly she dared not touch anything. Beads of perspiration popped out on her forehead. She sank down, leaning against a partition for balance. A bracing hand cradled her head and an arm enfolded her back, easing her onto the floor. When she settled there, two hands bent her gently forward to place her head between her knees.

Nora was not aware of how long she had been sitting by Joe's bed. She heard a soft contralto voice.

"Feeling a bit better now, I hope. No, no, don't worry. You've had a shock. Don't try to get up yet, just sit there and gradually take things in. It's better that way." The speaker's tone lightened. "I don't want you falling on my instruments after I've gotten them all rigged up." The joshing was conspiratorial, the you're okay-I'm okay kind of small talk Nora had spun years ago when Nell had her first stitches in an emergency room.

"My name is Caroline. I've been assigned to your husband for as long as he's in intensive care. The doctor will be in ASAP. We've been in touch with him by radio. Your husband hit his head on something hard, and he swallowed a lot of salt water. They pressed that out of him on the copter coming in."

Nora tried to speak through her swollen lips. "How is…?" She could feel warm blood oozing onto her chin.

Caroline took a fresh towel and gently pressed it to Nora's mouth. "He has a head wound plus a deep gash in his shoulder, and in both legs. He's lost a lot of blood, and he's in shock. The doctor ordered X-rays and brain scans. We won't move him until the doctor comes. I'll help you up so you can look at him. Then I'll have a nurse look you over. You have cuts and bruises as well."

Nora listened to his shallow breath, not rasping exactly, but fast, like panting. She stared at his chalky face, the sunburned skin of yesterday gone colorless, thin, almost transparent. She could see blue veins in his eyelids. His full generous lips that had shaped eloquent words on the nightly news were drawn back in a taut scream position, revealing blue gums underneath.

"Is he cold?" Nora stammered, reaching out to stroke his face. Before her fingers could touch him, Caroline's arms turned Nora gently and steered her across the room.

"Yes. That's part of what happens in shock. He's lost a lot of blood." Caroline pointed to the tube in Joe's nose and another in his left arm. "We're giving him oxygen and intravenous fluids."

Two young women came in, a nurse with a cap and an aide in the universal pink of the volunteer. They led Nora into an adjoining room and took her temperature and her blood pressure. They washed her face, hands and arms, disinfected her cuts and bandaged a few. The aide brushed Nora's hair, slipping the brush past the raised bumps on her scalp with practiced skill. They gave her dry clothes—a worn plaid flannel shirt soft from multiple washings and a pair of faded but clean sweatpants, also well softened with use. The sleeves on the shirt were far too long, and the aide giggled. "We usually get big boatmen in ER," said the nurse as she rolled the sleeves to Nora's wrists.

A green-coated doctor came into the room as they finished dressing Nora. Their ministrations had made her feel warm, stronger, more hopeful, but the doctor's solemn face brought her horrors back in full force.

The doctor did not look at Nora. He held out his hand, seeming not to notice when she didn't take it. "Brian Cameron." He barked out his report. "We gave your husband a scan and found swelling in the brain. His head was struck with force by something hard. Your husband's vital signs are weakening. I've called Dr. Simon, the University of Vancouver's leading neurosurgeon. He happens to be on a nearby island at a brain conference. We have transmitted the scan material to Dr. Simon. He'll fly right over."

Nora did not faint this time. She nodded and tried to thank him, but her words came slowly. "I am so gra…Please…don't stop…yes." Her speech faded out with another nod of her head.

The doctor leaned forward, cupped her hands in his huge fingers and half bowed in a gesture like a salaam. His silent expression of sympathy alarmed Nora more than his gruff manner. He left the room before she could say another word.

Chapter Three

Nell and Charlie. Nora needed to call them. She dreaded the conversations. They would be devastated. At this stage, before the pronouncements of Dr. Simon, she could do little but lay out false hopes, or worse, the vibrations of concern she had received from Dr. Cameron. They would ask if they should come. She must not hint to the kids that she wanted them far away.

If she called right now, four hours later their time, with luck, Charlie would be in class and Nell would be at her cub reporter job at the *News Daily*. Good. She wouldn't have to answer their questions. But what about the message on their answering machines? There was nothing she could think to say that wouldn't make them suffer, perhaps even galvanize them into action. On the other hand, there was an off chance that some emergency radio hacker had picked up the alert. "Joe McKeever, veteran news anchor for WSOL, rushed to emergency hospital after boating accident, Grant's Landing, British Columbia." *Joe isn't news like the world pundit, Walter Davidson. Or even like national news grabber Jacob Rolfson.* Joe, however, had followers, especially in the news business. Why hadn't she thought "we"? She noted grimly that her retirement had worked to destroy her ego. Had she already eliminated herself from the husband-wife news team known and revered by reporters who prided themselves on working alone?

Caroline had provided a phone in a small cubby near Joe's room. She tried to think. Of course, the children needed to know. Anyone else? Certainly, Bridget and Jordan at the office of McKeever and McKeever. She dialed the number, making a note to tell Caroline that she had made a long-distance call to the States. Jordan, the office manager was not in, but she gave the information to Bridget, the Gal Friday for everyone including Nora. Bridget's tears spurred renewed tears for Nora, but she gave the facts as best she could with promises to let them know more when she had the doctor's reports.

But every time Nora went to pick up the receiver to call the children, her doubts checked her dialing fingers. She couldn't admit to Nell and Charlie that she might have caused the accident that had battered, oh God, perhaps killed their treasured father. She had been so angry with him. She had even whispered "I hate you" under her breath, not long before he went over the side.

Had she stood up, rocked the boat, and tumped him? An accident, even if subliminal. Or had she stood up, grabbed the fish bopper in her right hand, and crashed it down on his skull? She had thought of doing that a bit earlier, right after he ignored her first fight with the dogfish.

She attempted to analyze the situation, as if she were researching a possible murder for a McKeever and McKeever news story. She could frame the report as a helpless abused woman. No, she would not play the role of victim, even in a self-protective scenario. She, the researcher of the team, would have to seek out the answers as best she could, even if she ended up proving she tried to murder her husband in the flush of overriding rage.

Nora knew she couldn't begin to think straight about these issues if the kids were here. They would disturb her effort to analyze. She would be far too protective of their family sense, their futures, and their self-esteem. If they were here, she could not face her guilt. It would be hard enough if she, they, and the world believed that her anger let her jump up to throw her husband overboard by accident. The law and the world might forgive an ignorant boat person, but would she? And would the kids?

She decided to call later, after Drs. Cameron and Simon had made some sort of diagnosis. That would give her time to think.

A nurse tapped lightly on the door. "Caroline sent me to put you to bed," she said. "You must rest now. Drs. Simon and Cameron will wish to talk to you after they have made their diagnosis."

Nora nodded with relief. She could call the kids later.

"Caroline wants me to give you a shot, nothing too potent, just a little something to help calm tension."

Nora nodded numbly. It would be good to get out of her head for a while. The nurse held her elbow as she moved Nora down the hall and into a spare room, little more than an alcove with a cot, pillow, and blankets. "The hospital is full. This is the space we use when resting on call. Caroline wanted me to promise you that we'll come wake you if any issue arises."

Nora recognized that the hospital personnel respected Caroline. If she gave her word, her word would hold. As Nora stretched out on the bed, she understood that these provincial doctors and nurses had no luxuries. The cot was hard and narrow. The room had little to offer but this one flat surface, a door to close and a light that turned off. She raised her arm for the calming shot and felt the needle slip in. Nora closed her eyes as the young nurse left the room.

Once more, she ran through the scene. Joe held his rod with one hand while he maneuvered the outboard handle with the other. Joe's grace and ease filled her. She drifted. There was Joe diving off a tall rock. "Come," he called. He stood with his arms wide, beckoning her. Joe, where was he as she floated on a board with water lapping around her? She could hear rhythmic pounding, like waves breaking on the shore. She dared not turn for fear of falling off this board, yet without kicking or paddling, she would crash onto the rocks. *Joe, where are you?* No, not waves breaking. Waves of cheers, the roar rising and falling, followed by silence. Joe stood at the throw line, all muscles tensed for the free throw. The scoreboard showed Hamilton High 96, Brandywine 95.

The clock ticked, three seconds to go. Joe bounced the basketball twice. In a move like a dancer, his body flowed upward, a liquid geyser springing forth, his fingers, hands, arms following the ball as it arched up, over, and down through the hoop. Nothing could be heard but the swish of the ball in the net, then roars from the crowd.

Silence descended, as the ref handed Joe the ball for his second free throw. Joe stared at the rim of the net, turned the ball in his hand once and bent his knees. The ball sailed into the air. A streak of light magnified the arc of the ball. The crowd's intake of breath sounded like an undercurrent pulling ripples back into the sea, the soft swish of the net and *clang*, the ringing of the bell. Game over. Brandywine 97, Hamilton High 96.

The crack of light grew larger. "Are you awake?" Nora heard the nurse's voice. "Drs. Simon and Cameron would like to speak to you now."

Half lost in her dream, Nora padded after the nurse to an office where Dr. Cameron waited next to a white-haired man with eyes and mouth rimmed in laugh lines and eyebrows like an unclipped privet hedge. Unlike Dr. Cameron, who had hardly been able to look at her earlier, the second man walked forward with his hand out. "I'm Gerald Simon, a neurosurgeon from Vancouver Hospital. Fortunately, I was nearby at a conference when Brian Cameron's call came in."

She managed the handshake, and he settled her into a chair by Dr. Cameron's desk. "We've studied the CAT scan and MRI carefully. The force that hit your husband's head passed through the surface of the skull and caused heavy bruising in his brain. You understand that all serious bruises cause swelling. Even if the damage itself is minor, with the brain being enclosed, swelling in it is serious. It causes pressures that can be even more damaging than the original contusion. We have placed a catheter in your husband's head to drain the fluid. We will watch closely. If the catheter does not relieve the pressure as rapidly as we believe necessary, we will want to open the skull to give room for the expansion. In that case, we would need your permission to operate."

Nora had researched enough tragic accidents to understand the theories. Yet she couldn't think what questions she should ask. *Will he live? Walk? Talk? Will he be Joe again?* She nodded at the men and then stared at her hands clasped in front of her. As if he had read her mind, Dr. Simon placed his hand gently on hers. "The injury is at the front of the head, the frontal lobe. This important area controls the things people do in sequence: getting up, brushing teeth, cooking food."

The silence stretched in front of them. "We have two children," she whispered. "Adult children. What should I tell them?"

"Do they live nearby?"

"No. Both are thousands of miles away, clear across the continent, on the east coast of the United States."

"You may need them to give you support. But there is nothing you or they can do for your husband right now."

Dr. Cameron briefly touched Nora's shoulder. Dr. Simon continued. "All we can say for certain is that he is in a critical condition. You can let them know that many have come through similar accidents to live good lives. However, we believe it is essential that you understand the risks. Also, with all severe brain injuries, the process of healing is likely to be slow. It will require great fortitude from the patient and support from his family."

"Doctor. They worship their father. I am frightened to tell them." Her voice cracked. "I think I may be able to call them now." She paused. There was something else she had to do. What was it? Dizziness returned. She leaned her head on the desk. His question came back to her. "Yes. Of course, you have my permission to operate."

"Good. We'll go back to your husband. You can go home, if you like. Give Caroline your phone num—"

"Oh, no, Doctor. I can't do that. We've rented a cabin way out near Grace Point. You may not know that area. We have no phone. We use a ship-to-shore radio.

I'm not good with the outboard. If the wind came up, I couldn't..." Her voice drifted off. "I'm sorry."

Dr. Cameron had been silent. He spoke now to Dr. Simon. "It is a long reach of open water between Grace Point and Grant's Landing." Turning to Nora, he said kindly, "Can you afford to rent a motel room? If not, the hospital may have funds. I'll call Social Services to help you make arrangements."

Chapter Four

The coastal region of British Columbia was Albert Mackey's first RCMP post after six months of training in his home province of Alberta. There, they were observed carefully on routines like traffic control, desk work, sometimes partnering with senior officers on minor robberies and road accidents. Since his arrival in BC, Mackey had received special training on boat maintenance and rules of the water. Books told him about the power of the tides, but like most newcomers, he thought of tides as simply a shift of the waterline throughout the day, not the vital, life-changing force that dominated coastal existence. Mackey had studied the coastal charts showing treacherous reefs hidden at high tide and giant boulders that lay under the water's surface. *Someday*, he promised himself, *I'll check out my theory that these are remnants of ancient floods filling rough mountain valleys.*

To become more familiar with the territory, he rented a twelve-foot rubber boat like the ones used by the Mounties and the Coast Guard. On his first free afternoon, he cruised Desolation Sound, the name given to a passageway by a British officer, Captain Vancouver, in 1792. He saw steep slopes covered in endless forests of tall spruce, fir, cedars and pines. Alders and an occasional red madrone tree peeked through the forest cover. He saw no signs of human habitation on these mountain ridges. Vancouver thought of these great fiords as barriers to human life.

Occasionally Captain Vancouver's exploring ships would pass some Indian village nestled on the rim of the water, or Indians paddling giant canoes, but the captain saw only desolation on those slopes. Mackey laughed to himself. Now sailboats clustered in the bays along the Sound, three, sometimes four rafted together with kids diving off the bows and grills going on the decks. *One man's desolation is today's chosen vacation destination.*

He passed seals basking on a rock uncovered at low tide. He switched off his motor to look more peacefully, and the slumberers immediately slid and flopped into the water. When he started the motor, the seals popped their heads up to study him as he had wanted to study them. He watched a bear cub climbing up a rugged incline and saw churning water, gulls flying into the spray, the fish-feeding frenzy he had read about. Enchanted, he vowed to go further.

On his next expedition, he swooped around Bradley Island, glorying in the shafts of mountains that plunged into water-filled crevices four hundred feet deep. Albert saluted three gulls floating on a log. *Thank you for showing me the deadhead.* Soaked with water, these half-submerged tree trunks, escapees from log booms, created navigational hazards up and down the coast. He laughed at the indifferent birds as he roared by at nearly full throttle.

His boat slipped to the side. Mackey adjusted the wheel. Waves mounted. The boat skidded to the side again. His engine bucked in intermittent surges. He pulled the wheel to starboard, concentrating on the changed sound of his motor. He slid down a hilly slope, steep like a ski run. His boat skimmed sideways once more, picking up speed as it skated down across the hill of water. Wind and current threatened to turn him sideways into a whirlpool wider than his boat was long. Pushed onto the rim of the maelstrom, Mackey looked into the concave vortex that plunged one meter down, swallowing a log into its gullet. He leaned hard on the wheel, forcing the skiff away from the sucking gorge into another churning mass of water.

Mackey took his eyes off the water just long enough to check his fuel gauge. Instantly the motor ground into a submerged log. The outboard safety pin snapped, cutting the motor's rotation. With power gone, he became a victim of the waves and tides pounding his rubber duck, threatening to hurl it onto rocky cliffs or into the guts of the gaping whirlpools.

He grabbed his oars and threw every muscle into his strokes. Gradually he pulled away from the mountain of water behind him into a widening channel. With the last of his strength, he beached his boat on a lonely sandspit. Lying on his back, panting with fear and exhaustion, he listened to the raucous screech of an eagle as it swooped over his head. *So, you spit me back, old Neptune. It's time to pay attention.*

After that incident, Mackey sought out all the old men of the sea he could find. On his off hours, he bought a six pack and took it out on the wharf. An offer of beer and an easy manner gave him good conversation. Bit by bit, he moved from rookie cop to accepted outsider.

"You'll never really belong, you know," Old John, a retired harbormaster, told him one day. "But you haven't been salted and dried like several of your crusty old officers. We'll learn you as best we can."

They told him about boat accidents and deaths. Alcohol inspired many a drunken fisherman who mistook the message of the channel marking buoys, or a soused bargeman pushing another off the bow into the churning power of the motors. More than once, a careless outsider viewed a towboat with its boom in the distance and pushed his rented yacht behind the tow, not realizing that a giant chain lay under the waterline. The old hands warned him about fishermen who had been stuck on boats for months at a time. All hell could break loose when they came to shore inflamed by gambling and alcohol. Mackey listened. He knew that poverty drove conflicts. He wondered if even the blatant murders were suicides of a sort. Poverty and despair in paradise.

This accident with McKeever, his first serious case, seemed out of scale. The degree of damage appeared larger than natural circumstances would have led him to expect. Mackey did not idle while Nora slept in the nursing station's hideaway. After the forensic team had taken all the fingerprints and blood samples from the motor and boat for DNA testing, he donned rubber gloves for his own inspection. He photographed the little boat from every angle, focusing on the motor and the bloodstains on the metal siding. The boat was a mass of snarled fishing gear, discarded clothes, and the soggy sandwiches and spilled tea of a picnic lunch. It appeared that Mr. McKeever's rod and salmon, if indeed there had been one, had gone into the drink with him.

Mackey stashed the metal fishing bopper in a plastic evidence bag to be tested for blood types. He placed the pliers and the gaff in other bags with precise and businesslike movements. He would soon know if there was only dogfish blood on the gaff and bopper. After every conceivable item had been inventoried, Mackey cut useful hooks off of tangled line and curled the unspoiled leaders back into their spools. He had grown up in hardship. He respected things. His whole life had honored order and cleanliness. Finally, he upended the boat and washed it from stem to stern.

The easy part's done. Now for the hard part, the interview. Poor suffering slobs. Even when innocent, they seemed to dwell on guilt. He had read interview notebooks filled with self-blame. "If only I had…" "I should have done…" "Why wasn't I the one, I was driving." He had doubts in this case about actions and motives. He would have to probe, dig, trap, snare.

He went back to the hospital to find Nora sitting in the waiting room, dressed in outsized fishermen's clothes. Unsure if she would remember him, Mackey introduced himself. "I'm Constable Albert Mackey, the RCMP who brought you here. I never asked your name."

"Nora McKeever."

"Do you live near Grant's Landing?"

"No. You may have guessed. We're Americans. Visitors."

"How's your husband?"

"Not good. Head injury. The doctors tell me there's nothing for me to do but wait."

"Maybe then you want me to take you home."

Nora explained they had rented a cottage near Grace Point. "I want to stay near the hospital, find a motel." Her eyes widened. "I can't do that, either. My money, my charge cards and checks are in the cottage."

"Let me take you to gather your stuff. My boat's fast, as you know. We can be back in a little over an hour."

Before leaving, Mackey took Caroline aside and asked her to keep a clever nurse in McKeever's room at all times, even when his wife was with him. "Caroline, I'm sorry. One last thing. Could you make sure the OD keeps a routine record of everyone who calls to ask about the accident, and, when possible, who they are. Need I add, no visitors, but a record of all who try to visit. I'd be grateful to know if you see anything unusual in or about the corridors."

Caroline raised her eyebrows, curiosity written all over her face.

Mackey answered the unspoken question. "Something somewhere is not quite right. Accidents happen. But this guy was—no, is—a competent fisherman. I'd swear it by his tackle box and boat. Your hospital records prove old hands fall out of boats. But we need more of the story to figure out why this guy got tossed out into his motor."

Mackey had decided that treating Nora like a suffering wife would be the best route to her story. He didn't enjoy being a cynic. He preferred to question all suspects slowly and gently, to the exasperation and sometimes outspoken complaint of the district commander. In Nora McKeever's case, he would take on the role of the friendly conspirator. He would help Mrs. McKeever find the truth for her sake and for justice. *Whatever the hell that is.*

He wound up his comments to Caroline. "There are a lot of summer residents we'd all like to do in, but I'm not sure this guy fits that bill."

Caroline stood with her hands on her hips. "Albert Mackey. I never thought I'd hear you sound like a cop on the Stateside tube. Go home. Get some sleep. Tune in tomorrow. Caroline will watch your little house hen and the salmon snatcher she married."

Sleep sounded good, but Mackey had no wish to go home to his small one-room apartment with a stove, refrigerator and television. He had come west to escape the memories of the family farm dying from drought. Here in Grant's Landing, he found water aplenty, but also aching poverty and death from drought of another kind. Nature's spectacles were diminishing: forests once filled with giant cedars and firs, now cut raw to the bone on mountainsides that plunged to the sea; giant logs, some eight feet across, dumped into the ocean and dragged off to factories and pulp mills; islands laid bare by giant bulldozers scraping thin topsoil to the channels below; runoff and refuse sinking to cover spawning beds; clear water becoming thick like mucus. On arrival from Alberta, he'd thought he had found perfection. Instead, he looked at a world filled with breathtaking mountain peaks, long fiords stretching toward the wilderness, spectacular beauty hiding areas of desiccated hope and increasing despair.

He knew something about narrowed dreams. His father's face flashed before him as he drove Nora to the harbor. Father had been a writer who never wrote. Rufus Mackey married a First Nations daughter, an assistant in a tribal center, his Ma Cherie, a mixed marriage frowned on by Rufus's parents and hers. When Ma Cherie got pregnant, they purchased forty acres of Alberta's semi-wilderness in an excess of hope and affection. Albert was four before he realized that Ma Cherie was not his mother's name but his father's endearment.

It had been the lovers' plan that Rufus would farm by day and write by night and in the wintertime when the work of planting and harvesting was done. Ma Cherie would work in a center after their baby was old enough. She'd play her violin in the evenings to accompany Father's writing. The baby was born in August, as they were harvesting their first bountiful crops. They named him Albert, a joyous affirmation of their dreams in this western province. But the lush summer of their dream was a fluke, a tease, nature's joke.

That first year, Ma Cherie kept urging Rufus to put his stories on paper instead of spilling them into her ears as they worked. "Later, later, Ma Cherie. When the work is done, then I'll write." But that winter, he had to chop wood to keep baby Albert warm. The next year he had to carry water to the plants, because the rains did not come. Ma Cherie began working by day, but Rufus never started writing at night.

Albert went everywhere with his father when his mother was at the center. At first, he lived in a pouch on his father's back like a papoose. Later he learned to put seed into furrows as he walked solemnly behind Rufus, who chanted endless rhymes. "Sit, little nestling while I hoe/Grow, little corncob in this row." Later, when green shoots began to sprout, Albert dipped a cup into the bucket from the yoke on his father's shoulders to water the seedlings as Rufus chanted more rhymes. "Drink, little corn seed, become a cob/Watering you is Albert's job."

Albert learned to listen as he had learned to breathe. At breakfast and lunch time, after putting Albert's food on the table, Rufus read portions of his agricultural journals aloud, everything from how to make compost from local weeds to saving water by slow-drip techniques. Between the farming information, he spun fantasies about witches and dragons. Albert absorbed all the stories that would never be written, sadness and love, anguish and sorrow, and finally bitterness in the teller's voice as the endless drought continued. Rufus never turned his rage on Albert or Ma Cherie, but when he spoke of himself, he spoke with the unforgiving fury of a guilty witness. Albert learned to hear it all with a patience as gentle as Ma Cherie's smile but as persistent, as relentless, as the old man's failure.

Nora sat silent on the way to Grace Point until they passed the McKeevers's boat. "May I take Joe's tackle box back to the house?" she asked. "Joe would want me to take care of it."

Mackey picked up the heavy box and carried it to his boat.

For Mackey, taking Mrs. McKeever to her cabin was a good plan. He could see their home as they had left it that morning without having to swear out a search warrant. He wanted to see her respond to reentering the place of her and her husband's life together. The home, even a temporary one, might have exaggerated meaning to someone raised on a farm, but he believed a sense of surroundings can give insight, much as listening for tone and pitch in verbal statements.

Joe McKeever's little rubber dinghy waited on the buoy. "Moor the boat," Nora said. "Joe doesn't like to beach boats on our rocky shore unless it's absolutely necessary."

Mackey rowed them to shore. There was something solid in her insisting on Joe's habits and maintaining Joe's things, though he knew he couldn't submit it as evidence. Wouldn't he want his wife to keep his possessions carefully if he were ill? Did he want a wife, someone to look after his tackle box? Someone to sit by his bed and worry about his recovery? Or maybe someone to push him over the side into a roaring outboard motor? *Keep your head on target, Albert.*

As they drew nearer, he analyzed the McKeever home place. A cliff-like ridge rose behind the cabin. Seals barked from giant boulders along the beach rim, alders clumped near the shore whistled in the breeze. Only boaters and the eagles who fished from their aeries high in the trees had access to this spot. What that meant, if anything, he didn't know.

Nora climbed out onto the stony beach. Mackey pulled the dinghy up above the tide line. He asked her if he had put the dinghy in the right place, but she didn't respond. She stumbled on a rock or two, waddling duck-like from boulder to boulder, moving about the beach without direction, as if she didn't know where to go.

Mackey watched her with concern. He worried that she might be losing touch with reality, separating from the situation. He had seen such moments in training films. People struck out or turned into automatons. They confessed in rambling talk as if they had no audience, no critical ear. He feared Nora McKeever was in emotional shock. She shivered as if she was cold. For all he knew, the soggy sandwiches in the boat indicated she'd had little to eat all day. He hoped he had pushed her to the edge without pushing her over. He wanted to see her expression as she entered the house without causing a mental breakdown or hovering like a spy over her shoulder. *Stalk her carefully,* he told himself. *Stay upwind. Move slowly.*

Mackey walked toward a worn path up the hill. Neither spoke. Nora began to move mechanically, as if from habit. Reaching the top, they crossed the short meadow. Still without speaking, Nora climbed the three steps to the deck, draped her wet jacket over the chair under the porch overhang. She nudged her left foot out of her boot by holding the heel down with her right foot and shaking the left foot free. She leaned on the wall for balance and pulled at the second boot with her hand. Then she turned to the door and opened it.

The place had collected heat throughout the afternoon. Mackey felt it sweep past them. The cabin was simple, couch and kitchen in the same room. The sink was empty, the breakfast dishes on the drainboard. There was a book on a sofa and tide tables lying on a sawed-off log next to a reading chair. The place was tidy except for a pile in the center of the room. A backpack, a wallet, a towel and a file folder lay loose in the mess, as if dropped or thrown. The door to the bedroom stood open, the bed covers pulled straight, clothes hung on hooks around the walls.

Nora continued through the room straight to the stove. She lifted the kettle and gave it a little shake and then turned on the gas. "Tea? Coffee?" She was the housewife playing hostess, nothing out of the ordinary, until she turned around and looked Mackey full in the face. Her eyes widened in surprise, as if she had expected someone else.

She crumpled, grabbed for the edge of the counter, leaned over the sink and threw up while her legs gave way under her. Perspiration beaded on her forehead as she rested her head on the refrigerator door. Mackey had leapt to her side to catch her as she went down, but he reached her sinking form too late. Nora heaved a thin brown liquid onto Mackey's shoes as the tears started.

Mackey felt helpless, as one does in front of a frightened animal. Nora heaved again and then scrabbled for a towel hanging on the refrigerator door handle. The back of her head bumped Mackey as she tried to stand. The kettle whistled. The familiar screech brought her head up. She crawled away, wiping at Mackey's shoe with her towel.

To Mackey's relief, she finally spoke. Her voice sounded almost natural. "I'm sorry. I throw up with bad news. Our son came to me once with a bad burn. I almost threw up while I bandaged him. Fat lot of help I was." She tried to laugh. "I don't think I've ever thrown up on a stranger before." She paused. "If you give me a hand, I think I can stand."

Mackey turned off the screeching kettle and helped her up. Nora staggered off to the bathroom. Mackey heard water running, tooth brushing and more water. Nora's absence gave him a chance to clean off the floor and look around a bit more. There were kerosene lamps hung on the walls along with water charts for decoration, Desolation Sound, Bute Inlet and Malaspina Strait. He noticed that they also had a few electric lights attached to makeshift cords. He had seen solar panels on the cabin's roof as they walked across the meadow. An open closet held an inverter that transformed power from the solar panel on the roof into usable AC current with two powerful storage batteries for the electric lights and a CD music player. He didn't know why, but it pleased him to know that their cabin for roughing it used multiple energy sources, propane for the stove and fridge, electricity for sunny days and kerosene for the cloudy ones.

Two sawed-off logs acted as side tables next to an old sofa with one chair near a homemade bookshelf. The cabin was plain with no frills, much like Mrs. McKeever.

When she returned, she wore a pair of faded jeans and a sweatshirt. She had brushed her hair and cleaned her face. "I'll have to ask you to fix your own coffee or tea. The stuff is all there on the shelf."

She sat down on the couch and kept on talking. Mackey stayed put and just listened. "That mess," she said, pointing to the pile on the floor, "I threw that down this morning, yesterday morning, how long has it been?" She closed her eyes briefly and pressed her fingers over the lids. "Shame on me. I had a moment's anger at my husband. He wanted me to hurry, and I hadn't finished packing our lunch. Joe started for the boat, telling me he would wait on the beach." She shook her head. "Standing in the room this morning, or whenever it was, I wanted him to think of my needs, to share what he was doing rather than giving orders. I sat in that hospital and reran—what do you call it, the accident? I couldn't remember what happened. One minute I was fighting that dogfish and the next minute Joe screamed from the water. Nothing at all in between. I didn't even remember being upset until I saw this mess."

She stared off into space. "I think I'll go mad if I can't remember what happened." She stood abruptly. "I need to get back to the hospital."

She ran to the bedroom, grabbed a suitcase from the back of her closet and threw in some clothes. She collected her pocketbook and her address book from the bedside table, returned to the front room and snatched her wallet from the pile on the floor. They were starting to leave when she set the suitcase down and dashed back into the bedroom. She emerged a minute later, her arms filled with her husband's pajamas, a sweater, a pair of his tennis shoes and a book from a bedside table.

"The doctor doesn't know when Joe will respond," she said, as she jammed his things into the suitcase. "He'll want his own stuff, if only he'll have the chance to use it."

They left the cabin and returned to Grant's Landing. Back in the harbor, Nora led Mackey to the car the McKeevers kept in town for errands and excursions. Mackey put Nora's suitcase in the trunk, then opened the driver's door. "Follow me back to the hospital. I'll wait there. Whenever you're ready, I'll lead you to the motel, so you'll know the way."

At the hospital, they went to the nurses' station. Joe McKeever's coma was unchanged. Caroline Hampton was reassuring and sympathetic with Nora. *Good move*.

"The doctor left a tranquilizer prescription for you, if you want it," Caroline said.

"No, no. At least, not yet. I need to call my kids. I haven't begun to sort out what needs to be done. Constable Mackey recommended the Harbor Inn. He said he'd show me the way there now. I'm sorry, I don't have the number."

"No problem. We have those motel numbers on record. We'll call you immediately if anything changes."

It had been a long day, but Mackey had more to do before sleep. He was eager to know how Nora would report the incident with her husband to her children. He had booked Nora's room with forethought. He could not tap her phone line officially, but he knew enough about the motel system to break into Nora's calls.

Standing by the bedside table in the adjoining room, staring at the phone there, he pulled on his ear, a nervous habit from childhood. Whatever he gleaned would not be admissible as evidence, but it could give him a window into Nora's behavior and perhaps her motivation. It might even suggest some ammunition for Nora's protection rather than her prosecution, if indeed she was innocent of wrongdoing.

Briefly, he felt ashamed of himself for capitulating to other people's methods, taking a step on the downward slope. A voice whispered in his mind's ear: *"Law enforcement is your field. You must do what you must do."* Then his parents' voices, yammering at him: *"Don't accept other people's methods and goals without question."* He had sworn to uphold law, order and justice. What was justice, and how did one find it? Right now, he felt too weary to get it straight in his head.

He wished he had a compartmental mind, the kind that worked until five and then went home to another life. This was a mind he found in his neighbors, good people all. They seemed to have a gift for the twentieth century, where work is work, and personal time is personal time. Maybe growing up on the farm, when work didn't stop by the clock, had set him apart. With effort, he set aside his internal battle. Caroline had been right. He should go home, open the door to his own small apartment, remove his boots from his sweaty feet and pop the cap off a cold bottle of beer. Instead, he carefully adjusted his connection to the phone in the adjoining motel room and then lay back on the bed and waited.

He had started to doze when the tapped phone registered a dial, and a pleasant male voice on the other end said hello.

Nora answered, speaking calmly at first. "Hello, darling," but quickly collapsed into silences between intakes of air. Albert hated himself as he listened to her anguish and despair. "Your father is alive. Your father is alive."

"Mom, what? What's going on?"

"There was an accident. The doctor says he's badly hurt, but he could recover fully." Her story tumbled out then, emerging in confused rushes. "The waves," "the dogfish," "your father overboard."

The other voice broke in. "I'll come. Where are you?"

"Charlie, darling Charlie, I'm sorry you had to know. He's not conscious. Grant's Landing. Oh, Charlie, for all I know they'll ship your dad to Vancouver. Wait, darling, don't come here yet. Goodbye for now, I'll keep in touch."

"Mom. Stop. How do I reach you? Where are you? What hospital is dad in? Mom???"

The agonized questions rang through the phone line. Nora's tear-choked voice followed. "He's in the Grant's Landing hospital. I'm in a nearby motel. Let me find the card…" A pause, then: "Phone 604-366-9989. That's the motel number. Charlie, don't forget for a moment how much he loved…loves you. I should have said that right off. I haven't reached Nell. I'll call her now. I love you."

Click.

Albert's face heated with shame. Yet he picked up the receiver again as Nora dialed a second number. An answering machine picked up, the message brief.

"Nelly, dear Nell," Nora whispered. "There's been an accident. Your dad is seriously injured in the Grant's Landing hospital. I didn't want to have you hear this on the radio. I'm in a motel." The dial tone buzzed. Nora dialed again. "Nelly darling, call me, 604-366-9989, Room 6. I love you."

Albert hung up, hating himself. *Serves you right, police spy. You learned nothing from that. Nothing.* He looked at his watch five or six times, irritated at how slowly time passed, before falling into a restless doze.

He was startled awake by another dialing and then his own voice on his answering machine. He sat up as Nora spoke, her voice sounding scratchy. "Constable, it's Nora McKeever. I've thought of something to tell you. It's probably nothing, but I can't get it out of my head. I'm going to a twenty-four-hour diner, if I can find one, then back to the hospital. Please meet me if you can." Click.

Albert got up and walked into the bathroom. "Now there's a pickle, police spy," he muttered to the mirror as he washed his face hoping the cold water would clear his head. "You can't go knock on her door and invite her to the Busy Bee. You'll have to let her leave and wander around town looking for food and coffee. You'd have been better off sleeping in your own bed. Fool."

Ten minutes later, Nora's door opened and shut. He waited another minute before turning off his room light and opening the curtains to look out. He saw Nora's car backing out and starting toward the parking lot exit. Mackey streaked out his own door to his police car, carefully parked on the other side of the motel building. He peeled out of the lot, hoping he'd catch sight of Nora on the empty streets. Luck was with him. She had turned the wrong way from the Busy Bee and town. Mackey spotted her car and let her drive for five more minutes toward the edge of Grant's. When she pulled over and began maneuvering her car to turn around, Mackey pulled alongside and rolled down his window, waving her to a stop. Mrs. McKeever had not brushed her hair.

She wore no make-up. Her face was red, from what? Crying, he supposed.

He took pains to relax his face and slow his speech. Now, more than ever, he needed to give Nora McKeever space. "I got your message. Let me lead you to the best all-night diner. It's where we cops and weary fishermen go."

Nora threw her hands in the air. He had frightened her, perhaps, or she was so distraught that everything set her on edge. "Do you want me to drive you?" he asked. "We could leave your car here until you've gotten some good Busy Bee breakfast into your stomach."

He waited and felt pleased when she got out of her car and walked over to the squad. She climbed into the patrol car without a word.

Chapter Five

August 3, 1998

Mackey guided her to a booth, the only empty spot in the whole place. She sat with her head drooped and her shoulders hunched, an old woman near collapse. She lifted her chin briefly to the smells of coffee, baking bread and frying bacon, then slumped.

Tiny Hannah followed right behind them with two mugs in one hand and a steaming pot of coffee in the other. Hannah studied Mackey and Nora for a brief moment. "Honey, you've never visited me at the Busy Bee before," she said to Nora, "so you may not know. We serve the best breakfast in British Columbia, maybe even all of Canada. Mackey here will vouch for it. Now, what'll you have?"

Nora sat silent.

Mackey spoke up. "You can have three eggs over easy, or a cheese omelet, or steaming oatmeal with walnuts and maple syrup, or steak with hash browns, or salmon burgers or crab cakes. I'll have my usual, Hannah, thanks."

"His usual is a tomato-cheese omelet with bacon, and hash browns, and toast, and orange juice, and coffee, and a fresh blueberry muffin or two," Hannah said, still focused on Nora. "I keep telling him he needs to eat proper at home."

Nora laughed, a good solid laugh. It was so different from her silence in the squad car, and her hunched posture of a moment ago, Mackey wasn't sure what to make of it. "I can only handle two scrambled and dry toast."

Hannah left to place the orders. Mackey saw Nora's eyes following Hannah's brisk movements. "Look around. She's the only one taking orders, delivering food, bussing the tables. She has a little sass for everyone. Next time you come in, she'll remember. By the time you're here for a third visit, she'll have a little sass for you, too. I'm told by the old hands that her hair gets a bit redder every year."

Mackey talked on about Hannah. He wanted to have the food in front of them and privacy from Hannah's good care before Nora told him what she'd called about. "That guy over there's a shrimper on the *Pot Holder*. He goes out two or three weeks at a time. Maybe you've bought some of his catch right off the boat. I do every chance I get." By the time he had nodded at a few other men in the diner and explained their roles in town, Hannah was back with a heaping plate for Mackey and eggs with bacon for Nora. "You haven't tasted bacon until you've tried ours," she said, and disappeared as quickly as she had come.

Nora dug in ravenously, then put down her fork. "I may have awakened you for nothing. But every time I remember the jerk of our boat and see the waves coming over the gunnels, I catch a glimpse of three men in yellow slickers with their backs to me, moving away from us fast. All the other boats came toward us to help, so that memory of the boat pulling away stands out."

"What kind of boat?"

"Another tin boat like ours and lots of the others."
"See a name?"
"No."
"Recognize anyone aboard?"
"No."
"Do you think you could spot it, if we went out on the water?"

"No." She sighed. "Constable, I dragged you out of your bed for nothing, I guess. Only it keeps coming into the frame, you know, my vision of, of, of… What should we call this thing that happened?"

"The accident will do. Anything else? Did you reach your children?"

"Only my son. I told him not to come yet. What can he do but sit in the dreary hospital and wait?"

He wanted to tell her that her son could keep her company, maybe help her unleash a few of her fears, but he kept quiet and finished his omelet.

She sipped her coffee. "I didn't sleep much last night."

"That figures."

"I guess I didn't realize how early it was when I called you."

"I told you to call any time. I meant it and still do." Questions. Now was a chance to ask some. "You told me your husband was away for a week. What did you do while he was gone?"

She changed the subject. "Let me pay for breakfast."

He thought about pressing her but decided it was too soon. Especially since he wasn't sure anything wrong had occurred. "I'll let you pay for yours. I can't accept gifts. Regulations. But thanks anyway. I'll take you back to your car whenever you're ready."

The sky had lightened while they ate. He brought her back to where they'd left her car, gave her directions to the hospital and drove back the way he'd come. Dead end. He had to admit he'd been hopeful. Now, he thought maybe he should let it go. Fishing accidents happened all the time. No one but this nervous woman would bother about the definition. She'd let it settle in time. *So could I. Maybe.*

After leaving Nora, Mackey started on his interviews with the fishermen at the scene. Speaking to each of them one-on-one might disclose more information, starting with Jacob, the flag-waving citizen constable. It was early morning, and the tide wasn't due to change for several hours. He hoped Jacob would be home. Happily, Jacob's boat was in the driveway. Mackey parked his squad and got out, crossed the few yards from the street to Jacob's house, climbed the wooden steps to the screened porch and knocked.

Jacob came out right away, a big man with big hands. He was wearing a navy watch cap, as he had been yesterday when the accident occurred. He held the door open. "The wife saw your squad pull up. She said you'd be comin' by today. How's it goin'?"

The porch was full of lumber, tools hanging on a peg board all neatly outlined with red paint, jars of nails and screws sitting in a tray on a workbench. Mackey entered the porch, being careful to step over all the lumber. "Looks like I'm interrupting a project."

"Nah, I need a break. The wife likes to keep me busy. She wants to winterize this porch into a greenhouse so we can have fresh vegetables most of the year. She and her girlfriends have become nature nuts. All they talk about is healthy food. She even asks if she should cook the fish I bring home. You know, toxins and junk in the water. I don't mind doin' the work out here, but I'll be raisin' Cain if she cuts out my fish. So, what's up with the guy?"

"Thanks to you and your friends, the poor man is alive, but tied to machines in the hospital. And thanks to your towing, we've gathered evidence of the accident. Forensics is doing the studies now. The sequence of events isn't clear. Can you fill me in a bit?"

Jacob snorted. "I get so angry with those tourists. The wife looked surprised that I helped fish the bloke out of the water. That's not the only time out-of-towners have ruined a good tide rip, that's for sure."

"So how did it start?"

"I was baiting my line when I heard a scream and saw this skiff running in crazy circles. I swear I saw the man holding onto the side of the boat, but it circled away from me and when it came back around, he was off bobbing in the water."

"And the woman, where was she?"

"By this time, other boats had pulled up as near as the broad would allow. She was yelling at us to stay away."

"Stay away? Why?"

"She kept pointing to the man in the water. Old Chester, the guy with the fishing dog, thinks she was worried we'd mow him down, but he sees good in everyone. Me, I'm not so sure she didn't push him off the gunnels. He'd been hanging on right smart." Jacob scratched his chin. "We told her to shut off her damned motor or we'd all drown. That snapped her up a bit. She sort of crawled toward the outboard and fumbled with the motor arm. Seemed awful slow to me, but she finally managed."

Mackey thought of the three men in yellow slickers Nora had described, in a tin boat moving away from her. "What else did you see?"

"Nothin' much. She waved an oar around. Wonder if that's what socked him over."

"Did you see a retreating boat?"

"Nah. Too busy watching out for the body in the water."

"Were you the one to call the Coast Guard?"

"Yep. I keep a walkie-talkie for that reason. Sometimes they make you wait for a long time, but yesterday they came real fast. It was slick. I'd never seen the op up close. Quite a sight, what! The wife made me tell the story to our kids and grandkids. She thinks they need to learn respect for government services."

He shook his head. "One son in particular goes around town raising a fuss. The wife argues with him all the time. He says all government folks are paid too much for doin' too little.

"Sorry, now. I hope I don't offend you. The wife would say I've been rude. You being a government official, too."

Mackey smiled. "I'm too minor to take offense."

Jacob looked relieved. "That boy of mine. I even had to bail him out of the pokey once because he yelled at a cop. You'll know him if you ever see him. He wears a t-shirt saying *Don't let the bastards grind you down*. His whole gang of friends wears the same slogan. Kids these days, even ours, I'm sorry to say." Jacob shrugged.

"Part of me says she was beating up on that poor bloke, not turning off the motor, raising the oar at us trying to help. Another part of me admits I don't know what she was thinking, or even *if* she was thinking. The wife says *she* wouldn't know how to turn off the motor, and she's been putting up with my fishing for thirty years. Course, the wife stays home most of the time. She'll cook my fish—who can tell for how long, but she won't pull them in or clean them neither. Sure I can't get you nothin' to drink? Coffee? A brew?"

"No, but thanks for asking. So, tell me more about yesterday."

"Truth is," Jacob continued, "fishing's changed. Or at least the water's changed. All those boats that crowded in yesterday. That's new, even in the last few years. After the war, it was slow up here. Guess it began to pick up in the '80s, with corporate-owned yachts, more resorts for tourists and all. Now it's government rules, and no-fish zones, and measuring each catch for keepers, but the worst is all those damned tourists banging around causing trouble.

"I been fishin' these waters since before I could hold a rod. My dad would take me out for hours at a time. It was paradise for me. Pa didn't hold much to school. By high school, he was pulling me out to hire out with him on a shrimper. In freezing winter, we'd hike up to the lakes for some ice fishing. Hauling in a big bass ain't like a twenty-pound spring, but it was better than sitting behind a school desk. Ma protested, and the school police came after Pa. But away we'd go until we got caught the next time."

Mackey wanted Jacob to keep on talking, hoping some fresh observation would spill out. "Yesterday," he reminded the man gently.

"I've told the family and neighbors about it. They all think that woman threw the man overboard. Why else would she try to hold us off from pulling him out of the water? But me, I dunno what to think. I'm only glad the guys helped haul him out."

So much for new information. Mackey changed the subject. "Did you have any trouble towing the skiff?"

"Not a bit. Water wasn't too choppy after the copter left. I hooked 'er up. She followed right along. I put in and out at the same harbor, so wasn't no trouble. I'm going to wet my line this afternoon. I'm hoping there'll be fewer Statesiders to mess us up."

After turning down Jacob's offer of coffee or brew one more time, Mackey said his goodbyes with another layer of thanks.

Chester came next. The old fisherman's dog was asleep on the porch, but roused, tail wagging, as Mackey closed his squad door. Albert's lucky day—if the dog was there, Chester might be at home as well.

It took three knocks to rouse the man, but Chester came to the door with a smile equal to his dog's tail wag. "Why, it's the constable. How d'ya do."

Mackey went into his routine of thanks and news from the hospital then eased into questions about the accident. "Poor frantic lady," Chester said. "She was screaming for help. Sam here," he patted the dog's head, "got pretty upset. He whined and whined."

"I'm told you all tried to help, but she warned you off."

Chester nodded. "She didn't want us running over her husband or buddy or whoever it was in the water. You asked what I saw. I don't see too good, but Sam here, he sees everything. That lady couldn't stop shaking. I remember they had to lift her into your boat. She was one sorry sight."

"How did Sam react to the Cormorant?"

"Oh, Sam didn't flinch a bit. You'd 'uv thought he'd seen a hundred rescues at sea. Maybe he did in his last life. He watched the line come down and go back up. That's his job, watching the line, just like he watches mine." Chester patted the dog's head and rubbed his ears. Sam wagged his tail and nudged Chester's hand for more.

More thanks, another farewell, and Mackey was back in his squad car, consulting his notes for the third fisherman's name before driving off. Unlike Jacob and Chester, William came to his door scowling. "Why are you bothering me? I done nothing wrong."

Mackey stepped back, a de-escalation move his training had taught. "No one is accusing you of any wrongdoing. I'm here to get your description of the incident yesterday."

"You call it an incident. Hah. I call it a murder. That woman pushed him in."

"Did you see that?"

"No, but it was obvious. She had that oar in her hands and yelling at us to stay away. Nobody but a fool would think otherwise."

"Please describe to me exactly what you saw."

"That boat circled and circled with the poor victim clinging to the side, and when the boat came round the last time, he was gone. The woman swung that oar around, trying to keep us from coming in to help the guy in the water."

"I need some evidence that she pushed him."

"Evidence? Ain't her yelling at rescuers to stay away, waving an oar like a club, evidence enough? I ain't got nothin' for evidence. I found a hat in the water.

Didn't see it until after Jacob pulled off with that murderer's skiff. Doubt if it'll do you any good, but I'll fetch it outta my boat."

William came outside and stalked to his boat parked in the yard. Mackey followed. William turned back the tarp tied down over the boat and pulled a soggy canvas hat from under a seat. "Tourists. Statesiders wear these things. See them all the time." He handed the hat to Mackey. "Be my guest. I wouldn't be caught dead wearing it."

Mackey had one more fisherman to find. The last guy showed more interest in his own removal from the incident than anything else. "Forget about me. I have no opinions."

"I'm only asking what you saw."

"Don't go putting my name in the papers. I'm a law-abiding man and I don't like trouble." He shut the door in Mackey's face and wouldn't open up again.

Chapter Six

Time to go to Old John. If there was any scuttlebutt around the harbor, he'd know it. Mackey grabbed a few beers and two crab rolls and went in search of the man.

True to form, John sat on an abandoned crate overseeing the docks, his baggy trousers held up with suspenders. Mackey handed John a crab roll and a brew. John reached behind the garbage dumpster and pulled out another plastic crate. "Here, pull up a throne and watch the fun."

Mackey parked himself on the crate and unwrapped his own crab roll, thinking how to ease into his questions about yesterday's incident. Old John was a talker hard to steer in anyone's direction except his own, but the old fellow's verbal wanderings often held nuggets of useful information. It was worth the time to let him come at things sideways to see what might turn up.

Mackey started with a friendly dispute that he and John had continued over many weeks about why the salmon were disappearing from the waters around Grant's Landing. "Bet no one's catching much salmon today. They're like me. They don't like all the crowds and water traffic."

John pooh-poohed that idea. "Fish follow feed, Mackey. Now, the whales and otters, I'll agree with you about them. Those orca like to rub themselves and each other up at Robson Bight. I've seen it year after year for thirty years now. The last time we went by during the mating season, the sound of the boat chased them away. They're acting nervous. Why, one day two years ago, I saw a pod down by Manson's Landing. A whole flotilla followed, a Southern California yacht in the lead, big as the Queen Mary with a cruising-size yacht slung on top like a dinghy, along with a water-skiing boat, a surf sailor and kayaks and who knows what other rich man's claptrap. After them came three big boats, charters, I presume, then a gaggle of maybe five or six little day fishers, and last, by God, insult of insults, the tail of the flotilla was a sea plane. This monster parade followed those poor devils all the way around Grant's Landing. Chased them down the Strait to the California coast, for all I know. I was plumb disgusted. Imagine how those animals felt. July and August, this place is like the Vancouver Aquarium with gum chewing, fat-assed tourists, flashes popping in their ringed and sunburnt hands."

Mackey smiled. His salmon theory had been given another line of proof. He loved Old John, he decided, really loved the old guy. Talking the town's issues with him was the right way to go. John received gossip from all over the area. If anyone had seen anything unusual yesterday, John would be as likely to know it as anyone.

John pointed toward the gas dock, where a big rental yacht was pulling in. The captain, in spanking clean sporty boating clothes, clearly had no idea how to manage a boat. In the summer season, the gas dock had vessels lining up for service, so the amateur backing and filling created hearty entertainment. Some drivers threw the motor in reverse, forcing the bow out away from the dock. Others, like this one, came crashing toward the boards in high throttle. John slapped his thigh in laughter as the yacht hit, and a fellow onboard threw a line at the gas attendants like throwing a stone. One younger helper ducked, while a pair of old hands backed off a bit and let the frustrated linesman try again. "Get a load of that one. It's good that dock is double lined with bumpers."

Mackey ate a bite of crab roll. "I'm too raw with my own boat stupidities to laugh at other poor blokes. I went out in a smelly inversion. Are they regular happenings? Pretty nasty stuff."

"Weather trick and bad chemicals. Happens more and more."

"How do the townsfolk feel about that?"

"I guess most shrug. A few complain." John bit into his crab roll, chewed and swallowed. "Trouble is, there's too few province or federal inspectors, and the local newspaper kowtows to industry. I guess you know about the explosion in '86. There was a heap of trouble back then. Some dead and wounded mill workers. Townies were damaged too. Lung problems, rashes from the chlorine, that sort of stuff, but none of the townies could prove cause and effect, so the ruckus died down. Now, there's hostility building, angry workers meeting in the bars, a few toughs I've never seen before parading about. Can't put my finger on anything, but tension is like mold, it sort of creeps up on you. Know what I mean?"

A large schooner floated past the harbor. John nodded toward it. "Now there's a sight. The captain of that tub bought into Grant's Mill a few years ago. Some say he's the major investor. It's rumored that he's looking to sell his shares, but who knows. Jeremy Foster. He comes here every summer on that boat. Ever since the purchase, he's funded the traditional summer festival here. They serve brats, fries and watermelon. His bossy wife gives out prizes. People go. Kids get faces painted, but I don't see much joy in it anymore. The mayor and Gallagher, the manager of the mill, stand around with smiles glued on. They look about as comfortable as rats cornered in a trap."

"I know about the festival." It was coming up soon, he realized. "All leaves have been canceled for the day and evening. Police and Mounties are on double shifts with overtime pay. Are they expecting trouble?"

"Don' know. More newcomers every year. Some look pretty rough. Now if I wanted to make trouble, I'd rob houses outside of town, as all you guys will be guarding the face painters. But what do I know?"

"Do folks like the Fosters?"

"Who knows what they think about him. He don't bump into gas docks. No fun from him. He glides in, waves to people on shore, smiles and gives big tips to the service boys. Mrs. Foster, now…" He took a swig of beer. "My friend, Mabel, she runs a food stand and promotes no-pesticide farming, was accosted by Mrs. Foster one day. Apparently, Mrs. Foster noised her doubts that Mabel's produce really is pesticide free. Anyway, Mabel tells me there's anger building around the festival. Mrs. Foster has taken over."

"What's she done?

"She hired a big-name band from Seattle, the Leapin' Lizards or somethin'. Seattle, mind you. Not just local strummers and street dancing at night, like there used to be. Everyone must buy tickets for these imports. And she's bringing in artists from Seattle too, for the booths. No more church-run craft fairs. Women round here been crocheting and knitting doodads for months, locals make homegrown pottery and stuff. They look on the work like a community effort, even if some of it is crap. No, she's asking the famous summer artists who live here to jury the entries for the booths. She says the tourists will spend more. It will be good for the school fund. Mabel says those longtime part-timers, ain't that an odd title, are too special to kowtow to outsider control. They've made friends in Grant's and hereabouts. Everybody gets along fine. That'll change if the longtime folks jury the locals out of selling their work. Friends'll break up. Mrs. Foster's idea is, no crap to be sold in Grant's Landing no more. Just high-falutin' 'real' art. Mabel and her friends are pissed."

Mackey couldn't help smiling. "Do you think we'll have a civil war over crocheting and strumming?"

Mabel says don't worry about the longtime part-timers. She calls them FFOs, Friends From Outside. Mabel says they love what we love about this place. You know—beauty, the waters, the mountains, sun rises and sunsets, the wildlife, and yes, they appreciate us locals with our mixed histories and heritage."

John looked embarrassed after these flowery comments. "Hell, she thinks they even trust old rummies like me."

John took a slug of his beer. "Pretty funny, Mabel talking like that. I says to her, 'Mabel, with that Scottish accent, ain't you an outsider, too?'"

"She came right back at me. 'We're all newcomers, John, except the First Nation folks, and they came from somewhere, just like us. You know what I mean. We got to be welcomers, not naysayers like Mrs. Nose in the Air Foster.'"

John took off his cap and scratched his head. "My

advice to you. If there's a battle comin' on, don't side against Mabel. Mrs. Foster may be in for more than a vegetable war.

"But we've strayed from the real issue right now. You're the story. Is she guilty?"

"Do you mean Nora McKeever?" Word traveled fast. "What can you tell me?"

"No facts, just blabbing. Everyone on the water yesterday has a story. And the scuttlebutt tells me you're asking around."

"That's why I'm here. I thought you'd have all the answers."

"No, but I seen you bring her in, then inspect the guy's boat, then take her out for a run in your Mountie tub, so what's up?"

"Guess nothing's up, at least not yet. Be eyes and ears for me, if you're willing." Disappointed that John had no information, Albert picked up John's empty bottle and stood to go back on duty.

A big guy staggered up to the quiet pair. He had blotches of paint and oil stains on his jeans and wore a t-shirt that said in bold letters, *Don't Let the Bastards Grind You Down*. Its chopped-off sleeves revealed bulging muscles covered by tattoos. "So, you're blabbing away with that Mixti, John. Why you pow-wowing with him? You know he ain't no real Mountie. He's a quota guy."

John rose from his crate. "You're drunk, Butch. Don't come into my space until you're sober and civil."

"Preachin' me, are you? You've downed a pint or two in your time. You only talk to this Mixti because he brings you free fuel."

"You got it wrong, Butch. The word ain't Mixti, it's

Metis, them people have been around for centuries, fine folk descended from fur traders and Frenchies. Anyway, he likes to learn, which is more than I can say for you. Now, walk off this dock before you fall off."

Butch turned to Mackey. "You, boy, are a 'designated.' It's the law. I learned that much in school. You know what that means? People designated for special government treatment, 'women, visible minorities'—now ain't that a silly phrase----'mental and physical cripples and First Nations,' all bunched together."

John's face turned red. Veins on his forehead throbbed. With the speed of a sixteen-year-old, he grabbed Butch by the arm. "Outta my sight and off my dock or it's into the drink with you."

Albert laid his hand on the old man's arm. "Let it go, John."

Before Albert could pull John away from Butch, the old man put his foot forward and pushed. The next second, Butch lay flat on his back on the dock.

John broke into a wide smile. "Didn't know I could still do that. Pretty neat, eh?" He laughed. "Thanks, Albert. I haven't felt so good in years." Grabbing his sides, he sat back down on his crate. "Ugly son of a bitch, ain't he? Ain't we all!"

His laughter vanished as quickly as it had come. He looked at the oiled planks of the dock. "Life is a bitch, a goddamned stinkin' bitch."

Chapter Seven

Mackey had to go for the dreaded interview with the 'suspect,' labeled so by a few tourist-hating fishermen. Innocent until proven guilty did not resonate with them. He wasn't sure how he felt, just that he needed to know more.

"Any news?" he asked when he found her in the hospital. He leaned forward and spoke directly to her, shutting them away from the accumulated audience in the waiting room.

Nora shook her head. His sympathy must have shown in his face, because she patted his arm. "The doctor said we wouldn't see any progress for several days, even under the best circumstances." She tried to smile, but her eyes filled with tears.

Mackey knew what he needed to do. He had to ask her to go over the story again, a routine he hated as much as the suspects did, but the second telling often revealed a little nugget hitherto unknown. As gently as possible, he asked her to come with him. "I want to review everything we know."

Caroline had found him an empty office. Mackey brought in coffee for both of them. Instead of sitting behind the desk in an unspoken position of authority, he pulled his chair next to hers. "We've tested the metal bopper for blood types," he began. "Mostly dogfish blood, though there's some of yours and bits of your husband's as well. His and your blood was found all over the boat." He smiled at her. "Tell me once more what you remember."

"I guess I should start in the cabin. Joe wanted to go fishing. That was routine, but the night before, he'd come back from a trip with a few friends, fishing way up at the tip of Vancouver Island. I'd been left alone for a week." She rubbed her face. "That's why I was angry. 'You're just home,' I said to him. Louder than I meant to. He told me, 'Come fishing, if you like. I'll wait on the beach.'

"I was in a state. I admit that. You saw the pile of junk in the cabin. I started grabbing stuff to leave. I even thought I'd ask him to take me to the main dock, so I could…." She paused. "You know, do some shopping. 'Calm down, Nora,' I told myself. I picked up the sandwiches and tea I'd made, grabbed my windbreaker, sunglasses, day stuff and met him on the beach.

"The wind had come up. The waves were choppy. You know our boat, only fourteen feet long, an old beater, open, perfect for potsing about. I felt secure in it, but we don't take it out when it's rough. The weather blew up as we reached the Narrows. Perhaps we should have gone home then. But the tide was changing. There were lots of others exactly like us out there and big boats, too. No one was catching anything. All the boats were hanging around, waiting. Then Joe caught a coho, good size, and boats around us began to catch fish as well. The nets came out, here, there, you could feel the excitement. More boats came in. Joe had to do some fancy steering with one hand, holding his rod with the other. He scanned the water, dodged boats, checked his line all at the same time."

Mackey kept quiet. He knew she was talking for

herself. He wondered if this was the power of the confessional, the relief, the joy even, of releasing burdens. He forced himself to stop these musings, to use his eyes and ears.

Nora's tongue moved across her top row of teeth, then behind the lower row. She pursed her mouth and looked off to the corner of the room. "I melted when he looked like that. I could hardly remember why I was upset that morning. He pulled in his line to rebait his hook. He cuts his herring just so. I marvel at the meticulous process even in calm water, but in bouncing conditions, it's like a miracle. I offered to take the motor. He set his jaw and ignored me. I felt rebuffed. How dare he ignore even my offers to help. That's what I thought."

Nora's face changed. Her lower jaw protruded, her brow furrowed tightly, her body grew as tense as her words. "Then I get all confused. I've gone over and over this as I sit in that waiting room."

She spoke to him and not herself. "Constable, I don't know what happened. None of it makes any sense. Everything came at once. Joe stood up, feeding out his line. Then my line jumped. I thought I had a salmon, but of course it was a dogfish, a big one. I laughed at myself, trying to erase my earlier fury. I told myself, 'I hate this dogfish even more than I hate Joe.' That sounds awful, but I talk to myself that way. I try to tease myself out of bad moods by writing them into a make-believe TV script."

She paused, folded, and unfolded her hands. "Scripts. I had looked up dogfish. There's a Haida story about a dogfish that stole a man's wife, linking a dogfish to lost love. I began to beat that creature. I now wonder if I was reversing the myth, bashing the fish and losing my husband.

"I grabbed the pliers and missed the hook four or five times. Those monsters scare me. I flummox getting them off. I put down the pliers and hung over the side of the boat, banging at the fish with my bopper. I gave the fish one good whack, hit the side of the boat a few times. I remember the thuds." She drew in on herself, tighter than before. "I leaned back to wind up for a major thwack, Joe gave a groaning shout—a low-pitched, 'Oh, my God…' and the boat rocked. I had to grab the gunnels to keep from going in. The dogfish almost washed into the boat. I turned around and Joe was gone. The boat was running in circles, other boats were all around, someone was yelling, the waves were rolling us up and down, and I didn't see Joe anywhere."

She swallowed hard. "I knew I had to stop the motor, so I sort of crawled to the stern and grabbed at the outboard handle. One of our motors has the stop button on the handle end, on the other it's next to the starting puller. It took me too long to find the button and push it hard enough to stop the motor. Waves were rocking the boat, but at least it wasn't careening in circles anymore. That's when I saw Joe in the water. I couldn't reach him. The oars were wedged under the gunnels. I finally wiggled one free and tried to do a lot of little strokes, drawing the one oar to the side of the boat. It was slow, oh how slow, but I got close enough to reach the oar out to Joe. He didn't make a sound."

A sigh escaped her. "I got the oar sort of under his armpit and leaned on my end. I could only lift him slightly. By this time, other boats had realized something was terribly wrong with us. Several boats surrounded Joe. There was lots of talk back and forth, and then they pulled Joe from the water. He was covered in blood. I know I'd been screaming because my throat was raw, but I can't recall anything I said. I was standing up, the boat was rocking. You know the rest better than I do. I guess they called the Coast Guard. Who called you? Does the Coast Guard automatically report to you, or do you only get called in when things look wrong?"

"The fishermen nearby thought they saw your husband hanging on to the side of your boat."

Her eyes grew wide in alarm. "Didn't I tell you that? There he was, his face contorted with pain, his skin gray except for the bloody streaks. I tried to pull him in. When I grabbed him, both of us on the same side of the boat, it tipped and started to roll. I thought it would turn over on top of him. The boat was going in circles. I had to turn off the motor. That's when I crawled to the stern, pushed the button. When I stood, I saw Joe floating away." She began to cry. "That's when I pulled the oar out from under the gunnels and paddled to get closer to him. I got the oar under his arm but couldn't…couldn't lift him. The other boatmen were coming close. I screamed at them to watch out, not to run over Joe."

Nora collapsed across the table, choking and sobbing, her raised arms spilling the two cups of coffee.

Mackey stood beside her, not knowing what to do. He turned to open the door and call for help when Nora lifted her head, dry-eyed, her sobs in check. "I'm sorry, Constable. The memories have been playing in my head over and over. First, I can't remember anything, and then I remember too much."

Mackey knew he'd broken all proper police rules. He had attempted to interview her alone. Wrong. Even police procedural fictions had at least two witnesses in the interrogation rooms. If she had destroyed her own case testimony by omitting this part of the story, it was now gone forever. Whatever came in subsequent interviews would appear to be manipulated.

Why had he proceeded on his own this way? Was he torn by his sympathy for her? He had become too involved, that was clear.

Mackey realized he had been assuming her innocence. This change in her story filled him with doubt, doubled by her controlled hysterics. And what about the men in yellow slickers she'd mentioned at the Busy Bee? Was she confused? Had she made them up?

Nora tilted her head. "Do you want to continue with your questions?"

He changed his tone, cooler with her now. "No, that will be all for the moment. I'll speak with my colleagues and make an appointment for completing our discussion later." *This is the way I should have been all along, the professional, cool cop.* "You may go back to the waiting room or to your motel, whichever you prefer."

Chapter Eight

Time dragged in the waiting room. Why had the constable's tone shifted after she told him what happened? What was the truth? How had things gone wrong?

Now, looking up at the hospital ceiling, Nora realized these memories only increased her anxiety when she needed calm. She went and found Caroline at the nurses' station. They went together into Joe's room.

Caroline stood beside Joe's bed and went about her nurse's business, checking his charts, feeling his pulse, and watching the drip on his IV. Nora sat with her hands in her lap, trying to piece together this strange trip. She had spent her professional life pulling stories together. What was missing with this one?

Nora sat quietly, looking at Joe and letting her mind drift. Her thoughts kept bouncing from the shape on the hospital bed—a stranger with tubes and wires attached at the wrist, in the nose, on the chest, under one arm—to the man she had known. Joe's face normally had a rounded boyish look, the cheeks filled out and ruddy. Now he was gaunt, the skin tight and pulled back, all the firm flesh vanished.

The real Joe, the old Joe, had a mobile mouth. It was one of the things he used on his programs to pull out feeling and character. The lips could bell out softly in an admiring pucker or draw in to curl or scowl. Those lips could express rapt attention to a new scientific theory. The cameraman once kept a narrow focus on Joe's mouth throughout a reading by a renowned author. "Cosmic error, an unforgivable TV sin," Joe said to the cameraman when they viewed the rushes. But Nora knew, the cameraman knew, maybe even Joe knew, that following Joe's mouth was the best response to a reading that novelist would ever have. The mouth sighed, wept, laughed. It responded so sensitively to the author that it sometimes seemed Joe was mouthing the words in harmony. In fact, it was Joe's way of listening intently. His whole body connected, especially his full lips. Now they were narrow and passive, stretched so taut it seemed they might break if he attempted a smile.

Thinking about these details, her sense of Joe the man began to penetrate the tubes and the blue-green lights on the monitors. The wide-angle camera lens in her head switched to full vision as she dove into memory.

Joe. The Catch. The high school hero. The teachers thought they had met a natural poet, the original, the spirit of the earth rising up through a lean, muscular body to a head full of exuberant curls. The cheerleaders and other future prom queens, the trim and expectant narrow-thighed beauties, blond or brunette, all dreamed of placing themselves on his arm for the prom, the graduation waltz, the wedding march. The football coach watched Joe's run, his loose joints loping down the field. He grinned when Joe broke the pattern, reversed direction, and zagged to the center. Joe seemed to anticipate the opposition's plans, moving to block a drive to the left when everyone expected a fourth-down kick. He had everyone enthralled but the math professor. In fact, even that human stick loved Joe, but he couldn't deliver math to him. Which was why Old Static had hinted that Joe should go to Nora Spaulding for tutoring.

Nora's reveries turned up feelings she'd thought long buried. Until the spring of junior year, she had led two high school lives. One life was an opening, an enlargement. Every idea led to a bigger one. The first rock in geology class was a rock. But then it became a sedimentary rock, then a relic of the time when a hilltop was an ocean floor, then a marker to the climate and the habitat of creatures. Some of them crawled from the sea to the land where they changed body structure and learned to breathe oxygen from the air instead of the water. Every subject had such expanding horizons.

Social life, the other part of high school, was a closing in, a retreat. Nora ran her fingers through her hair. Long face, straight hair when the prom queens had bobs neatly curled. *I had curves, but I was too shy to exaggerate them as they did. Worst of all, I was serious.* Loving the work was bad. When the class had assignments, she went to the library. She handed in work on time, often several pages longer than requested. Sin of sins, she found some questions in the research that encouraged talks with the professors before and after class.

Her ears burned as she remembered standing by her locker door one day, overhearing the conversation between Joe and Janice Hardwick, the perfect prom queen in the making. "Come over this afternoon, Joe. Mom's gone to Boston and Dad'll be at work."

"Can't. Old Static has me all set to go over formulas with Nora. Bad math score, no game on Saturday."

She'd sensed rather than seen the other girl's petulant shrug. "Okay, if you prefer her, you can forget movies Saturday night."

"Come on, Janice. Don't be stupid. How can anybody be jealous of that walking math book?"

Years later, Nora would throw that "walking math book" up to Joe as their private signal of a moment when her feelings were hurt. Joe caught it, gave her a tender, funny response, or some special look. *Year after year, until last year when...* Her breath caught. *I don't know when, or why. Year after year, until our private code broke down.*

She shifted in her chair and scratched her nose. Her injured hand ached. She knew she was plain, or, at least, not glamorous. Indeed, she had taught herself to be proud of her unfussy looks. Recently, Nora had observed that she wasn't alone in this. Many women habitually wore armor for self-protection, being fat, being weak, whatever little foibles one needed to prevent a robust competition. Nora's plainness was the outer shell of her armor, the inner shell her steady manner. Miss Dependable. At an early age, long before many American children are expected to do chores or understand adult problems, Nora's mother had turned to Nora.

"Darling, the boys are fighting. Please do something about the noise."

Nora, age six, would dash into the boys' room to quiet them with entertainment. She told them stories. "Once upon a time," she chanted in a singsong voice. The twins stopped their tussling. Once upon a time was a good start, but what next? Even then, Nora understood that she could catch the boys' attention by talking about them. "Once upon a time, there lived two blond boys. They were the same age. They looked alike and talked alike. A big giant came to their door when their father was away. 'I'll eat you for my breakfast,' said the giant."

When the boys were quiet, Father could go back to typing his reports, and Mother could unfurl her brow. Mother often had a worried face when Father worked on his reports. Sometimes she looked like the deer they'd startled one morning when picking black raspberries. The fawn, nestled in the bushes, was too frightened to do anything but widen its eyes, too frightened to stand, too frightened to move. Nora remembered that moment often when she thought of her mother. The deer was so exposed, so defenseless, that Nora and her mother had turned away from it. Years later, thinking back on that scene, Nora wished she had looked at the fawn more carefully. She wanted to know the color of its lips, see the tongue. Was it pink like hers, gray like the cow's or sort of black like the dog's? Nora knew she had turned away with too much haste. It seemed all she could do to spare the deer the indignity of discovering its weakness.

Fabric rustled and soft footsteps retreated as Caroline moved about the room. Nora barely paid attention, instead focusing her mental camera onto her mother. Why was she so fearful? Yes, Father had developed bad habits. He laughed at Mother or, worse, paid her no attention. There were pictures that showed her dad looking at her mother with tenderness. When had that changed? There was the time when Nora was…how old? Eighth grade, perhaps. *Father stood up at dinner while Mother was telling a story and walked out of the room, as if he didn't know she was there.* Mother paused before continuing in a softer voice. Then Mother's voice stopped altogether. She had been telling the story for him, that was clear. She tried to keep going, but she'd lost the plot. The story trailed away like seeds caught in the air. With seeds, some would root in rich soil while others might come to rest on a rusty car roof and be dried out by the forces of nature.

Nora knew the stories had rooted in her. She felt them nudging her in her sleep, so that she woke up surrounded by friends, enemies, intrigues, domestic scenes, or dramatic confrontations. Drifting from sleep to wakefulness, she had a hard time separating the stories from her real life. When she realized she was lying in her own bed, she felt as if she had been turning pages in a new and cherished book. What was this? A curse that inhabited her mother and had been passed along to Nora?

The story, the great gift from her fawn-eyed mother, was a disease to her busy father. Yet, hadn't her mother entangled him in her net by weaving stories, in the same way Nora calmed the boys when Mother furrowed her brows?

The awful dinner scene faded back into the story hour. In Nora's tale, the boys made the giant retreat. "You can't eat me. You don't know my name. Am I Samuel? Am I Joshua? You can't eat what you don't know. 'Sam is poison,' said Sam. 'No, Joshua is poison,' said Josh. Sam or Josh, by gosh. Josh or Sam, by damn. Name us if you can." The twins were laughing. Mother's lilting voice, calmed by the fact that she'd cooked another perfect meal, called everyone to dinner.

Her father told stories too, though he would have denied they were stories. He spoke about facts, the real world, he called it. He probed details of highway engineering and transportation reports, or public safety issues. He never spoke fiction, only fact. Truth, his truth, was a force for good. *He may never have actually said it, but we learned at his knee that fiction is immoral. But what is fact? What is fiction?* Mother's tales evoked the facts of atmosphere, the sense of place, of feelings, of moods.

Growing up, she rarely saw her mother and father touching. They didn't greet with kisses. Nora realized she'd never thought about sex at all back then, even when schoolgirls clustered to whisper and smirk about who was hot.

In senior year, when she and Joe spent hours together for many weeks, she looked forward to the tutoring afternoons with her nice, bright student. He wasn't good at math, but he loved stories, especially stories about people like him who struggled against problems.

Then, at college, in that turbulent year of 1968 when riots followed Martin Luther King's death, they partnered on news stories for the campus *Bugle*. Aroused by the angry crowds, they interviewed distraught King admirers, searching for words to capture the sorrow of heightened hopes now dashed. They grew into an impassioned news team, delving further and further into the backgrounds of their stories.

A few months later, torn by Bobby Kennedy's murder in June, Nora remembered that she'd collapsed sobbing after they posted the last line for the first *Bugle* report. As they walked back from the *Bugle*'s press office, Joe put his arms around her, a comforting move perhaps to help her stop her crying jag. She tucked her head into the space between his shoulder and his chin, shaking with sobs. He lifted her chin, kissed her gently, then more deeply.

By the Democratic convention in August, Joe had

moved out of his scruffy apartment into her only slightly larger walkup. *Both of us were caught in the wave of ardent stirring of ideals, mixed with anger, fatigue, skipped meals and the comforts of a shared bed. Yes, Joe, you and I discovered the excitement of covering the news and making love. We reveled in both.*

Nora shifted her weight, restless. Facts, facts, facts. One time, she had driven miles to advance an interview with storm victims, so Joe and the team could pull viewers into a story that would play on the nightly news. She searched for little things the camera could pick up: the mud on the baby's crib, the piano on the dog pen that showed the tornado's force. And like the calm fixer of her brother's fights, she soothed the weary TV crews as each fussed over his camera angle or placement in the van.

Nora, plain, competent, unflappable, ego free, was the producer of McKeever and McKeever Independent News. Joe, the handsome charmer, arrived on the scene to entertain gawking children with his magic nickel trick, or brace a frightened accident victim with a tender pat on the back. Joe, the center of her world, the center of McKeever and McKeever, never asked why or how this particular assortment of people had come together to talk with him. He looked in their faces and responded to the facts she had found. He asked the right questions, not *where were you on the night of,* but *how do you feel? What will you do?* They answered him from their hearts and through him to the hearts of their viewers.

Once, he stood in dusty, drought-scourged fields pulling stories out of the grime. Men sitting in their dens with sprinklers going *whoosh, whoosh, whoosh* on their suburban lawns wept, watching little plants shrivel and die. They looked at Joe in black and white or full color and saw the world as he brought it to them. Fact, fact, fact, a whole series of small details piled together to turn fact into story, story into understanding, and understanding into caring, even if only for that precious moment frozen in time by McKeever and McKeever Independent News.

Chapter Nine

Nora sat with her hands in her lap, trying to piece together this strange trip.

They had come to British Columbia several times, the first when Joe suggested a romantic interlude, a break from work and their kids, ages two and four. *We rented an isolated cabin, put out crab and prawn pots, roasted oysters on the rocky shore, swam naked by moonlight. We explored fiords as far as Bute Inlet, an excursion into a part of the world that felt like wilderness, unbothered by multiple resorts and tourists.*

We passed mile after mile of cliffs, some so steep that only occasional clumps of mosses clung to crags on the surface, clear waterfalls tumbled down their ridges and deer grazed on lofty fields. Other hills looked softer with pine trees standing straight like sentinels. Yet, again and again, packed brown dirt covered the crests with road remnants like scars decorating the surfaces, an occasional bulldozer abandoned on the hilltop.

Bradley Island, then and now, could have been two different places. Then, a simple lodge provided rental boats and fishing guides who understood giant rapids and ways to navigate huge whirlpools, some thirty feet wide. Masses of water released by glacial melt in the high peaks above Bute Inlet flowed into an area where wide fiords narrowed suddenly into a tight space, enhancing the tidal forces. This combination made these waters world famous. Fishermen plotted the tide changes for fishing paradise.

She'd been curious about the whirlpools, so Joe invited her to come along in his piloted rental boat. The guide steered them down toward the rapids, the whirlpools building all around the little craft. As the guide deftly swung the boat around the edges of a whirlpool, Joe's line went taut, his catch leaping into the air several times, trying to shake the hook. The salmon and the line shed sprays of water, pink and purple in the early rays of sunset. The feisty fish dove deep, making a run almost to the end of Joe's line. Perhaps the churning waters stimulated the fish to extra fight, or the atmosphere of danger stirred both fish and fisherman. Whatever the reason, Joe said that catch had been the most exciting fishing he had ever known.

Nora jerked herself into a standing position. She left the waiting room and paced the corridor, wanting something to, to…what? To erase yesterday and today, to put Joe back on the beach waiting for her and the picnic. She wasn't alone. Others in the waiting room murmured, perhaps sufferers from other family dramas.

Momentarily distracted, she continued trying to figure out how this trip differed from that first one. Then they had rented a rustic cabin, and the lodge restaurant cooked Joe's salmon. They shared a bottle of local wine and talked late into the night before stretching out on the cabin's deck, hoping to see the famed Northern Lights. *Neither of us quite believed the stories we'd been told. A loon called. The sound echoed across the quiet water. I nestled against Joe, resisting its aching cry.* Streaks of green and purple flashed in the sky. They had lain entwined as Joe's hair reflected silver and gold. *Our bodies mirrored the sky's electricity. My skin tingled as Joe gently traced the lights across my back, shoulders and thighs.*

A child sitting down the hall bounced a ball, *thump, thump*. The sound brought her back to the hospital. Nora halted her pacing, trying to quiet the tremors of longing that raced down her arms.

The thump of the bouncing ball pulled Nora from her reveries. She forced herself back to that first trip to British Columbia.

The next morning, Joe had hired another boat and guide. Nora walked a trail above the channel toward another rapids, a narrow waterway opening at the top of Bradley Island. Deep woods flanked the island side, with a row of trees along the channel's edge, eagles fishing from their branches. They swooped down toward the whirlpools to snatch salmon from the raging waters, much as Joe had done the night before. A heavy rush of air from thrusting eagle wings brushed her cheek; the eagles' piercing cries echoed. One eagle grabbed another's salmon mid-air. Another dropped its catch, only to have an attacker swoop underneath to retrieve the prize.

From then on, they had thought of British Columbia as their own secret world. They brought the kids back several times on summer vacations, though they never ventured with them as far as Bradley Island. They explored the coastal area, Thunder Bay, the towns of Vancouver on the mainland and Victoria on Vancouver Island.

So, Nora, that was then. This is now. What am I missing? She went over the narrative as if writing a script. After her retirement, things had been tough.

McKeever & McKeever's most reliable cameraman, Greg, was undergoing chemotherapy for colon cancer. Only the supremely fit could lug those behemoths, but muscle was not his only skill. He had a sense of story. He didn't need to be told when closeups or light filters were needed. Better yet, he cared about the quality of each story. Greg's illness was only one of multiple staff problems.

One night, Joe dragged into the house, two hours later than expected. Nora took one look at his drooping face and curbed her complaint about a spoiled dinner. Joe dumped his coat on the chair by the door and sagged into his reading chair.

"I've had it. We messed up. Arrived late. Missed the interview with the senator. The other cameras were packing up and leaving."

Nora held her tongue. She brought him a vodka on ice with a plate of smoked salmon and cream cheese, a special treat. Then she sat down and picked up a novel she'd started.

Joe was quiet for a long time.

"Too much, too much," he finally said. "I'm surrounded by incompetents. We've never had these problems. Tomorrow, I'll cancel the interview with the floundering housing inspector. People are tired of hearing his same-old, same-old excuses."

Again Nora held her tongue.

He brightened. "Let's go out on the town. Tomorrow night. We need a break." He went to bed not long after, his dinner sitting untouched in the kitchen.

The next day, he called with the restaurant's name and the time of the reservation, a fancier place than their usual, what the children would call a white-tablecloth restaurant.

They started dinner with stories about Greg, his tears at every funeral and his anger when they covered a modern-day lynching story. Too saddened by Greg's condition to keep going, they started in on Alex—what in the hell was his last name?—who dropped the new camera in a puddle and, Lord-a-mighty, who disappeared into a bar as the President walked over for an interview. Story after story of difficult moments and funny circumstances followed. They were laughing so hard Nora grabbed her napkin to dab at her tears.

Joe pulled her up from her chair and they walked over to the three-piece band. "Do you guys know 'I Could Have Danced All Night,' you know, from *The King and I*?"

He'd named the wrong musical, but it didn't matter.

Joe and Nora had not danced in years, not since Charlie was born and two kids on different schedules made sitters harder to manage. Their first steps were a bit clumsy until they caught the rhythm and twirled as of old. A couple from another table joined them on the little dance floor. Then another. Nora was breathless after a while, but they danced on.

Finally, a waiter came into view and gestured at his watch. "I'm sorry, sir. It's closing time."

Nora looked around. She and Joe were the only remaining customers.

That night, Joe curled around her, cupping his arm around her waist, breathing gently on the nape of her neck. It had been a long time since they had nestled like this. She looped one leg between his, pulling him closer. She placed her free hand on his hip, circling his hip bone with her fingers, then slipped her hand to caress his groin. They turned toward each other slowly, slowly, as if they had all the time in the world. His eyes followed his hands, moving gently to cup one breast, then the other. She arched her back and opened her thighs for him as she murmured, "Yes, Joe, yes."

They both slept late the next morning. It was over coffee and eggs that Joe suggested she look for an isolated cabin to rent in British Columbia over the coming summer. The kids were in college and would be taking special courses and internships for those months. It would just be the two of them returning to their personal Shangri-la.

As the weeks passed, Nora decided Joe had given her the job of planning the trip as a way to make amends for her retirement. She didn't understand why he had insisted, really forced her to step aside from the work she loved. When she asked, he merely repeated that she seemed stressed and overworked. And why wouldn't she feel anxious with stories piling up? The kids going off into their own lives hadn't helped. She missed the family dinners, their camaraderie and laughter. With the kids gone, it was only work, research, and more work in between managing the schedules of a growing team of reporters and technicians, cooking dinners for them, packing equipment plus food for assignments. She knew it upset her when the team struck out with their own ideas for stories and didn't follow her plans. Maybe she had yelled at them on occasion. In remembering, Nora felt her anxiety mounting. Perhaps she had been losing her cool. But retiring her?

Reviewing all this in the hospital, her cheeks flamed with a sudden realization. *No, not retiring her. He had fired her.* She folded her fingers inward, her nails biting into her palms. She paced, pounding her feet on the linoleum floor. *Could it be?*

At the beginning of their partnership, she had not paid attention when they signed the business contracts. It never occurred to her to read the fine print about management decisions. They had shared the hiring and firing. Nora had been in charge of scheduling and research. Joe had made the artistic decisions. She never interfered with those. Well, she occasionally made suggestions about the artistic parts. And Joe often made suggestions about scheduling. Suggestions, not decisions. So why? She worried the issue of her dismissal like a dog licking a wound. *Stop it, Nora. It keeps the sore open.*

She'd found them a cabin to rent near Grace Point. They would return to a propane stove and refrigerator, reading at night by kerosene lamp, or by solar power after sunny days. The vacation started well. Joe wanted to go to Bradley Island, a romantic rerun of their first adventure there. He rented a larger boat for the long trip. He could fish, and she could re-walk the path she had named Eagle Trail. But this excursion was different. The lodge served frozen salmon and shrimp for dinner, not Joe's catch, or the glorious fresh prawns of the area. That night, Joe didn't suggest looking for the Northern Lights. Perhaps he had forgotten the spine-tingling experience.

At dawn, Joe went off with a guide, and Nora set out looking for the Eagle Trail. Everything had changed. A sign pointed out a path to a golf course. Another sign read *Rapids Overlook*, both arrows pointing in the same direction. Nora walked toward the roaring sound of the rapids, but there were no trees along the channel edge, no piercing cries of eagles on the hunt, or beat of eagle wings, nothing but a bank with a drop-off, and the sight of rushing water far below. On the inland side, there was a smooth stretch of golf fairway where once forest had stood. The wild woods had been destroyed by the creep of what many might call civilization.

Disappointed, she trudged along, growing increasingly hot and thirsty. The path had been undermined here and there with runoff gullies, the result perhaps of clear-cutting to build the golf course. She stepped off the path to walk on the smoother fairway, but a golf ball came whizzing past, scaring her back to the path.

Around a bend, she looked down on a fantasy scene. Behind a line of what appeared to be newly planted trees, she saw two giant barges pulled up to the shore, one with a house, tennis court and a swimming pool, the latter complete with a long-legged, topless female lying in the sun with a towel wrapped around her head. The other barge had no structures or bathing beauty, only a wide deck with painted lines.

She leaned through the tree branches to see better, pulling out her camera to record Hollywood in the wild. A hand grabbed her arm as the camera strap around her neck pulled tight.

Nora screamed and turned her head. A bearded man no taller than she stood close, holding a rifle aimed at her head. Following the pull of her camera strap, she turned her head further. The person who'd grabbed hold of her was a woman dressed in combat boots, camouflage shirt and trousers, with a gun belt across her chest.

"Please put the camera down and give me your film," the woman said.

Shaking with fear and anger, Nora somehow

managed to speak quietly and firmly. "Take your hand off my arm. I've done nothing wrong."

"You are intruding on private property. You and your camera have no business here. The film, please. *Now*."

"I borrowed my husband's camera. If I lose his photos, he'll be upset. I haven't even pressed the button to photograph that lovely pool. Please, don't take the film."

The woman's eyes glinted. "Hand it over."

The guy with the gun waved it at Nora. "Better do what she says. It's bad luck to disobey Jasmine."

For a minute, Nora wanted to laugh. *Jasmine. In camouflage. Joe will never believe this story.* Her smile was wiped away by a harsh tug on the camera strap. It banged her nose as Jasmine pulled the strap over her head, opened the camera, unspooled the film, and dropped it into a pouch at her waist.

"Turn and march down that plank," said the gun-wielder. "Now."

He gestured. Nora saw a steep board with no railing leading down toward the first barge. God, what were they going to do to her? She wanted to scream, run, anything except obey orders, but the rifle gave her little choice. She moved slowly toward the house and pool, as fearful of slipping off the narrow plank to the roaring water below as she was of these two guards.

They reached the barge without incident, and a man stepped out from a covered portion of the terrace. "It's okay, Franz. Bring her over for a glass of something. She must be thirsty in this heat." The man caught Nora's eye and winked as he nodded toward the woman who'd taken her camera.

"Don't mind Jasmine. She likes being bossy."

Nora wanted to say, *is that what you call being bossy?* But she kept her silence.

Blinking in the bright light, the man held out his hand. "Let me help you." He led her to a drinks table—bottles, glasses, wine in a cooler, plus a bottle of vodka, and a tub of beer on ice.

"Water would be lovely," she stammered. She studied him as he poured her a glass. His body showed not an ounce of extra flesh, long and lean like a long-distance biker, or a professional tennis player she'd met while covering the US Open. It was hard to guess his age; sun-bleached, almost white curly hair with creases around his eyes hinted that he might be older than his fit body suggested, maybe in his late 50s. He had an iron jaw and teeth as white as his pristine trousers and short-sleeved polo shirt. Something about that affable smile combined with his hard jaw put her on edge.

He handed her the tall tumbler filled with ice and water. "You seem interested in our little nest," he said after she'd sipped. "Let me show you around."

He took her arm and guided her into a room filled with radios, three televisions, a row of computers, two large screens and several microphones. A board with dials and other strange instruments lined one side of the room. Floor-to-ceiling windows made up the far wall with white leather couches arranged in front of them. A long table, set for four, sat in the middle of the room.

His fingers pressed hard on her upper arm, but his voice remained calm and quiet. She dared not flinch, though the pressure of his fingers hurt. Nora couldn't relax. Her protector was too handsome, too smooth, and his grip on her arm too strong.

"We have guests coming for lunch," he said. "Would you join us? It's easy to set another place."

She choked back her concerns, trying to sound normal. "No, no. I have to be getting back to the lodge. My husband will worry if I'm not there."

As she squeaked out her response, the sound of a helicopter reverberated. The man led her to a window at the end of the room. A copter with a bright-green logo stamped on its side, *EnerGy Inc.,* landed on the second barge, stopping neatly at one of the painted lines. Two men climbed out and walked to a ramp between the two barges. One of the men was tall, muscled yet slim, with dark, slicked-down black hair, deep-black eyebrows and an equally deep-black mustache. *Movie star handsome. The kind of man who plays the villain in Grade B westerns.* The second man, walking slightly behind, was bald and heavily built.

Her host steered them back outside to meet the newcomers. "Who's this?" the mustachioed man asked.

"A thirsty hiker who stumbled onto our little hideaway. I've invited her to lunch, but I can't introduce you, as I haven't yet asked her name. Unfortunately, Jasmine got overexcited and took her camera and film." He smiled at Nora and finally let go of her arm, leaving dents in her flesh where he had pressed with his strong fingers. "I apologize for such poor hospitality."

Nora wanted to rub the spot where he'd gripped her but gulped water instead. Her host stepped to the side, pulling the mustachioed man with him. A flurry of whispers ensued. She could catch only a few phrases: "Don't…know nothing…danger." Mr. Mustache slapped his thigh, then swatted the host's hand off his arm.

The host grinned. "That's more like it, Harry. Come join us for a drink."

Nora's reporter curiosity throbbed, but her gut told her this could be a moment for escape. She broke into the conversation. "It's very kind of you to offer lunch. I'm grateful for the water, but I need to leave. My husband must be frantic with worry, not knowing where I am." That was true, she realized, as the words slipped out of her mouth. Joe would be worried and maybe angry as well. He did not like to be kept waiting by anybody, least of all his wife.

The host smiled. "In that case, John, here"—he pointed to the bald man—"will fly you back. It won't take a minute. Before you go, here's your camera. I'm sorry about your lost film.

Nora, grateful for the return of Joe's camera, still protested the transportation to no avail. Once again, her host took her arm. His hard grasp made her wince. He led her across to the upper barge. "No problem at all. The blades are warmed up and spinning. Hop in, lady."

The firm grip on her arm changed to a rude two-handed boost under her bottom into the helicopter. The pilot buckled her in, then settled into the pilot's seat. She was lifted up and over the channel. In what seemed like mere seconds later, the copter landed on a platform near the lodge. She climbed out on shaky legs, and the copter lifted off and was gone while she tried to yell *thank you* over the noise.

She found Joe pacing furiously in their cabin. "Where have you been? I searched the dining room, the picnic area and the little store. I was about to call out the boaters to search the waters."

"Joe, you have to hear what happened. I—"

"There's no time to talk now. If we don't leave immediately, we won't reach home before dark. You know as well as I do, it's dangerous to drive a boat without lights at night." He stalked out of the cabin with his overnight bag, leaving her to pack hastily and follow after him.

The ongoing *bleep-bleep* of the machine by Joe's bed pulled Nora from her reminiscences. A realization struck her, like the clarity that comes when you put egg white and shells into broth to settle the particles. All her life she'd been trying to merge her mother's feeling and her father's facts to tell some more-solid truth. *Or has it all along been the little girl trying to please everybody? Maybe that higher truth is a pathetic fiction. Now I need facts, hard evidence about a real story, and I don't know where to turn.*

She stared at Joe's face, so pale and stretched and unreal-looking. She didn't remember pushing him overboard or bashing his head. She had tried to minimize it when talking with Constable Mackey, but she had been angry. *I wasn't going to tell him about our fight. I guess I still haven't done that.* Seeing the mess on the floor of the cabin had reminded her how angry she'd been. So angry, she had thought of asking Joe to take her to the airport. She wanted him to see how it felt to be left alone. *I was furious because Joe had been away fishing with friends. No, I guess I'm really angry because I've been retired—face it, Nora, fired—from our business, the business we've run together for thirty years. I suppose I thought I was indispensable. When we used to come up near here for a break, for two or sometimes three weeks, I could justify playing with the kids or reading. But now I've been doing nothing that matters at home, so coming here was a vacation from my permanent vacation.*

She tapped the arm of her chair in time with the rhythm of Joe's monitor. Perhaps she could find some truth by reviewing her activities in the week Joe was away. His absence, after all, was a motivator for her rage.

She let her head loll against the chair back and closed her eyes.

Chapter Ten

July 24-August 1, 1998

Joe helped plan for his departure. He insisted on loading up the larder in case the weather was too rough for their open fourteen-foot skiff. He tried to make her comfortable with their ship-to-shore radio, insisting she not use Channel 16 for unimportant calls, but leave Channel 12, the channel used by friends, fishermen and tugboat captains for conversations, open all the time in case he needed her. *Needs me. Fat chance. Needs me so much he goes off on an adventure without me on our vacation together.* She hated listening to all the boat chatter, mostly about fish caught or not caught in places unknown to her. The first thing she did after he left was turn off the damn radio.

At first, she'd started knitting a sweater. She enjoyed knitting. When she was young, she and her mother made socks, scarves, even a sweater or two. But the wool she found in a Grant's Landing store cost more than a beautiful, handmade sweater in the local tourist shop. She knew this project was a minus, economically and artistically.

Outdoors was better, where she could ramble alone. She studied the grass around the cabin. It had shriveled and browned with lack of rain. The few herbs she planted soaked up her daily watering. She recognized the surrounding signs of serious drought, discovered by her preparations for many McKeever and McKeever news stories.

She'd learned to time her life by the tides. Swims before the tide ebbed were the best, the water warmed by the sun. She preferred beachcombing after the ebb when more beach was uncovered. She loved the first days of exploring, turning over rocks to see little rock crabs scurry sideways from sight. She delighted in searching for the five-armed starfish, deep purple like the last light of day or wild fuchsia like coneflowers in a prairie, or large circles, flat orange stars with twelve to fifteen arms. Once, she found a helpless clam in a star's five-armed grasp, the tubelike feet pushing the large, hard-shelled clam toward the small mouth at the star's core. She wondered how the starfish pushed a big, hard clam into its small orifice. She skirted the big orange jellyfish, not even liking to poke them with a stick as kids do. Back in the cabin, she looked up starfish in her field guide and read that a starfish can extend its stomach outside its own body into the clam shell, eat the goodies inside, and leave an empty shell behind. She lifted several starfish after that, hoping she would see the process in action, but that never happened.

She watched the red-beaked oystercatchers chattering among themselves as they patrolled the wave edges for choice tidbits. On evening walks, she came upon them settled in quiet waters, still murmuring in a clutch like mothers at a playground watching their children. Steep cliffs and boggy high bushes blocked her from exploring beyond the bay's rim, but her small sea world opened an ever-changing window to another life, low tide providing feasts for birds and beasts, high tide bringing renewal with fresh food and water.

Two days down. Interested as she was with all this, the days and nights alone remained long. She painted a few ugly pictures, but she knew she needed a bigger project. She swam before the outgoing tide, twice around the boat buoy or maybe three times, then back to the cabin for reading or supper. It was enough for the first days, but then began to pall.

She tried studying a history of the coast, but their library at the cabin was inadequate for research. She didn't even understand the boat traffic. Sometimes a tow, pulling two or three barges laden with wood chips, ran north to south toward Grant's Landing. At other times, similar tows pulled chip-filled barges south to north. That made no sense. Frustrated with her ignorance of the area, she decided that on the first clear day, she'd brave the distance to Grant's Landing for new reading material.

Most days, the exhaust from the stacks of Grant's Mill floated white mist into a picture-book sky, yet those same stacks could belch sulfur smells and eye-watering fumes. Nora's news nose told her there were stories here. Facing days more of boredom, what better pastime could she have than to probe the real life of this vacation playground?

The next day was clear, and she packed up for town. Dressed in casual tourist clothes, she rowed out to her skiff with a small duffle bag, planning to stay overnight in some motel while she explored. She'd brought along her wallet and her journalist's badge, her professional notebook, her laptop. The day was picture perfect, the water calm. Old energies and curiosity stirred.

She reached Grant's Landing without trouble, docked the skiff, and spent a short while checking in at the first halfway-decent-looking motel she found. Taking her laptop to the public library, she sat for hours examining governmental environment reports and various Mill Public Relations messages. The chemistry posed a confusing challenge. In the old days, she would have gone to a friendly university professor who could be trusted to explain it to her in lay terms. One mill bragged that new chemical substitutes had been discovered for chlorine bleach, yet the chemicals listed looked to Nora like letters for chlorine. She had a lot to learn.

She typed a formal request for an interview with the manager of the Grant's Landing paper mill, using jargon from the past. *With outlets in 156 stations across the United States, the independent firm of McKeever and McKeever wishes to explore the history of the Grant's Landing Pulp and Paper Mill. With decline in demand for newsprint equaling the decline in new building in the United States, how do lumber and paper mills adjust to economic pressures? We would like to demonstrate the innovations you have made to manage your success.*

She listed several in-depth studies made by McKeever and McKeever of other industries. Pulling out all the stops, she ended the letter with her request for an interview. *I am visiting Grant's Landing for a brief stay. It is my hope that you will be able to meet with me July 28th or 29th, in preparation for a profile of your work and achievements. As I have no local phone number, I will call in the morning in the hope of making an appointment.*

She signed the letter with a flourish and inserted her card in the business envelope.

After delivering the envelope to the mill's gate

attendant, she drove around Grant's Landing to lay the groundwork for her interview by learning more of the town's environment. Garden borders with neat rows of plants, more formal than most in the U.S., greeted her on every street. Yet many of the houses had peeling paint in good neighborhoods and bad. Back on the main drag, she spotted a crowd gathered around a small makeshift platform plus speakers with bullhorns. Tables had been set up along the sidewalk. She parked her car, got out, and walked over to listen.

A speaker with a bullhorn was addressing the crowd. "Can't breathe? Does your tap water smell? Want clean air and clean water? Join us."

Nora's gaze shifted to a woman, not fat, square from feet to shoulders. With rubber-soled, leather-topped garden boots like Nora's at home, wearing spotless canvas trousers and a multi-pocketed smock, she stood at the edge of the platform looking at a clipboard, the edge of a plaid notebook sticking out of one large pocket and a trowel in another. Nora searched her brain for why the notetaker looked familiar until the woman spoke. In a strong, gravelly voice, she named the jobs that needed volunteers. Her accent, perhaps a Scottish lilt, took Nora back to a garden stand she and Joe discovered on their first day in Grant's Landing. She recognized the notebook and the aura of authority that had made the vegetable purchase memorable.

"Tomatoes ripened in an Okanagan field; peaches from an Okanagan orchard," the woman had said. "No pesticides. Picked by local farmers. Order now for next week." Nora had asked to taste a peach. With a rapid movement, the woman had pulled a long, sharp knife—more cleaver than paring knife—from her ample pockets, cut off a slice and held the slice out on the tip of the sword-like blade. Nora carefully eased the slice off and popped it into her mouth. Sweet juice sluiced down her chin. Yes, this was the best peach ever. Nora had ordered a half dozen along with tomatoes and fresh green beans. All had been as perfect as the peach.

Having placed the notetaker, Nora listened with gathering interest to her commentary. "How many friends and neighbors now have mysterious ailments? How do you feel in the mornings? Do you wake up tired?" The woman waved her pen in the air. "The sludge the mill gives Grant's Landing parks is polluted. When they offer it to you as examples of the mill's generosity, don't accept it. That sludge poisons our land. The poison moves up the food chain into our bodies. And that's not all. When the Grant's Landing mill burns its hog fuel made of sea-soaked wood, the carbon and the salt combine to make dioxin. All that coats our lungs, making them stiff and heavy."

The crowd was rapt, silent, as the woman went on. "Mills are using thousands upon thousands of gallons of our precious fresh water every hour of every day. They tell us they can't use less, as it would make heavier concentration of chemicals in the effluent. Hear that? The mills complain that closed water systems cost money. Weigh those costs.

"But you all know me, Mabel Joiner, and my spiel. You don't want to listen to a lecture from me. Make your own decisions. The future of Grant's Landing depends on all of us working together. Join us. Be a Sludge Buster. Dear volunteers, we thank you." She stepped down with a quick jump, belying her gray hairs and girth.

Nora walked on, reading hand-painted posters. One

with a portrait of a bicycle said, *Ride for the Forests, July 30, Sign Here*. There were pamphlets on the tables. Idly, she picked one up and stuck it in her purse.

Her eye caught a three-piece painting, a triptych, she would have called it in art class many years ago. The first panel was everything she wanted in her own paintings: a watercolor with shaded washes for the sky, a pink golden glow as the rising sun cleared the mountains, a cliff on the right, a waterfall plunging through a crevasse. The water's edge led to a hill covered with fir, cedar and pine trees, each with its distinctive bark, cedar with its strips ready for peeling, the pine's bark curled like fish scales and on the hilltop, a red-splotched madrone tree. The sea, pictured like a botanical cut with oysters at the mid waterline, clams a bit deeper, and snapper, salmon and even a hated dogfish next to a crab pot, the thief ready for action.

The middle panel held the same rock cliff but with the trees needleless and leafless, bare branches here and there as if peeled, the red of the madrone toned down to a dull mauve. Small dots throughout the water, perhaps the remains of organic life floating like flotsam. The final panel's water level was green-black and shiny with slime. The pink-gold glow of dawn had been replaced by a thick orange streak across the sky. No gulls dipping their wings in giddy flight. Tree branches littered the ground. Dead birds lay on the rocky beach. No salmon to be seen, not even a dogfish. Nora shivered. The artist's mastery had hit her harder than reading pamphlets.

She trudged down the street and turned at random into a laundromat, hoping to lift her spirits with sights of ordinary activity. Two guys came in with huge duffles, talking of pulling near-empty prawn pots. A few minutes later, a frazzled-looking teen came in, along with a chocolate-smeared toddler. Sister or child? The teen lugged three pillowcases stuffed with baby clothes, crib sheets, ragged bath towels and a few pairs of jeans. The toddler sat on the floor fondling a stuffed teddy bear. After filling two machines and plunking in her "loonies," Canadian dollar coins, the young woman pulled out a dog-eared magazine with a picture of a half-naked couple kissing on its cover. The toddler threw her bear at the older girl. "I wanna go." The girl didn't look up. Nora dangled her car keys at the little one to distract her. "I wanna go."

The older girl turned to Nora. "Is she botherin' you?"

"No, I thought I could make her laugh."

"Forget it. I told Ma not to send her with me."

"Do you live in Grant's Landing?"

"Why do you ask?'

"I'm new in town and exploring."

"I'm going for Ma." She grabbed the toddler and left the laundromat.

Shortly afterward, an angry woman stalked in with the toddler under her arm. "You, lady, are you some kind of government snoop? You got no business questioning my kids."

Taken aback, Nora stood. "I'm a tourist, here from the States. I thought I could keep the baby distracted with my keys."

"Where's your laundry? Janie didn't see any."

"I didn't bring wash."

"Then why ya here?"

"I wanted to talk to folks about living in Grant's Landing. My husband and I are planning to move here."

She hadn't thought of that before, but she found she liked the idea.

The woman pursed her lips. "Looks to me like you should go to one of those island resorts for your information. Now, get out of here before I call the RCMP to report harassment."

Dispirited, Nora wandered for another block, then went into a local bar. Conversations roared all around her. She ordered a beer and held a magazine as if reading, in order to eavesdrop without drawing attention to herself.

One rowdy bunch of patrons pounded beer mugs on their table. Nora raised her eyes above the magazine's rim and watched as one man climbed onto his chair. He wore dirty, torn jeans and a shirt that said, *Don't Let the Bastards Grind You Down.* "We'll not let those do-gooders stir up trouble. Let's storm those protest meetings. They need to be put down by force."

His companions waved him down, amid laughter and scattered comments. The man stumbled from his chair and staggered out the door, while the group ordered another round of beers.

Discouraged, Nora left the bar without bothering to finish her drink. She went to the local museum, bought a book on the old days in Grant's Landing and headed back to her motel, a dreary but clean spot on the main drag.

She spent the next few hours reading oral settler histories from the 1930s and '40s. Back then, men were cutting giant trees with axes and hand cross-saws, using teams of horses to pull the fallen giants to water chutes. Grit, poverty, rhapsodic descriptions of community dances, rowing across the Strait to neighboring islands, fishing and hunting for food and fun filled the pages along with fatal accidents and tragedy. Nora ached with empathy for this raw physical life and the tough folk who had settled here.

The next morning, she called Grant's Mill at eight-thirty. She netted an appointment with the manager, Mr. Gallagher, at ten. She dressed carefully for her interview, not in the tourist clothes of yesterday, but in her most professional business suit with a colorful scarf at her throat.

Gallagher's assistant, a standout blond beauty in a wraparound dress met Nora at the factory gate. "My name is Gloria Hobart. I'll lead you to Mr. Gallagher's office." Her outfit showed off full breasts and accentuated her small waist. Her hair was swept back from her forehead but hung loose so it swung in the breeze. Nora decided Ms. Hobart could have been entering the Santa Barbara Golf and Tennis Club for lunch with its president.

Mr. Gallagher's office overlooked the bay's expanse, bright-blue water dotted with sailboats leaning into the wind, white clouds scudding across the sky. Gallagher rose from his large business-like desk to greet her as she entered. He was dressed casually in slacks with an open shirt, loafers with tassels, and a curious ring on a chain around his neck. Nora noted that the desk held not one visible paper, nor a telephone.

He led her to the office centerpiece, a table made of one piece of wood fourteen feet wide and four inches thick, its rim curved like its mother tree. It must have been a treasured specimen, a slice from an old growth cutting. Nora gasped on seeing it.

"You have a good eye," Gallagher said. "I inherited that table with this office, a symbol of the glories of

British Columbia. If ever a leader of this company were to lose interest in its produce of lumber and paper, this table would restore his commitment."

He settled them at the table, the light from the bay bouncing on the water glasses delivered by Miss Hobart. Nora began the interview, and he responded easily to questions about mill policies and the company's plans to reduce emissions in air and water.

At one point, he caught Nora looking at the ring on the chain around his neck. He tapped it with his right index finger. "You've noticed."

"My husband has a ring somewhat like that. He was given it for his prowess on the football field. He never takes it off," she lied. Joe's knuckles had broadened with age. His ring stayed in his bureau drawer.

"I used to wear my ring night and day. Then my hand got caught in a log chain." He laid his left hand on the table. Two fingers had been cut off at the first knuckle. "Fortunately, the man who released my hand knew how much that ring meant to me. He picked it off the floor from the remains of my bloody fingers."

His voice hardened. "One thing you must know for your story. Ours is a dangerous profession. Only real men survive it." He waved his gnarled hand for emphasis. "People are squeamish about safety. We are asked constantly to build shields, create barriers, design new hard hats. We don't top trees as my father did in the '40s. He climbed on springboards, planks notched into the trunks like steps, up the tree with a hand saw until he was a speck in the sky. But it's hard work that demands sacrifices. Pain to create beauty, to create product. Men, real men, to fill jobs."

He stroked the table with his good hand. "Years ago,

I interviewed individual mill workers. I don't do that anymore. At some point, I'd be sure to wave my crushed fingers in the prospective worker's face. 'This job requires courage,' I'd say. I'd hire the men who came through that interview without blanching."

Nora longed to take out her tape recorder but dared not interrupt this monologue.

"I no longer interview individuals, but I do go to trainings. I make my point then, the same way. It gets their attention." He laughed, then stood. "Come with me. The regular tour doesn't go up to the log selection area because of its dangers. Your film will have to show this."

He led Nora to an elevator that carried them up to a high platform above the ground and car park, overlooking a series of gutter-like alleys. Chains pulled logs, peeled of their bark, one by one along each alley. Gallagher gave running commentary. "Cameras inspect each log. The ones without disfiguring knots or soft places are guided into the planer, the others go to the chipper."

Nora could see the alleys, running in curving patterns like toll-road interchanges over vast open space with buildings or water below. Gallagher rested his hand heavily too low on her lower back. Nora felt the little finger a bit below her waist with the forefinger on the top of her buttock. She wanted to jerk away from him, but the platform was narrow, her fear of falling greater than her fear of the pressure of his hand.

He leaned close to speak in her ear, his wet mouth touching her ear lobe. "We have jokes about this process. Misbehave up here and you go to the chipper."

Determined not to react, Nora watched as a log was guided from the planer alley to the far right. She listened to the growl of metal teeth slicing a once-proud tree, a high popping and groan as the tree disappeared into the maw. The grader sent another log to the chipper. Nora smelled a spicy cedar scent and thought she felt dust from the tree's remains on her eyelids. Her scarf, blown by a gust of wind, wrapped around her throat, suffocating her, or was she imagining her fall into the mound of chips slowly swallowing its new victim?

Back in Gallagher's office, Nora tried to regain her professional demeanor. Certain he had noticed her fear, she sipped at the water she had abandoned for the tour. It sparkled in the light bouncing from the harbor below, ice still clinking in the glass. She had not been up on the platform for the eternity it had seemed.

As if sensing his new power over her, Gallagher's monologue became more intimate. "There were three children before my grandfather went off to the war. That was World War I, mind you. My grandmom had to feed them and make do for four long years. She became an ace shot, wielding my grandfather's old shotgun like a toy. He came home to create three more kids. Bang, bang, bang, just like that, my pa, the eldest of the second bunch. The story goes that one day, baby Pa was lying naked in the yard, kicking his heels and enjoying a warm spring morning when my grandmom spotted a cougar crouching in the tree beyond the edge of the yard. She picked up her husband's gun, kept nearby, and shot that cougar right through one eye. Cooked it for dinner, mind you, but my pa was too young to know for sure. He used that cougar story as a part of his mantra. 'I was a man from the start, saved from the cougar's mouth. You have to be a man to survive this world.'

"He raised us up to be hard. If we wanted to go to

Campbell River across the Strait, we rowed there. If we wanted fish for dinner, we went out to catch them. If we wanted duck or bear meat, we shot it. Pa was eight when he shot his first bear. The bear cub and he were both berrying, and luckily for Pa, the momma bear was far enough away that he had time to reload before she came roaring into the berry patch. You better believe he told that story until we shot our own bears. Most often, he told it again anyway.

"But you don't need to hear about my past. You have a question you haven't asked. You all do eventually, you Statesiders. Some ease into it. Others come out straight with anger and superiority." His eyes narrowed, and a sneer colored his mimicking voice. "'Tell me, Mr. Gallagher, the steam that comes out of your stacks. Does the government test your emissions?'" He took a breath and continued in a high singsong, "'Tell me, Mr. Gallagher, what do you do for public health?'"

He leaned back in his chair and slammed his gnarled hand on the table. "I'll tell you about public health. This mill is the health of Grant's Landing. Without this operation, there would be no restaurants—well, maybe a few expensive tourist places down on the wharf, but no real places for workers to eat. They'd be out of business. The hardware and the Supermart, maybe even the liquor stores, would close, though the liquor would be the last to go. Schoolteachers would walk the streets. Dress shops and bookshops, all with bars over the windows, closed. This mill is the engine of the community. I told you, I'm tough on discipline. The workers have to follow my rules. They know that if they don't, I'll fire them, and that means their kids will starve. They can't go out with a gun and shoot a brace of ducks the way my grandmom used to do. They might catch a few fish, sneak some gull eggs from a nest, but flour, sugar, cooking oil? Nada, zilch, nothin'."

He lowered his voice. "I'll give you our latest reports. We do what the government requires. Every year, the rules get tougher, but we keep up. It's basically self-regulation. Inspectors don't need to come around. Once in a while, a new government relaxes a few clauses and we relax with them, but you'll see, we do what we must."

He opened a desk drawer and punched a button. Seconds later, Miss Hobart appeared. "Give Ms. McGruver the latest mill newsletter and the B.C. government's Ministry of Environment Report on Pulp and Paper Mill Effluent. Ms. McGruver will need to explain to her audience that our plant is environmentally sound." He stood. Clearly the interview was over.

Nora thanked him for his time, smiling to herself about his scramble of her name. She had the presence of mind to ask Miss Hobart for her card, thanked her for the volumes of paper that were pressed into her hand and walked out with as much dignity as she could muster.

Drained and weary, Nora trudged back to her car. She felt as if she'd been dragged by her hair through the streets of Grant's Landing. She knew there was a story here, but for the moment, digging it out wearied her.

Back at the cabin, she marked another day off of the calendar. Joe would be home in three days. She went for an evening swim to wash away the hostility she had encountered. The woman in the laundromat, Mr. Gallagher, the men in the bar, all belied the smiling polite Canadians she had met everywhere else. There was a secret burden here, something that hated her tourist know-nothing questions. She swam twice around the buoy, enlivened by the cold of the water, the sight of the red-beaked oyster catchers inspecting the water's edge, the eagle that swooped over her head. This was why she and Joe had come here.

Home, she put a Mozart concerto on the player, poured a stiff vodka and took it onto the deck. With her book on the old lumbering days and her drink, she watched the breeze stir the water into a swirling fabric box of patterns: Italian flame stitches here, Japanese silken kimono clouds or pleated petticoat flounces there, until a royal purple cloak descended on the view and the mosquitoes came out for their nightly feast. As she went into the cabin, a loon called. She copied its cry with a lonely call of her own.

On the last day before Joe's return, she decided her historical research was useless. Time to take her painting more seriously. Feeling self-conscious, she'd brought art supplies with her on this trip. *Retirement means watercoloring,* she told herself. *That's what elderly ladies do between bridge games.*

She had painted the view from the cabin porch many days last week, but her renderings were sugary sweet. She'd tried slashing scarlet lines to outline the mountains in a more robust manner, but the slashes looked like jagged sores. They added no meaning, no truth. There was too much beauty here for the beginning artist. As with the news, perhaps it would be easier to paint ugliness than the delicate, tender refrains of beauty, peace or awe. She would follow Monet's lead. She would paint the steam of the mill, instead of his steam in a railroad station.

She exulted in her project. The boat trip would take

her to the pulp mill. There, she could work on the jagged lines of the conveyor pipes, the various shapes of the silos, warehouses and trailers.

Nora prepared. She covered her face with sun goop, chose a long-sleeved work shirt from Joe's shelf, put on her floppy white sun hat, assembled her supplies for the day: from camera, to paints, to water for the paints, water for herself, and a sandwich. She felt adventurous and foolish, even childish in her detailed planning. *My trip to the North Pole*. She knew she was playing games, thinking up projects to keep herself going. She was supposed to be thrilled with retirement from McKeever and McKeever. In fact, it made her feel cut off, separated, disengaged even from Joe. How could he resent her help, push her out like this? She mustn't think about that. *Think watercolors.*

Still a bit frightened of running the boat, she carried the little rubber dinghy to the water's edge, put her bags and bottles in, then stepped in herself as carefully as possible. The small dinghy folded inward around her and she could feel the outline of the rocky beach under her bottom. By hunching with the oars, she made little crab-like motions into the calm water. One half-hearted wave and this whole enterprise would sink, but the calm prevailed.

Nora's rowing was as awkward as her ship launching. She had practiced starting and stopping the outboard with Joe barking orders. *Tighten the screws every time you go out. Slow the motor before you shift. Start it on the first or second pull, or it will flood. Never take your eyes off the water. You'll be in real trouble if you shear a pin. Don't. Do. Remember.* It all buzzed in her head. But she was going on her trip today, as she had gone to Grant's Landing.

The water was smooth as glass. Snug in her body-fitting dinghy, her eyes were almost at water level. She could see the intricate patterns, swirls and half circles, the Italian flame stitch she had seen the night before that turned into a tanned old lady's wrinkled skin with a little puff of wind. Nora was enchanted with her craft, her adventure, herself. She reached the skiff and climbed in. The outboard started with one pull. She picked up speed until the boat planed. She slowed, stopped, took photos of the mill, tried painting in her sketch pad. When that palled, she went home, swam around the buoy twice, fixed dinner and went to bed.

The next morning, she cleaned the cabin for Joe's return and prepared a welcome-home dinner. He seemed appreciative, relaxed, until she joked about his week's "escape." He got angry then, for no reason that made sense. "I have to fish with friends. You'll never understand about boats, fishing and real action. You live in your head, Nora. I can't do that all the time. You should've figured that out by now."

He got up abruptly and stalked out of the cabin, leaving her to wonder how their romantic vacation had gone so suddenly wrong.

Chapter Eleven

August 3-4, 1998

In the evening shift, the hospital corridors echoed only with the occasional swishing of a nurse making the rounds. Caroline, keeping her promise to Constable Mackey, took this shift to spare her staff. Nora sat quietly, comforted by Caroline's presence, her competent medical routine providing an air of confidence.

Nora thought about *My Week Alone*, the title she had given her adventure. What had she learned? She'd found hidden anger in Grant's Landing, perhaps different in kind but not in intensity from her own. She had lost her enthusiasm for useless hobbies, painting, knitting, even studying local history. And what about that strange experience on the barge off Bradley Island not long before Joe left? She thought of the happenings almost like short stories. Joe's anger was another one. He gave it importance with his illogical explanation for his week away. All that about needing real action, how she wouldn't understand. *Your fantasies are raving nonsense*, he'd said. She groaned. The memory hurt like a bleeding wound. Her whole life of fact-gathering for stories had been reduced to fantasies.

When Caroline stepped over to check a monitor, Nora whispered, "Are you married?"

"Yes, with two kids, though mine aren't as old as yours. One's three, the other five."

"Who minds them when you're here?"

"My husband. He's jobless now. Laid off from the mill, so it's easy."

"I went to the mill last week. Interviewed the manager. Tough man. Do you mind my asking why your husband was fired?"

"Tough guy is an understatement. Gallagher runs the mill like a prison warden."

"He waved his maimed hand in my face and said he didn't hire people who blanched when they saw his cut-off fingers."

Caroline shook her head. "Frank didn't blanch. He's worked at the mill since he was a kid. His brother and cousins too. Unlike me, they grew up with chainsaws, grinders, slicers, planers. They talk lumber like some people talk baseball. You know, 'Remember that old cedar devil tree. My back aches thinking about it.' Then there was the fire, or the story of the two town drunks wrestling on the high platform. Things like that. They can talk all day and night about such stories."

"What did Frank do wrong?"

"He sent Gallagher a work memo. Warned him about a possible leak. Warned him three times. I guess that was his mistake."

"Gallagher says he wants workers to follow safety measures."

"Doesn't feel that way to Frank." Caroline eyed another monitor, then stepped back and smoothed the thin hospital blanket over Joe's chest. "There are two factions at the mill. One group wants the mill to take advanced measures to fight pollution. Mills up and down the Sunshine Coast dump toxins into the air, water and onto the land. The other group scorns the go-green efforts. They say change will cost jobs. The enmity is fierce. Frank gets a lot of grief for being a leader of the Greens. Even now, men who are out of work swear and shake their fists at him. He gets notes in the mail. 'Are you watching your kids?' 'Better get a food taster.' That kind of crap."

Despite her numb exhaustion, Nora's instinct for story stirred. "That's terrible. What happened?"

Caroline settled into a chair, taking a rest for a change. "The government asks about water emissions, started with an explosion of chlorine dioxide back in '86. Nowadays, mills are supposed to self-regulate, keep records about water disposal. Frank spotted signs of leakage, stains around pipe joints and sent the memo. He figured someone would take care of it. A week went by and nothing happened. So, he wrote a second memo. Next day, Gallagher calls Frank into his office, says he sent a team to study the 'so-called leak,' and they saw nothing. 'That's not your section,' he tells Frank. 'Are you meddling in another department? You're a troublemaker and I don't want trouble.'

"Frank told Gallagher one of the fellows that works the water hose thought the pressure was down. They use a powerful water jet to debark the logs when they come in. Frank checked it out off-hours, because the guy asked him to. Gallagher says to him, 'You take care of your job, McDonough. I'll take care of mine. Now get back to work, or I'll dock your pay.'

"Frank let it go for a few days, then checked off-hours. Sure enough, the water stains around the holding tank had grown bigger than on his last check. This time,

Frank reported it to the safety inspector. The next day, Frank was on break at home. Gallagher called him to come into the mill. He had to hire Emma, she's a neighbor of ours, to watch the kids. Gallagher met him at the mill gate office, accused him of planning a union revolt, handed him his stuff that they'd cleared from his locker and told him he was fired. He also said he'd make Frank's 'insubordination' public, so he couldn't find work in any mill on the coast.

"Frank hates the guy. Also, he's afraid for his friends. They used to meet every few days. But Frank thinks he's being followed, so he sent word to stop meeting. He's fearful that Gallagher will fire them for knowing him. Frank's coiled like a bed spring waiting to snap."

Nora reached out and touched Caroline's hand. "I'm so sorry. Here you are, stuck in the hospital, unable to help. How did you meet Frank?"

"It's a small town. After I moved here for work, I bumped into him and his buddies all the time. Wasn't impressed. Frank was one of those easygoing guys, all the time joking around. My friends tried to match us up. But I saw this big hunk, a partying type, arranging picnics, kayaking parties, and clambakes on the beach.

"Then one day, he came to the hospital and very politely told me his sister was dying. Doctors gave her up years ago. He asked me to come see her for medical advice about her care. He sat me in the living room and ducked out. A couple of minutes later he pushed a wheelchair with this child-woman into the room as gently as any mother with a toddler. He talked to her in the same voice he uses talking to me, no baby coos. 'Katherine, this is the smart nurse I've been telling you about. Maybe she can help you.'

"He sat by her, holding her hand while I checked her pulse and felt her head for fever. She choked and drooled a little. He wiped her mouth, then pushed the chair in small motions back and forth, rocking her as he softly sang an old Irish ditty. When Katherine drifted off to sleep, he took her back to her room and closed her door halfway. He told me they left it open enough to hear, because she could gasp and choke anytime, day or night. He and his other sisters helped as best they could, but the worry and the hours were wearing their mom down. Him too, though Frank didn't say so. I could tell."

Caroline stood to check the monitor. She continued talking with her back to Nora. "I started visiting. Sometimes I could care for Katherine when Frank was at work. His mom is fragile as a moth caught in a box. She frets and flutters. She'd make special puddings to spoon into Katherine's mouth, but teared up whenever she was washing Katherine or brushing her hair. That wasn't good for either of them. Frank was such a gentle bloke, I fell in love. We married six months after Katherine died."

Caroline paused, took a breath, then swallowed. "Trouble is boiling up. Frank's not the only one who's been fired. The guys go out in their fishing boats at different hours when they can, meeting by arrangement on vacant beaches. Could I ask Frank to stop by and talk to you about your interview with Gallagher?"

"I'd like that. Ask him to come. Is breakfast too soon?"

Nora drove back to her motel when Caroline went home from her shift at 11 P.M. The next morning, early, both were at the hospital again, sitting by Joe's bed.

Frank arrived at 7:00, and Caroline waved him into Joe's room. Frank spoke before Caroline could introduce them. "Caroline told me about your husband. I'm so sorry. Waiting, worrying takes its toll on a person. We know about that."

Nora managed a quiet thank-you. Caroline showed them the back door to Joe's room with stairs down to the hospital's rear lot. "You two can talk on the steps for quiet and privacy."

They ducked out of the room, Nora following Frank, and halted partway down the stairwell. Half uneasy and half invigorated by the clandestine feel of it all, Nora gave a full report of her meeting with the mill manager. Frank laughed when she reported Gallagher's use of his mangled hand.

"So, he even gives strangers the treatment, does he? If he hadn't had that accident, he might have had to slice off his fingers himself. It worked on all of us once. These days, we debrief new hires with the question, 'Did you get the hand?' Wonder if he flaunts it at his wife when she burns the toast. Anyway, the mill doesn't operate at full tilt now. The toughs fighting our efforts for change have a point. They say our requests would make paper prices go up. The market won't pay more. Mills will close.

"With me it's personal. I'm certain mill pollution killed my sister, Katherine, and will eventually kill the rest of us. But there's no proof. Other illnesses crop up all over the area. Skin rashes, throat problems, not to mention shrimp dying and fish not spawning. We fishermen would like to see fewer salmon-eating seals around here, but we don't like finding dead ones on the beaches."

Nora spoke up. "I don't know if you know, but Joe and I came to Grant's Landing in 1986, back when the chlorine exploded. We did a story that ran in the States. The coverage sank pretty fast. U.S. mill owners didn't like the subject, and newspapers didn't seem to want questions about their newsprint sources. Do you Greens have a solution?"

He shrugged. "Solution may be a strong word. We've suggested improvements. Mills use tons of water. Creating a closed loop where water is cleaned and reused is expensive. But released water is dirty, even when chlorine use is limited, and it heats water temperatures, which is bad for prawns and salmon. We want a closed loop for water usage and no chlorine in the system at all."

"I went to a street rally. Mabel...something with a J., the garden-booth woman, she said some of the same things," Nora said. "I've thought about my interview. Could it be that Mr. Gallagher is a very insecure man?"

"Yeah, well. He's made me pretty insecure, too. I hate putting all the load on Caroline. Her sense of mission is special. She's trained to save lives. I just fell trees, wield a chainsaw, haul nets, or do a little welding at the mill. Being with her gives me a piece of her purpose, her dignity."

"She says the same about you. She fell for your sense of community and family. Sounds like a match."

He smiled at her. "Thanks for that. I've got to go. I asked Mom to look after the kids."

After Frank left, Nora called Charlie and Nell, even though she had nothing new to report. She wanted to hear their voices. It seemed strange that the gloomy talk with Frank made her more hopeful. Maybe it was only the idea that people could share worries, get by. That new sense of hope enabled her to leave the hospital for exercise, the first time since the accident, if only for an hour or so. She took a walk along Main Street, poked around the harbor, finding boats from all over the coast, Vancouver, Seattle, San Francisco, Port Hardy, one from Cabo san Lucas and another from Puerto Vallarta. *And I thought Grant's Landing was nowhere. It's part of the world.*

She bought a crab sandwich and walked back to the hospital somewhat refreshed to sit in Joe's room. Caroline was off duty, but a pretty dark-haired young woman named Angelica had taken her place. The other nurses called her Angel. Repeatedly, Nora jumped up to ask Angelica if she'd seen changes on Joe's monitor. Each time, Angelica went to the machine, studied the chart and shook her head, then settled in her chair again.

Nora had just finished her sandwich when she saw Joe's hand move. Once more, she leapt from her seat. "Did you see that?" she whispered.

"See what?" Angelica moved to Nora's side.

"His hand. It moved. I'm sure of it, Angel."

Angelica stared at the heart-rate monitor. It bleeped as before, its arc pulsing steadily through its rhythmic hills and vales. "I'm sorry, Mrs. McKeever, I don't see anything different. Maybe, when I adjusted the drip, you know." Her voice faded. In her too-calm tone, Nora could hear Angel's dismissal of Nora's repeated worries.

Nora sank down. Defeat had returned. She ached with weariness. Her feet were swollen, every muscle in them screaming for release. The monitor sounded through the silence. *Bleep, bleep.* She crossed and uncrossed her knees, fidgeted with her watch strap, rolled her shoulders.

Angelica broke the silence. "Can you go lie down, Mrs. McKeever? Or take a walk? I'll be having to take care of you, too, if you don't take a break."

"You're right. I'm not helping Joe, and I'm not helping you. I'll run up to the cabin and pick up a few things. I might be back before your shift is over."

The sudden resolve to *do something* put a spring in Nora's step. She didn't feel expert driving the boat, but she'd run it all the way down from the cabin to the mill the last day before Joe's return from his fishing trip. It had been sitting at the dock since Joe's accident. *Besides, from now on...* She shuddered and let the thought float away.

A short while later, standing at the dock, she untied the line before getting in and starting the motor. Like a novice, she went through her memorized instructions. *Pull.* Nothing happened. She waited a minute. Pumped the bulb for the second time. Pulled. The motor turned over and died. She turned off the choke and tried again. On the third pull, the motor chugged. She hastily turned the handle from high acceleration to slow. Cautiously, she pressed the gear into reverse. The skiff hurtled backwards past the end of the dock. She said a silent prayer and turned from reverse to neutral to forward. The boat lurched. She'd revved the motor by mistake, but she was moving in the right direction.

Out beyond the breakwater, her stomach clutched as she bumped over wakes. She dodged a shrimp pot buoy too hard and slipped into a circle, the skiff tipping onto its side until she slowed the motor. The boat lost speed as it came down from its plane. *So, we go slowly,* she thought, *but we're going. That's something.*

By the time she saw the cabin, she'd fooled herself

into imagining she could handle the boat, but she rammed their buoy instead of coasting up to it slowly as Joe did. She had crawled into the dinghy before remembering to lift the motor out of the salt water. *Never mind, I won't be but a minute.* With the jerky curves of a novice rower, she paddled to the beach. As she pulled the dinghy up above the tide line, she gloated over her exploit. *You wait, Joe. My boat skills will surprise you for sure when you're well.*

She spotted a boat, much like theirs, anchored at the edge of the bay. *Must be fishermen hoping for salmon. Joe never fished there. Funny, that's a first.*

Nora puffed up the hill to the cabin. The door was open. Wary, she stepped cautiously inside. Chaos met her gaze. The bookshelf had been emptied, clothes pulled off hooks, even blankets pulled out of their plastic sacks. A teapot lay shattered on the floor, the cookie jar turned upside down with broken cookies all over the counter.

The back door, too, stood open. Still stunned, she walked over automatically to close it. *No mice allowed.* A tarp came flying out of the shed a few feet away. Spurred by sudden fury, she stalked toward this fresh destruction. She suspected a search by the RCMP and prepared to yell. Mounties weren't supposed to behave like this, even with criminal suspects.

A man wearing a red-checked lumber jacket stepped out of the shed. This was no uniformed Mountie. Another man joined him, carrying her and Joe's carefully packed tent bag. Neither man had spotted her. The intruders ripped the bag open with a knife, shaking out the tent, sleeping bags and pillows in ferocious gestures. Nora's fury turned to fright. She backed into the cabin and out through the front door, then turned and ran toward her boat.

She could hear them yelling at her or at each other. She didn't know. She did know she could never haul the dinghy down to the water, row out, get into her boat and pull away. Instead, she ran down the beach, stumbling from boulder to boulder. Sometimes her foot landed on a roller, and she came close to falling. Sharp oyster shells, clinging to rocks, cut her ankles. A *ping* of something metal hit a near rock. A bullet? Oh God, they were armed, and they'd seen her fleeing. Gasping for breath, she rounded a mound with a few alders and high grass growing on it. For now, she'd pulled out of their line of sight.

Lovely silence followed. Nora kept on going, crawling into a patch of ferns and salal that clung to the rocky shore. A rustling noise and a sudden movement on the stones directly in front of her made her jump back. A tiny, wet mink scurried up the rocks from the water. It had not seen or smelled Nora. She watched it for a few moments, willing her heart to slow. *If I stay stock-still, maybe they won't find me.*

The mink jumped from rock to rock. It turned this way and that, then loped off once more to the water's edge. With a jerk, it grabbed something from between the stones. There was a moment's flapping, then silence. The little fellow skipped forward. This time when it jerked to a stop, she saw a crab larger than the mink's head in its mouth.

The mink came galloping back toward Nora, lifting the crab proudly in the air. Nora eased slightly upward to see more clearly, but the motion betrayed her. The mink hissed with panic as it accelerated its dash. Nora pulled herself back into the salal. She regretted the movement that made the crab fisher as frightened as she was now. *We're both on the run, little guy.*

Nora sensed the vibrations of steady movement on the rocks. A stone beach has its own music. The life that goes on under the rocks creates a chorus of small half tones, shells opening, the squirts of clams emptying their siphons, the flap of the small eel-like fingerlings, the slight motion of a stone as a starfish curls itself over a clam lunch. All these reassuring noises of life halt with a footstep. The whole beach waits, as Nora waited, still crouched in the salal, anticipating danger.

The footsteps were slow and quiet. A deep voice barked out, "We've got you, la-aa-dy. The tide's rising. There's only cliff above you at full tide. We may not see you now, but we'll see you floating, cold and stiff, when the tide comes in."

Cliffs rose above her, too steep to climb. Staring up at them, it seemed to Nora that they leaned out and over her, as if the shelf had been carved out by the sea. Looking around, she saw the incoming tide creeping closer. How stupid she'd been to run down the beach. Now she had two choices. She could go back straight to the intruders who'd shot at her, or she could keep on as fast as possible and pray to find a break in the cliff.

Chapter Twelve

The cliff stretched for a distance equivalent to maybe six or seven city blocks before reaching the point. She couldn't remember what was beyond it. The water could be 55 to 65 degrees Fahrenheit, even in midsummer. Cold now, she recoiled from the thought of submerging herself in icy water. Nora began writing a script—her way of thinking herself out of jams big and small. *Take off your shoes, tie them together and hang them off your neck the way the kids did last summer. If you do find a beach around the corner, you'll never walk any distance without shoes on the sharp oyster shells strewn all over. Get rid of those long pants and shirt, too. They'll weigh you down. Headline: "Burial at sea without honors. Foolish woman drowned by her own clothing."*

Stripped to her underthings, shoes bumping her collarbone, she held her breath and plunged into the cold. Anything was better than standing there freezing to death. She nudged herself further out into the water, swimming as strongly as the need for quiet would allow.

The movement after waiting was a relief. Action beats inaction. At first, she felt warmer. She swam every day. She told herself, *this is no different*. Then the cold began to throb in her feet. The point looked as far away as it had when she first entered the water. She stayed close to the cliff, looking for breaks as she swam. Here and there, fallen trees left great gouges of broken land near the cliff's rim. Nora tried thought games to keep herself going. *When I get to the next fallen tree, I get a C. When I reach the madrone on the outcrop, I'll get a B. What grade do I get if I round the point and the cliffs continue as far as the eye can see? An F for Frozen.* This gloomy thought took her to the fallen tree, C. By the time she collected her B, her movements were mechanical. She could hear seals bark and the high whistle of a fishing eagle.

The tide was coming in fast, bringing food for the animals and maybe a corpse for the two-legged predators behind her. Just as Nora decided she could no longer lift her arms for another stroke, she realized the shoreline had changed to the steady build-up of rock and sand that developed into a point. She moved toward shore and put her feet down. By stretching, she could touch stones. With flagging energy, Nora unwrapped her shoes from around her neck, hoping her stiffened fingers could undo the bow knot that tied the shoelaces together. With shod feet, she dog-paddled for a while, half swimming, half walking. She figured the men stood waiting for her to walk out near them. Like many who live near the sea, they had likely spent their lives trying not to be caught in the water. *They think boats, not swimming*, she repeated to herself like a mantra.

Rounding the point, Nora saw the cliffs stretching on into the distance. But here was the miracle she had only dared dream of—a long row of wooden steps arching up through a tiny ravine. The steps were moss-covered, very steep. They tilted down sharply on one side, clearly old, possibly even abandoned after being undermined by landslides. Water poured over one step, a little waterfall, picturesque perhaps, but not promising for safety.

Nora did not hesitate. Half delirious with exhaustion, she imagined that these steps had been lowered for her, Jack and the Beanstalk in reverse. She reached them and crawled slowly up. Her feet slipped on the mossy, slime-covered boards. Once, both feet slid completely off, leaving her suspended by only the tight grip of her hands. Grimacing, she placed her feet back on the step. The jerking motion caused the entire contraption to sway away from the hill. As the stairway bumped back into the loose dirt of the hillside, the rung broke free on one side. Once again, Nora dangled with all her weight hanging on her aching hands. She forced her feet onto the step above and stopped to breathe. With her ladder swaying, she couldn't rest long. Pushing her right hand and her left leg up at the same time, she boosted her body to the next step. Left hand up, right leg up. Right hand, left leg, slowly up. Finally, she neared the top. She thrust one hand forward, feeling only loose dirt. Desperately, she ran her hand over the unseen ground. She didn't have the energy to climb further.

The steps swayed. Her hand bumped something round…a branch, or root, or a loose log. She had to take her chances. She grabbed it and pulled. It didn't give way. Using the branch as a lever, she lugged her body onto level ground and found herself looking into a monster face with blazing eyes. Nora pressed her mouth to the dirt to muffle her scream.

Nothing happened. Slowly, she raised her face and eyed the monster more carefully. She was looking at a cow's skull, eagle feathers blazing from its brain pan, bright beach-glass eyes, one Coke-bottle green, the other eyewash-bottle blue. A makeshift shrine or a child's delight. Maybe a grandfather's joke. Gradually she released her aching fingers from the tree root she'd used to pull herself off the cliff ladder.

Nora lay for a time under the benevolent gaze of the monster. Her legs could hardly move her. She crawled forward like a baby, rested, crawled again until she found the strength to clamber to her feet. She pushed one foot in front of the other, heading down a grassy road leading away from the cliff and the stairs. There was a cabin all boarded up on her left, but she saw no sign of telephone lines or life of any kind.

The grassy road turned into a dirt one which had been traveled enough to develop first-class ruts. It would eventually go somewhere, she hoped, knowing full well that abandoned lumber roads lay all over the mainland. Nora stumbled along, thinking about Joe, the children, her mother now long dead. Her steps faltered. The cow skull totem had been her last companion. She didn't even hear the screech of an eagle or the croaking of ravens. She looked down at her scratched legs, her ragged underpants wet and dripping. She wanted cover and warmth. Trees stretched above her, so tall they arched over the road blocking the light and the sun's warmth. She came to a downed cedar that had begun to decay. Soft strips of bark with tufts of wood pulp lay near its stump. Nora lay down in the peat-like pulp and pulled bark over her body, a bed and blanket of sorts.

Her mother was advising her. "You need a hot bath with Epsom salts, then a hot toddy and bed. I'll read you *Lassie Come Home*. Now, why are you crying? I haven't even opened the book." Mother patted her gently on the shoulders. "It's all right. It's all right." She was being wrapped in a blanket, but the voice was no longer her mother's.

She peered up at her rescuer, an embarrassed Constable Mackey. "I'll call the station at once and tell them you're found," he said, raising a hand with a radio in it. "We've been searching for you."

"No. Danger. Don't call. I had to swim. Cabin. Men. Gunshots. I ran." She was babbling but couldn't stop. "The beach. The tides. The cliff. Cold. Monster cow head."

Mackey lowered the radio without pushing any buttons. He hung it back on his belt and helped Nora to his car, where he turned on the heater and reached for his thermos. He poured her a cup of coffee and pushed his cap back on his head. He stroked the car's steering wheel. He looked down the road and up into the trees without once glancing at Nora in her bra, underpants and tennis shoes, wrapped in his blanket.

"I have orders to find you, bring you in and charge you with attempted murder of your husband." He poured some coffee for himself. "I saw the cabin. It was the first place I looked. Mess all over. I don't know what happened, but I doubt you scattered books and clothes all over the house and pillow feathers in the yard. I can't take you back there. If I take you to the hospital, you'll have to go to the station for booking and questions. Is there anybody you trust?"

Nora's thoughts were clearer now, warmth and temporary safety eclipsing her fear. She realized he believed her, at least about the danger. Her story had hit a nerve. He might also suspect she had pushed Joe out of the skiff in a surge of rage, but what happened at the cabin was something else, something he didn't understand.

"Yes. I trust Caroline to protect her patient. I think she believes I care about Joe, and I think you can be trusted to search for the truth. But no one, including me, knows how the accident and this thing at the cabin fit together. Who were those men? What were they doing there?"

Mackey started the car. He never took his eyes from the road. "Get down in the seat, out of sight. I'm taking you to someone special."

Chapter Thirteen

August 4-7, 1998

"You can sit up now," Mackey told Nora.

The patrol car pulled up to a mound of brush. Nora made out a fence of alder trunks and cedar branches. On closer inspection, she realized the fence was not a haphazard bunching of limbs, but an intricate pattern with three slim alder trees, followed by a sturdy cedar branch, its base buried in the ground. A stout rope wove in and out through all the branches like a bracing wire. The fence, perhaps ten feet tall, reached over her head.

A slim gap opened, a swinging gate of the same construction braced top and bottom with tied-in cross branches. A woman stood framed there. Mackey got out of the patrol car. "Wait here," he said.

Mackey and the woman faced each other. Nora could not hear their brief conversation. The woman watched Mackey's movements and gestures intently, not turning to look at Nora in the patrol car until she opened the gate wide and waved at Nora with a come-in gesture. She strode back through the gate in an athletic swinging lope. Mackey followed her. Nora gathered up her blanket and trotted after them.

Nora stepped across the fence line into a garden catalog. Planters made of old cans painted in raucous colors hung from the trees. Stumps filled with flowers lined a cedar bark path that led to a house made of found objects. One window, arched at the top, looked as if it might have been part of a church, another window could have been the porthole of a boat. Tired and frightened as she was, Nora knew she had stepped into another world.

The woman had not spoken. She was tall and lithe with coppery-brown skin and straight dark hair. She held open her cottage door, a triangle cut into cedar boards. Nora entered and found herself in an open room that had a fireplace, sink and a pot-bellied stove nestled under beams made of peeled tree trunks. Hand-woven baskets and bunches of lavender, salal, fireweed, and yarrow were strung along the beams, hung far away from the wood stove.

Mackey spoke to Nora while facing the woman. "Nora, I've brought you to Sedna, fisherwoman and healer. I should have explained before we arrived. Sedna is deaf from an illness of her childhood. She'll understand you if you look at her when you talk. She reads and writes. You can see she plants and creates." Mackey shifted from foot to foot, then stammered, "I've brought you to the most beautiful living person I know."

With that, he turned abruptly and walked out of the cottage. He opened and closed the gate and was gone.

Nora's knees gave way. She sat down abruptly on a stump-carved chair. She hadn't the strength to decide what she would do, or how she would communicate with Sedna. Idly, she wondered if she shouldn't have simply let go when the wooden ladder swung out from the cliff. Being here now, in this unfamiliar place with this unfamiliar woman, demanded too much.

She felt shy in Sedna's presence. She had never spent time around First Nation people, as Indians are called in Canada. *What does one talk about? Colonists taking their land? As in the U.S., the army killing them by bringing them blankets used by smallpox victims? Or by straight gunshots in so-called Indian wars.* Had Canadian colonists done the same things? Nora was ashamed she didn't know.

Sedna went to a cabinet on the wall. She took out several pairs of sweatpants, held them up, examining them for size, then handed a soft gray pair to Nora. Rummaging in the cabinet again, Sedna pulled out a slipover shirt. "Put these on. I find clothes on my beach from time to time that I wash and mend for emergencies."

Her speech was clearer than Nora had expected. She must not have gone deaf before she learned to talk. Nora choked back a laugh at herself. What a strange thing for an accused murderess and fugitive to think about.

Sedna stepped away briefly, and Nora dressed in warm, dry clothes. When she'd finished, Sedna approached with a mug in her hands. The woman raised it slightly, indicating that Nora should drink, so she did. The liquid tasted of spearmint and something else, something unfamiliar, bitter. She swallowed a few sips and started to set it aside. Sedna stroked Nora's forehead. "Drink it all."

She did as she was told. Sedna spread a quilt on the floor and motioned for Nora to lie down. Then she opened the triangle door and went out. She came back a few minutes later with small, thin branches of something in her hand. She scraped them and pounded them in a mortar, two rocks shaped as bowl and pestle. Soon a pasty liquid formed, which Sedna spread on Nora's cuts. The liquid burned warm on Nora's cold skin. Gentle fingers spread the burning sensation onto her face, her throat, her upper arms, chest, legs. All turned hot. Nora tried to rise but could not. She sank back onto her quilt. "Settle, sleep," Sedna murmured.

Nora felt her body swelling, then shrinking. She lost the sense of her fingers, her feet, the pulsing cramps in her legs, the heat, and the smell of sweating flesh. Drowsy now, she watched Sedna's movements. The woman's footsteps made no sound. Her feet wrapped in leather coverings more like socks than moccasins, Sedna glided across the floor. When she reached up to take down some of the herbs tied onto the beams, her arms moved like a ballet dancer's.

Nora drifted in and out of sleep. She couldn't keep her eyes open. Like her fingers, toes, arms, and legs, her eyelids were too heavy to lift. She saw flickering lights dancing around her but couldn't focus on them. She floated up above the ceiling beams and down through the hanging herbs, gazing at her own body lying on the quilt. Then she was down on the quilt looking up at birds swooping in and out around the baskets, small white birds like miniature seagulls.

Everything grew dark. Nora lay in a tunnel deep underground with the sound of water running like a river rippling over stones. She tried to think of words: *creek, river, stream, ocean. No. Aquifer, that's it. I'm down next to the life-giving aqui....* She lost the word and the thought as she floated on the water, dipping her fingers in the cool waves. She must be out in the rapids during a tide change. She saw the mouth of the dogfish gaping at her, its teeth gleaming as it grabbed her hand. Nora screamed.

She opened her eyes to see Sedna leaning over her

in an almost dark room.

"Don't worry. You are safe." Sedna gave Nora a cool cloth. "Here, wipe your face. When you are ready, you can sit up. You haven't eaten in a long time."

Nora wiped her face twice. The cloth smelled of lavender. "Why is it dark?"

"It's night. You have slept. Now you need food. I have chowder for you." Sedna handed Nora another mug, warm like the first one. "Clams from the beach, potatoes from the land, milk from the goat, seagull eggs from the sky. Gifts from sea, earth, sky, and beasts to make you strong."

This time there was no bitter taste. Nora ate the chowder and held out her mug for more, but Sedna shook her head. "You've had a shock. Your body must slowly be reintroduced to food and drink."

That made sense. Certain she could not sleep, Nora stretched out on her quilt again and woke sometime later to bright midday sunlight. Strong enough to sit at the slab of wood that was both kitchen counter and table, Nora ate scrambled seagull eggs with salmon roe and toasted slices of wheat bran blueberry bread. A pot of honey was on the table, and Nora spread some on the toast. This time, Sedna let her eat her fill.

After breakfast, Nora reeled off a heartfelt, "Thank you," but Sedna had her back turned while she worked near the stove and made no response. Remembering, Nora placed herself in front of Sedna, and thanked her, feeling a bit shy. "Will you show me your garden?"

Sedna's smile spread across her face. Soon they were out the back door and walking in the garden, nibbling blueberries from the bushes, plucking crisp peas here, pulling a weed there, heading down a gradual slope to a rocky beach and a floating dock with bags of oysters hanging from its boards. "I sell oysters for bits of needed cash. I live off the plenty of the region," Sedna said.

With the eagerness of a child, she answered Nora's endless questions about the plants and their medicinal uses. "Yes, I gave you sedatives in that first mug. I mixed valerian, baneberry and black cohosh with a little lemon balm to improve the flavor. The dressings for the wounds gave you a burning sensation because I added cayenne, along with the common salal that grows profusely around here, yarrow, also common, and baneberry root."

Nora started to ask another question but faltered. "I'm sorry. I feel faint."

Sedna slipped her arm around Nora's waist and led her back up to the house, Nora stumbling most of the way. "What's wrong with me. I can't…"

"Shush. Shush. Shock takes a toll on the body. Come back to your quilt and sleep."

When Nora came awake, the setting sun cast a pink-golden glow across the ceiling. She listened to waves lapping on the shore. She waved her hands in front of her face and realized her fingers had stopped tingling. She wiggled her feet and toes. The numbness had disappeared. Nora sat up slowly and looked around. *I'm in one of my childhood fairy tales. This is either the witch's castle or the gentle godmother's cottage in the woods.*

Suddenly, her fears flared. *This is a trap. I need to find out what's going on. I'm losing control. Others are taking over. For all I know, Mackey is trying to keep me away from the truth, to find me guilty and take credit.* Her breath came faster, her heart pounding. *I'll leave tomorrow at the first light of dawn.*

Sedna was nowhere in sight. Nora gathered a half loaf of the bread left from breakfast and put it in a sack. She took a few apricots from a bowl and added them to her stash. She located her tennis shoes, now dry and sitting near the wood stove. As Sedna's footsteps sounded outside the little cottage, Nora stuffed the sack behind a stump-chair in the corner.

Sedna produced another miraculous meal, salmon covered in dill, parsley, and a berry Nora didn't know, baked on a pouch of green seaweed. Mounds of steamed chard glowed green on her plate against the coral of the salmon. Sedna had scattered pink, yellow and deep purple nasturtium blossoms and seeds over both. The hairs on Nora's arms prickled as she savored the crunch of the peppery nasturtium seeds and the succulent salmon tipped into the creamy deep green chard.

Nora asked about the berries she had never seen before.

"They are salmon berries, sweet and a bit tart. They grow all along the Coast. Generations have gathered these, also the more common salal berries, used for jams. They dried them and saved them for winter. I do the same."

After dinner, certain that she could not sleep, Nora nonetheless obediently lay on her quilt again. She awoke well after dawn. Peeking out the back door, she saw Sedna on her knees weeding in the garden. *She won't know I'm gone for a little time, at least. I can slip down the road and into the woods*. She scooped up her sack and shoes, crossed the room to the triangle-shaped front door, stepped outside and headed for the fence with the gate where she'd first entered. The gate of alder branches opened without a sound to a grass-covered alley under the trees, more a path than a road. Nora walked down it, turning, she hoped, away from the ocean and the cow skull at the top of the cliff ladder.

A slight breeze ruffled her hair. She threw back her head and laughed. *I'm free. I escaped the witch's cottage.* She whistled as she had as a child, to keep herself from fears and protect herself from bears, as was told in her books. Here there could really *be* bears. She whistled louder. The path led on and on. She went around a curve, saw another straight stretch and another curve beyond that. She walked up a slight hill.

Twigs broke in the woods. Nora stopped, catching her breath. A deer burst from the trees and leapt across the path. Three fawns followed.

"Nora. Don't be frightened," she said out loud. Peering up the tall trunks, one branch lapping over another, she couldn't see the sky. The forest was closing over her, pressing down.

The heat mounted. Her throat was dry, so dry she couldn't swallow. She pulled an apricot from her sack and bit into it, letting the juice trickle down her throat. She felt a moment's release from thirst, and then her mouth felt sticky. She tried to wash the stickiness down with saliva, but saliva wouldn't come.

She lowered herself onto a rock and bent over, resting her hot head on her knees. The position let her see the ground from another angle. She stared at a garden of shapes and colors she had never examined, a blanket of bright yellow-green like the color street workers use on their vests to draw attention, another patch of darker green with slender stems riding above the carpet, miniature red globes at their tops, and on the tree trunk flat gray oak-leaf shapes. She rested her hand on one of the acid green clumps. It felt springy, like a sponge. She longed for books to tell her more about this new world. Somewhat invigorated by her discoveries, she uncurled, stood, and pressed on.

At the top of the hill, the path wound onward down a slight slope and into another curve that barred further view. A giant log lay across the path right at that second curve, a log too heavy for one person to move. Constable Mackey could not have gone this way. His car would have been blocked. *I've taken the wrong road.*

She sat on the log and listened for sounds of water lapping the shore or a breeze in the trees. Nothing. The silence seemed to engulf her. Why was she here? What on earth made her plan an escape from Sedna's gentle healing? She had balked at Sedna's provisions, helpful as they were. *It's me. I want to control my life, the way I controlled McKeever and McKeever, the way I liked taking over entertaining the boys for my mother. I want to tell stories my way, no allowance for others' thoughts.* Sobered by these realizations, she knew that right now nature, the woods, and her thirst had control. Not her.

She walked down the path and into the woods to move around the giant log. Tangled plants grabbed her ankles. She tripped on branches buried in the cedar bark and leaves, landing on her knees. Wounds from the oyster cuts opened on her ankles. *I'm lost. I'll have to go back. I must have water. I'll die here, my punishment for trying to kill Joe.*

She stood with some effort, then walked around the tree where she'd fallen and into a patch of nettles. Slapping her arms and legs to arrest the stings, she searched for a trail, or any slight indentation that might be one. She followed what she thought might be a path to reach a hill. Still, she recognized nothing.

Panting, hot, staggering, she pushed on. She thought of calling out, but what good would that do? She looked down at her feet as she walked to prevent tripping on sticks and roots. She pushed one foot in front of another, trudging like those pictures of prison slaves marching in road gangs. *No ankle chains. That's a good thing.* The thought, meant to cheer her spirits, only made her trudge more slowly.

She lifted her eyes through the canopy of cedar trees, their bows drooping downward like the weeping forests of her childhood picture books. The sun was no longer straight overhead. *It's afternoon. What will I do here after dark?* She looked in vain for signs of her footsteps. No prints in the sandy places. No flattened grass in the soft patches or snapped-off tendrils where blue-green moss covered the path. She turned full circle, looking for other tracks to follow, and then she saw it—the tall alder fence woven together with vines and rope.

Nora feared she would meet anger from Sedna when she slipped through the gate. She opened the cabin door. Sedna stood at the kitchen counter, bent over with her back to Nora, filling a basket with spiky plants. To Nora's surprise, Sedna greeted her without turning.

"I went for a walk," Nora said hastily from the doorway.

Sedna half turned and caught her eye. "Are you thirsty? I have some cool tea."

Nora nodded. Sedna poured tea for them both, and they drank together.

Trying to keep her voice level, Nora said "This is lovely. Thank you." She pressed the cold cup to her face, then held out her mug for more.

She didn't want to keep thinking about her stupid escape, Joe's injuries or her fears. "Tell me a bit about yourself. You live alone. Did you build this house, these fences?"

Sedna shook her head. "My grandfather started all this. He raised me. Grandmother, too, though she died while I was still young. A great man, a shaman, Grandfather taught me with patience and wisdom as much as I could learn about healing the body and the spirit with herbs and ointments. I thought I would die when he did. In fact, I wanted to die."

Without conscious thought, Nora reached for Sedna's hand. "What gave you strength?"

"He did. I knew that if I let go, all his teaching would go with me. I drank the same potion I gave you the afternoon you arrived. I slept for a few hours. That night, there was a full moon. Grandfather and I often sat in the moonlight in silence together, and so I sat with him that night through the flood tide that comes with a full moon. The next morning in the low, low 'minus' tide that follows, I gathered clams and shells, and found trader beads glistening on the beach." Sedna got up and fetched a lovely hand-coiled pot, smoothed with a shimmering blue-green glaze. The pot held bright iridescent beads.

"Grandfather and I often searched for them in the minus tide. Rarely, we found one. That morning, I found two. I'm certain to this day that was a gift from him, a sign."

Nora marveled at the beads. "They look like Venetian glass that I saw once on a trip to Italy."

"They may be. The Spanish came to these waters in the 1700s, bringing gifts to bribe us Indians, or so we are told. They are beautiful and worthless, except as joyful treasure hunts for a child with her grandfather."

Nora reached for one of the beads. "May I?" Sedna nodded. Nora held the bead up to the light. Swirls of color made patterns on the table. After a few moments, Nora put the bead back. "Please tell me more about your grandfather."

"He was a storyteller. He told stories as we weeded, stories as we ate, stories as we wove the cords for the fence. If I started to make a wrong move, he'd tap my hand lightly to catch my attention before showing me the correct way.

"There's a variety of lines on that fence, mostly woven inner cedar bark and nettle fiber. Stinging nettles are gathered in the fall when they are tall and strong. Stripped into strands with fingernails or a sharp knife, the inner core is removed so only the fibers remain. These are beaten and cleaned and finally woven together, first into a two-strand rope, then sometimes braided into thicker ropes. It's time-consuming work, great for telling and listening to stories."

Nora rubbed her arms. "I walked through a nettle patch today. How could you stand the stings?"

Sedna smiled. "We dry the stems, then scrape off the leaves. They don't sting when dried. But we also used other plants. When storms washed them ashore, Grandfather also collected bull kelp stipes—"

Nora stopped her. "Stipes? Do you mean strips?"

Sedna smiled. "You are a good listener. No, I mean stipes, the name for the strong stems above the roots before the hollow kelp branches. We'd splice them, soak, steam and stretch them, then weave them into rope. They swell in water, making strong fishing lines and tie ropes for the docks. If it was a tough stipe, he'd help me with it by re-soaking it in fresh water and re-steaming. They can want to misbehave."

Sedna laughed. "Sometimes he would thrust the strand back into the water, saying, 'He needs more coaxing to let his juices flow.' Grandfather believed everything has a spirit: stones, trees, roots, the gulls that give us eggs, the salmon that swallow our hooks."

She sat looking up with her hands in her lap and her head cocked to one side, nodding, as if her grandfather were speaking to her. "He told me, back in the time when creatures and humans spoke the same languages and talked together, as Grandfather would say, we came to this land with abundance of every kind: fish, octopus, even dogfish; ducks, geese, gulls; forest wealth in wood, food and medicines. He worried that all this plenty had spoiled us. We held feasts where tribal chiefs tried to outdo each other in giving splendid gifts. He understood that the tribal feasts had a purpose. These same fests brought distant people together. We could have become isolated in clusters with no ideas from outside and a narrowing gene pool. He also liked the goal of feeding people, but he despaired over the fighting between villages and the bragging of showy hosts. Perhaps because Grandfather talked to the creatures as in ancient days and knew things others did not, or perhaps because his visions reached beyond into the future, he tried to help his community live in balance with nature. He wanted us to use only what we need and leave the rest for others while also clinging to our traditions, songs and dances."

Nora looked at the beads, letting the silence hang in the room.

After a long pause, she asked very quietly, "With

your deafness, how did he tell you stories as you worked and weeded?"

"The disease that took my hearing came late in my childhood. I was eight or nine. I don't remember. He had taught me names and words and told me stories for years. After my hearing was stolen, he would place me across from him and continue the familiar stories. He shaped words for me: whale, salmon, deer. He spoke slowly at first to let me lip-read with gestures to explain his meaning. He was a very good teacher. I learned."

"Did your school teachers help?"

The light left Sedna's face. She stood and walked away. Nora could see her body quivering. She rushed to Sedna's side to embrace the woman, then checked the impulse, fearing Sedna might resent such intimacy. Instead, she walked around to face Sedna head on. "I'm sorry. I've said something terribly wrong. Can you forgive me?"

Sedna took Nora's hand and sat them both down on a nearby bench. "You can't have known. It's a hard story. Even Grandfather found it difficult to tell. My father was very young when he and his friends were forced to leave the village and go to a residential boarding school. This had been happening for years, the sons and daughters of the Salish and other tribes taken away to learn English, to be trained away from native languages and practices. Some parents never saw their children after the removals. All the village elders protested, with Grandfather in the lead. He was so loud—his word—that he was jailed for a few months. After his release, Grandfather and Grandmother left their village and came to live here, remote from the world, to commune with the spirits. He told me it was the trees, the deer, the eagles, even the raucous croaking of Raven that pulled him back, made him the gentle man I knew.

They sat in silence for a few moments. Nora glanced toward the garden, a haven for her now as it must have been for Sedna's grandparents when they created it from the wilderness. Her nose for a story made her want to know more, but she hesitated at the thought of adding to Sedna's pain. Hadn't she done enough already, even without meaning to?

Sedna resumed speaking, and the decision was out of Nora's hands. "After a few years, Grandfather began working in his home village to teach the Salish language. He traveled up and down the coast, learning other stories, and other languages. Some say we First Nations have twenty-five or more. He kept teaching what he knew, asking his listeners to remember, find their songs, and hold tightly to the best of their traditions. Then one day, my father found him here in the woods. My father had come with my pregnant mother, the two of them closest friends from their early years.

"Grandfather had tears in his eyes when he talked about my mother. He said she had been a mischievous sprite, laughing, climbing trees with my father, both of them swinging together from great heights. She imitated bird songs, a goldfinch song to express pleasure, or the flycatcher's for 'Come see, come see,' and made everyone laugh when she scolded a misbehaving young sister with the black-capped chickadee's fast-repeating squawk. Her presence made people smile. But after residential school, when my father brought her here to my grandparents' hideaway, she didn't look at them or speak. She ducked behind my father and covered her face. The school did not allow them to speak together in our native language or wear remnants of our village clothing. The students had to drop all of our traditions. Both my parents had sores and wounds, my father's from regular beatings with a gnarled whip. My mother..." For a moment, Sedna's voice faltered. "My mother had been tortured in ways too horrible for me to tell.

"My mother gave birth with my grandmother's help. My parents both stayed while my mother suckled me. Grandfather said her face began shining again with hints of her old spirit. But one day, when a tree in the forest fell with a loud crash, they grabbed me and ran frightened into the woods. My mother retreated into silence again."

Sedna's face clouded further. "Not long after that, they left me here. Grandfather said they had escaped from the Residential School and wanted to be certain I would never be caught in the misery they had endured at school, never tortured by punishments and hunger and never bereft of the customs and family that had once been the center of their lives and the lives of their classmates."

Tears flowed down Nora's cheeks, and she realized she'd been squeezing Sedna's hand with ferocity. Sedna smiled at her. "Grandfather didn't tell me all this when I was small. He and my grandmother lavished me with love. Grandmother weakened, but she taught me about plants and ways of healing that even Grandfather didn't know.

"After she died, when I was older, perhaps ten or eleven, we sat in the moonlight. Grandfather stroked my hair and told me the story of how I came to live with them. 'We all must know our past,' he said. 'I failed to protect my son. I was prevented from teaching him the songs of our people or the ways we build from the bones of trees, seals or the gifts of land and waters. It is my lasting sorrow. But your wise and caring mother and father gave us the gift of you, our forever joy.'" Gently, Sedna wiped Nora's tears away. "Do not weep for me. Few have been so well loved."

Later, as she helped chop onions for their dinner, Nora pondered Sedna's words. How did societies recover from that kind of deprivation, everything they knew and loved taken away from them? What would she do if Charlie and Nell had been ripped from her arms? Her thoughts shifted to the tribal chiefs and their lavish banquets using up resources for status or ego. She had thought the First Nations, those who evolved from Raven, had lived in harmony with nature. Was it possible that they too, or at least some of them, diminished the gifts of abundant life? Settlers flooded in to abuse the land and waters. Governments added to the depletion. Were two-legged creatures destined only for failure? Or were there more leaders like Sedna's grandmother and grandfather who held visions of a different future?

After supper, when they had said goodnight, Nora lay on her quilt, struggling with mysteries deeper than the sights she had seen these last weeks, mysteries that embraced the past and present. Mysteries that shaped the future? She couldn't frame proper questions that could lead her to answers. *Do other animals hoard, or only humans? Why do we clear forests to oversupply warehouses with unused lumber?*

She fell asleep into dreams of nets overflowing with fish, and the long reach to her cabin clogged with logs.

Chapter Fourteen

August 8-10, 1998

That night, a ferocious storm came roaring up the coast. Nora awakened in the dim light of dawn to see Sedna closing the windows of her cabin. When she saw Nora sitting up listening, Sedna said, "Come look, if you don't mind getting wet."

They went out to the top of the garden where they could see the water below. Lightning flashes showed them brown and gray waves with white rims of foam. The waves pounded ashore. The oyster dock bounced. "Will the storm shake the dock loose?"

"I doubt it. We're in the backwaters of a fiord. That gives us a certain amount of protection. But, out on the Strait, storms like this have unleashed many a boat from their moorings."

"I've seen wrecks all up and down the coast on the long reach to our cabin. Joe and I stood once to watch a storm come in. Joe was kicking himself for not hauling our boat up onto the shore, but I'm ashamed to admit that I was enthralled. We saw a huge stump, complete with long roots, thrown into our little bay by the currents, waves and wind. I could hear the grinding of rolling stones, perhaps the turbulence that once created our rocky beach. I felt I'd been given a gift of seeing, hearing and feeling that big untouchable thing called nature, a power beyond our control."

Overcome by the storm's beauty, Sedna and Nora stood silent until soaked through by torrents of life-giving rain.

The next morning, a car pulled up near the gate. Sedna, unable to hear the motor sounds, continued with her morning jobs until she put aside her watering can and turned toward the door. "Albert's here," she said, and sure enough Constable Mackey opened the door.

"How did you know?" Nora asked as Sedna greeted Mackey.

"I see through walls," she said with a mischievous grin. Then she pointed to a branch hanging in the middle of the room. "My doorbell."

Mackey explained. "My touch on the door makes that branch wave. An ingenious alarm system."

Nora laughed. "So that's how you knew when I came in from a walk."

"Another Grandfather innovation. Of course, it doesn't tell me who's there. I only hoped it was Albert. Tea, Albert?"

He nodded, and the two of them kept conversing as if Nora wasn't there. "Twelve to fourteen eagles are fishing on the point, young and adult," Mackey said. "The storm must have stirred up a generous feed."

Sedna busied herself with the teapot. "A full moon tide plus a storm. Nature giving and taking."

"The doe on your road has three fawns with her. They followed me for a bit."

"They think you have handouts. I'm ashamed to admit I feed her."

Nora thought she could have been back in Grant's Landing for all their attention on her. Mackey turned her way, as if he'd read her mind. "You're looking better than the last time I saw you. Sedna's magic is working, yes?"

"Yes. And her delicious food."

He held up her backpack, as if reminded only now that he was carrying it. "I brought this for you. When we landed that first afternoon, I carried it to the squad, stashed it in the trunk and forgot it." He handed her the pack. "I'm sorry."

"I can't even remember what was in it. Probably nothing much." She opened the pack and pulled out her camera. "It seems a century ago. I drove our boat down to the mill to take photos. I'd been obsessed with the mill all during Joe's absence, took a tour, even interviewed the manager." Her face creased with remembering she'd used Joe's camera on the day they went to Bradley Island. *I wonder what photos he lost when Jasmine ripped out the film. Poor Joe.* He probably lost numerous pictures of great fishing trophies. Her voice faded as she thought about Joe's pained face looking up at her from the water. "I'd totally forgotten my camera."

"I'll take the film for developing if you want. I came to tell you my sergeant is mounting a search party with the whole force engaged. Your disappearance has pretty well convinced him you're guilty of something."

She fought down her fear. "Of course, I'll go in. Do they know about the cabin and the three men who were there?"

"Have you thought of any reasons for that break-in?"

"No. It seemed like they were looking for something. If it was hidden treasure, they were wasting their time, unless they wanted Joe's stash of double dark

Swiss chocolate, one of his passions." She tried to laugh, but recalling the horror of the scene made her slump down onto the stump chair she had first sat on three days ago upon her arrival at Sedna's.

Mackey pulled on his ear. "The sergeant sent a search party to your cabin to record the damage. They found nothing. The cabin was neat. No books and clothes all over the floor, no torn-up camping gear or pillow feathers anywhere. My sergeant's worried about my veracity. Even worse, he may think I'm protecting you."

"Can't you look for her a little longer?" Sedna suggested. "I like the company."

"Thank you, Sedna. I like being here, too. But I'm a threat to Al—Constable Mackey." She had almost called him Albert. *I can't do that with other people around. My being on a first-name basis might make them think we're colluding.* "You'll have to turn me in now, to save your career and get beyond this whole horrible event."

They talked it over a little longer and agreed Nora could risk staying with Sedna another day or two while Albert took the film to be developed. It wasn't much, but an excuse to extend the hiding period. By day, Sedna gave Nora herbal and cooking lessons. Nora, in turn, helped with the weeding. At night, Sedna told traditional tales.

Two days later, Mackey came back with the developed photos. "First, a hospital report. There's some good news. Your husband hasn't come out of his coma, but the brain swelling has gone down, and the doctors are more hopeful. Sorry to be slow getting back. Grant's Landing had its summer festival. Fewer people showed up this year—my friend John, the retired harbormaster, says folks were upset that Mrs. Foster, the mill owner's wife, pretty much took over—but all the Mounties and the police were ordered to extra duty anyway. That shut the search party down, but they're starting up soon. Today, probably."

Nora half listened to Mackey describing the festival to Sedna, something about a craft fair moved to an abandoned warehouse. Mackey laughed. "Mabel Joiner, a friend of John's, predicted that the FFOs, Friends From Outside, you know, residents who come here regularly, stuck with the locals by going to the warehouse, buying doodads, dancing to the strummers. People spotted Mrs. Foster's husband on the speakers' platform with a sexy woman who wasn't his wife.' Sedna, nodding at Mackey's tales, spread the photos on the table.

Nora rose to join Sedna and Mackey leaning over the photos, almost a dozen shots of the mill, taken from the skiff on the last day before Joe's return. They included a few shots of the big cargo ships in the harbor and a photo she'd taken of herself with the camera held at arm's length. The close range flattened her face, made her nose larger than life. The silly image displayed her rigged-up sun protection, her hat with a cotton scarf hanging down to cover her neck. Another photo, on the day of the accident—incident, whatever she ought to call it—showed Joe concentrating on baiting his fishing rod. He wore her sun hat, with the same scarf hanging down to cover his neck.

Nora pointed at her husband's headgear. "Joe came back from his trip with a ghastly sunburn, so I loaned him my sun-protection rig. It kept me burn free after hours in the sun the day before. Does that mean anything?"

Mackey sat silent for a bit. "One of the fishermen I

interviewed gave me a white canvas hat," he said finally. "Said he found it in the water after you and I left the accident scene. No scarf, but that could've floated away. He'd forgotten all about it until I turned up. What were you doing out by the mill that day?"

"I was trying to keep busy. I'd spent a few days in town at the library, and then walking around, exploring. The day I took photos, I went out to paint, you know, like Monet. I think the steam and Grant's Mill are sort of icons for the region." Mackey's face went blank. Nora tried to explain. "Monet painted a railway station filled with steam. He made the ugly beautiful. I once took a painting class, and the teacher suggested we take photos of scenes. The photos would be a crutch when back home, easier than 'plein air'. I didn't expect to come back by boat for sketching."

Mackey scratched his head. "Makes sense to me, but would it make sense to an observer?"

"Who'd bother to observe a little tin boat sitting near the harbor?"

"Think about it. Folks here are used to routines. Guys sit on boats for hours with a rod in their hands. You had no rod, and you weren't signaling distress like you were stranded. They'd wonder, what could you be doing?"

"Spying," said Sedna.

"Exactly." He tapped the picture of Joe baiting the rod. "That hat didn't seem important at the time, but now…well, maybe from a distance someone thought you and Joe were the same person. You're in the same boat. He had that same white hat on his head with your scarf hanging down." He paced the room. "What else did you do all week?"

"Picked up starfish on the beach. Read. Dug a few clams. Really nothing."

"You said you spent a few days in town. What did you do?"

"I took a tour of the mill and interviewed the manager, Mr. Gallagher. I thought maybe McKeever and McKeever could do a mill story. It was silly, and on reflection I gave it up. I spent a listless night in a motel, and then came back to our cabin. Like I said, nothing."

"Maybe so, but do me a favor. Sit down and write up everything, I mean everything you can remember. Let me and Sedna read it over and see if we can find something. Somebody broke into your cabin for a reason. Somebody may have been after you or Joe."

His final words made Nora shiver. An image flashed through her mind of a tin boat, three figures in yellow rain slickers, heading away. *Was that real?*

Sedna had gone over to shelves on the wall. Now she came back with a pen and a pad of paper. "Here. Mackey will help me gather vegetables while you write."

Nora started to protest, but then saw the look between Mackey and Sedna and decided to keep herself occupied. They needed some time to be together.

After they left the cabin, she started an outline but crumpled the page in dissatisfaction.

She scrawled a title, hoping it would give her story momentum: *Nora's Week Alone*.

Where to start. *Remember, Nora. Think of the highlights. The beach combing, the loon calls at night.* She started writing as memory took hold. Day Two or maybe Day Three, she had finished a novel, a vivid read into another world and stepped out onto the deck. A full moon made a shining path in the sea. A loon called its plaintive song. *I called back. The loon answered.* The tide had risen to the edge of the hill, as it does in full moons. *I slipped on my swim shoes and walked from the shore, letting water lap my feet and ankles. I stepped out of my baggy pants, laid them on a high boulder and swam on the moon path toward the loon's call.* Caught in the spell, she wrote on. The water felt warm. Smooth as glass. It slid over her bare skin, tingling like Joe's stroking, raising her longing for Joe. *I circled the buoy, came back to the shore, then swam out again. I slept that night, wrapped in total peace.*

Pausing from time to time to stare at the baskets hanging from Sedna's ceiling, Nora plugged along, writing as much as she could remember, even retelling the tale of the mill and its manager that she had shared with Caroline's husband Frank. Her fingers cramped, but she kept on. When she finally finished, she put her head down on the pad of paper. She felt foolish, having written the story in the third person. She was about to crumple the first page into a ball like the others when Sedna and Mackey re-entered the cottage. They seemed totally at ease together. He carried a large basket, and Sedna held a bunch of flowers. Nora turned her head, fearful they might see the envy on her face.

"I'm going to tear this up. There's nothing here, not even a good story."

Mackey moved fast, snatching the pad from her. "No, you don't. We'll be the judge of that. Sedna, will you read first?"

"No. I'm going to put these in water." Sedna motioned to her armload of flowers.

Mackey sat by Nora's side. He'd brought the fresh air in with him, plus a lingering scent of spearmint.

Lonely, roused by thoughts of Joe, she wanted to lean into him as he studied what she'd written. He sucked in his breath as he read, whistled once, and then sighed as he put down the manuscript. He stared off into space for a moment, then shuffled through the pages, rereading parts.

Finally, he said, "May I give this to Sedna to read? It's very personal."

"Of course."

Sedna was standing at her sink preparing vegetables. Mackey walked around her so she could see him, then touched her arm. "Please, read. I'll finish the vegetables."

Sedna read differently than Mackey. She sped through a page, then turned back to reread it. She moved her fingers under certain words, then went back to reread a paragraph here or there. When she finished, she laid one arm across Nora's shoulders and took Nora's hand. "Albert, you must find the rest of the story." She squeezed Nora's fingers gently. "Let's study those photos."

They got up to study all the photos in a line on the counter. At first, they all looked the same to her, save a few that were blurry.

"How long were you sitting out there in that skiff?" Sedna asked.

"An hour, maybe two. It was hot. I decided to go home."

Sedna pointed to one photo. "Look at this. The stern of the departing boat says *Sea Climber, Seattle, Washington*. It's sitting heavy in the water. That means its cargo is loaded."

She touched the photo next to it. "Here's the stern of

a ship with the same name, *Sea Climber*, sitting light in the water. No cargo. How could a ship leave the harbor, go to another port, unload, and return empty in such a short period of time?"

Nora picked up the photos of the *Sea Climber*. "I paid no attention to those ships. I focused on the mill."

Mackey paced. "Good question, Sedna. Next question. What was the cargo?"

Sedna stepped away briefly and brought each of them a glass of spearmint tea while Mackey kept pacing. He stopped long enough to thank her and take a sip. "We've a few issues to solve. The first is that soon, all the squads will be looking for you. It could be serious unless you turn yourself in and ask for protection. With the ransacking of your cabin, and me backing you up about it, you can justify the request. You should be safe in police custody, and that gives us time to observe the comings and goings at the mill."

"And if I don't turn myself in?"

"Then they'll accuse you of attempted murder, or manslaughter."

The thought made her feel shaky. She sipped tea to wet her dry mouth. "Those men searched my cabin for something. Could it have been the photos? If it was, that means they matter a lot to someone."

Mackey shrugged. "But we don't know why or to whom. The sergeant already thinks you're guilty; I doubt he'd accept that the photos mean anything, and even if he did, whoever's behind all this would try even harder to hide whatever they're hiding. I'd like to set a police watch on the mill and the tankers in that part of the harbor, but I don't see a chance of making that happen. There's too much we don't know."

Nora felt a desperate need for action and to see Joe once more. Surely, they'd allow that before putting her in a jail cell. She stood and marched over to Mackey. "Constable Mackey, I am turning myself in. Please take me back to Grant's Landing. Put these photos in a safe deposit box or somewhere else that's secure." She glanced at Sedna, who stood watching them with concern. "We should keep Sedna out of it. I'll walk down the road a good way, and you can pick me up somewhere in the forest or near the cow skull on the bluff. That might make the most sense."

"What will you do for clothes? You're dressed in Sedna's now."

"Yikes. Sedna, do you own anything that's not neat and clean?"

The woman nodded. "I'll look through my stash of found clothing. Things drift in from time to time. I collect and save them."

Sedna showed Nora her clothes cupboard. Everything in it was washed and folded. Nora chose a pair of lumberman's jeans that had been mended. Pulling out the stitches, she gave Sedna an apologetic glance. "After you rub this in the dirt for me, it should do. That and the good t-shirt will be perfect, also nicely dirtied."

"Do I need to scratch up your legs with brambles as well?" Sedna asked with a laugh. "You look awfully good for an escapee."

Chapter Fifteen

August 10, 1998

Plans made, Mackey went out to his squad car and reported to his sergeant. "I found her, sir. At that old cabin up near Grace Point. She's coming in willingly. She's eager for news about her husband and requests permission to stop at the hospital to see him on the way in."

The sergeant's gruff voice crackled over the radio. "Permission granted, Mackey. Give me your ETA. Two officers will take over at the hospital. As soon as you arrive with your charge, you're on relief for twenty-four hours."

After Mackey signed off, Nora frowned. "On relief? Does that worry you?"

Mackey sidestepped her question. "Repeat the same stories you've told me. You don't remember what happened the day of the accident. You want the truth. Tell them about your escape from the thugs, the swim, and the climb up the cliff. They'll ask you the same questions at least twice, trying to confuse you. They might tell you they found the cabin clean and neat to see how you react. Don't worry about that. If they start with a new person, don't panic. Just repeat."

"I'm not scared of finding out I tried to kill Joe. I don't think I did, but I need to know for sure. If I flunk,

I will have ruined your career and maybe destroyed Sedna's privacy forever. I'll end up involving you and Sedna. I can't let that happen, Mackey." She buried her face in her hands.

"We do what we do by choice. Remember that. We're getting close." He picked up his radio and thumbed it on. "Mackey here. Expect to arrive at Grant's Landing Hospital at 12:10. Over and out."

Albert saw the police van as he pulled into the parking lot. He drove his squad up to the van, but there was nobody inside. He felt Nora shrinking against the car door. Briefly he wondered if he should have put her in cuffs, but it was too late for that. "Can you walk in okay?"

"I think so."

"I'll escort you inside, but I won't put you in cuffs. Okay?"

"That's kind."

"Actually, it's stupid." He tried to smile.

He moved the squad to the hospital entrance and parked with his light flashing. They walked in side by side.

The two policemen from the van were talking to Caroline in the corridor next to Joe McKeever's room. Mackey nodded to Caroline and introduced Nora. They were experienced officers. She'd be in good hands. As he turned on his heels and left, Nora's quavery voice asked if she could see her husband before going to the station.

Mackey had the next twenty-four hours all to himself. He dropped the squad and the white canvas hat off at headquarters, explaining to the desk sergeant that the hat had been found at the scene of the accident. What to do next? Put the photos in his safe-deposit box and then sleep a little, perhaps...but it was midday, and he felt too wired for a nap. Still wrapped in the case, he decided it was time to talk to John. He might have picked up a tidbit or two about the cargo ships at the mill. At least it was a place to start.

He stopped at his bank to secure the photos and then at a convenience store. He picked up a six-pack and two sandwiches and walked to the wharf. John sat there, watching the incoming harbor boats, same as usual.

John greeted him. "So, you've been bumped from your case."

"Word travels fast. I thought I was being given a day off for good behavior."

"Maybe."

Albert set the six-pack down and handed the old man a sandwich, then sat down himself. "Why's everyone so damned concerned about a simple fishing accident?"

"Why're *you*? That's the question. You talked to all the guys. You drove her to her cabin. You went back there and reported goons had destroyed the place, but scuttlebutt says not. She's too old for you, Mackey, and she's no looker."

"Oh, for God's sake, John. You don't think…"

"No, I don't, but gossip's gossip. It's a small town."

Mackey stared across the water. "No, it's me. The outsider."

"Maybe." John tugged a beer from the six-pack and popped the can. "I'm hearing Sergeant Biddle sent a crew out to that cabin. They found a bit of a mess, but no stuff thrown out of the shed, no feathers or anything on the steps. Inside, there were a few pieces of a broken teapot on the floor, but that's all."

"I saw that mess with my own eyes."

"That's the problem. It was only *your* eyes."

"God damn, John. What gives?"

The old fisherman shrugged. "Tell you the truth, I'm puzzled. The talk all seems a bit phony, you know what I mean?"

"Not really."

"Can't put my finger on it. But why would someone from the mill come by and ask me questions about the accident?"

Mackey sat up straighter. "Did they? Who?"

"Yep, a new guy, not an old hand. Don't know the name. In fact, there's a bunch of new guys at the mill, and the locals laid off. Don't like it a bit." John swigged beer. "Then one of Sergeant Biddle's detectives wanders down here to ask if I'd seen you around? Lots of mill guys are jobless. They're milling around." He grinned. "Hey, Mackey, that's a good one. Hee-haw for me."

Mackey forced a smile. "Hee-haw. What do you mean, milling around?"

"On the water. One after another takes out his boat without fishing rods. Maybe nobody else sees that, but I see it. They look angry. It reminds me of the time after the explosion before you came to Grant's Landing. Bad, bad period that was."

Mackey grabbed a beer, more for something to hold than because he wanted any. "What do you know about the tankers over at the mill?"

"They come and go out of my view. They never put into this harbor. Now if you want to know about the ferries, I know heaps about them. Why?"

"Nothing. Just asking. I haven't paid much attention

to the freighters that go up and down. I should keep on learning stuff about this area."

"If you ask me, Mackey, you're too serious. Why not take a rod and go fishing?"

"Who'd cook it for me, if I caught anything? Nah. My kind of fishing is a fly rod and a river stream. Not trolling in the middle of a hundred other boats." Mackey's face drooped. He looked at his watch. Two o'clock. He had all afternoon to kill.

"Guess I'll take a boat out without fishing gear. But I'm not milling around, I'm trying to go on vacation for a day, and I'm not good at vacations."

Mackey did as he'd told John. The question of the tankers nagged at him, but he wasn't sure where else to seek out information, and he needed to clear his head. He rented a small boat and headed for a sandspit between Joshua Island and Campbell River, a pretty spot with relatively warm water trapped in between the spit and the island. By the time he'd gone home for his swimming gear, rented the skiff, driven to the sandspit, chugged three of the beers in between three swims and motored back to the dock, the sun was low in the sky, and he imagined he would be able to sleep.

His phone rang as he walked in the door. When he picked up, Sergeant Biddle bellowed, "Where is she, Mackey?"

"Who?"

"You know who. Your little American friend has disappeared."

Mackey pulled on his ear. "Do you mean Mrs. McKeever? I dropped her off at the hospital. Hugo and James took over."

"Yeah, well, they let her see her husband before they

took her in. They waited for half an hour at least, then went into the hospital room. Nobody there but the patient and a nurse standing by. When they asked where the hell Mrs. McKeever was, the nurse said Mrs. McKeever left a while ago. She presumed they'd taken her to the station. So, the woman's gone. Now where in the hell would she go? Where've *you* been? We've been trying to call you for hours."

"I turned in my radio along with the squad for the day. I've been swimming from that sandspit near Joshua Island."

"The hell you have. You've been hiding Mrs. Attempted Murderer."

"Ask Old John. We had lunch together, and he saw me go out in a rented boat."

"That old drunk wouldn't know the truth if it was packaged in ribbons."

Mackey struggled to keep his voice level. "Mrs. McKeever came in with me willingly. She's afraid the people who roughed up her cabin might be after her, but I promised her she'd have protection in RCMP custody. She may be in danger."

"The same damned danger she professed to find in an allegedly wrecked cabin? None of the things you reported were there. No damage. No ripped tent and pillow feathers in the yard. Protective custody, my eye. She's on the lam. *Again*," Biddle added with emphasis.

"Have you tried her cabin?"

"Either you think we're all stupid, Mackey, or you're being sarcastic. Of course, we checked her cabin. We checked her skiff. It's moored at the cabin. We've started questioning the nurses, but they all act like they know nothing. Of course, we can't question the husband.

He's in a coma and hasn't been of sound mind since his wife ran over him in the water."

Mackey pulled on his ear, hoping he could keep himself from rude responses. "Is there anything you want me to do?"

"Yes. Find her. You did it before. Now do it again."

"Starting when?" *You told me to take twenty-four off. Bastard.*

"Now."

"Yes, sir." *Bastard. Make up your mind.*

He hung up and tried to think things through. If everyone knew everything, as John had implied, he'd better stay as far from Sedna's place as he could. Also, he didn't imagine Nora could get to Sedna's sight unseen for the first leg of the journey, then through rough terrain from there on. He hoped she had not attempted that route.

Fool. Start from the beginning, the point where you dropped her off.

He went to the hospital. The work schedule sat in full view at the nurses' station. He knew that Caroline had been on duty when Nora came into the hospital to see her husband. He had faith in Caroline's smarts and her attention to details. He doubted Nora could slip through Caroline's fingers unless she pulled something really strong. He needed to hear Caroline's story.

He also learned that someone he didn't know was watching Joe on this shift. Caroline was off duty. She used her maiden name on the job, so her home address would be harder to find. Nora had said the husband's name was Frank. Mackey didn't know Frank's last name.

He struck up a conversation with the nurse at the station desk. After some chatter about his first swim at the sandspit near Joshua Island, he asked her about her life. "Are you married?" *Lord,* he thought. *She'll think I'm making a pass.* He quickly added, "I mean, I know Angel has a baby, and Caroline has two kids. How do they manage?"

"It's tough sometimes," the duty nurse said. "Angel's baby is so young, four months old. Angel will be on duty tonight and jumping out of her skin over leaving her with a sitter. Caroline's lucky. Frank's a nice guy, a really good parent. I've seen him with his brood. He plays with them, doesn't smack them when they get rambunctious. I guess he knows kids. The McDonoughs are a big family. He's probably been around children all his life."

Last name McDonough. *That was easy,* but now he had to continue the chatter a bit to cover his tracks. Small talk was not Mackey's strong suit. He tried a question about how she liked nursing.

"It's okay."

"Where did you train?"

"Victoria."

"Beautiful city, Victoria."

"It's okay."

He'd gotten what he wanted. Time to bail. "I have to be going now. Hope you have a quiet shift."

"That would be a change. There's been nothing but questions all day long. Strangers, police, everyone is jumpy as cats." She gave a little chuckle. "Why did I say that? My cat never stirs unless I put out food."

Mackey could only remember the feral cats of his childhood, mean bird chasers dumped off on country roads. Scratching his ear, he stammered, "Well, you're lucky to have a calm one. Hope you can get home to feed him soon. Goodnight."

McDonough. Frank McDonough. Now to find the nearest phone booth.

Information listed two Frank McDonoughs. He asked for the addresses of both. Driving past the first, he noticed all lights were out. A few blocks away, the second house had a light on the front porch and, best clue, a swing set in the yard.

He walked up the porch steps and knocked on the door. After a long pause, a curtain moved on the window next to it. Seconds later, Caroline opened the door a crack. "More questions, Albert? I've told the police all I know."

He decided to take a big chance. "I'm not here as a constable. I'm here because I last saw Mrs. McKeever eager and willing to turn herself in. She wanted police protection. I think she knows something that puts her in danger."

Caroline opened the door a little wider and stepped back so he could enter. She thrust her chin forward, pulling her lower lip over the upper, all the while blinking rapidly. She closed the door and pushed her hair out of her face, and he noticed her hand shook.

"Protection. For whom? That new patient, Joe McKeever, brought trouble. You asked me to look after him. Now you're asking me to look after his wife. Who's asking to look after Frank?"

"Frank? What's up with him?"

"Two officers came to the hospital to take Mrs. McKeever to headquarters for questioning. She asked to see her husband, and they said they'd wait. The minute she walked through the door of her husband's room, she asked me to contact Frank. She said she might have information for him. I'd brought him to meet her a few days ago, and they talked for a long time about conditions at the mill. Then she vanished. And now here she was wanting to talk to Frank before the police took her away. Against my better judgment, I agreed to call him.

"He knew there were search parties looking for her. He asked me to bring her to the back door where they could talk. Like a fool, I agreed. Five minutes later, I led her out the side door of the hospital room. She'd been on the steps of the back corridor once before to talk to Frank. This time she went down the steps to the lower level where there's a back door we use for garbage containers and the like. Frank was there with his truck. I left them alone so I could be back in Mr. McKeever's room if anyone came. I waited and waited, but she never came back."

"About when was this?"

"A little after a quarter of one. All hell broke loose when the police knocked on Mr. McKeever's door to tell her time was up, and then found out she'd gone."

"What did you tell them?"

"I told them she stood near his bed while I checked the monitor and instruments. That's the truth. I also told them that's been her routine since he came here. That's the truth, too. I tried to stay as near the truth as I could."

"Then what? Those are two experienced officers."

"They searched the closet in the room, found the side door, followed that to the back door downstairs by the garbage cans. They pressed me about what happened. I said I assumed she'd left, though it puzzled me that she didn't say goodbye. Gave them my best innocent look and said, 'Did she walk past you guys?'"

"For an honest person, you're a good liar."

"I regret it all now. Frank hasn't come home. I don't know what to do. I called Jason, one of the Greens who was also fired from the mill. I don't know what you know about the situation. There's Frank's group, the Greens, who want better environmental practices, and another bunch who want to keep things as they are. Anyway, I tried not to sound worried. Jason's wife answered. I asked for Frank, but she said he wasn't there. Then I asked for Jason. 'He's not here, either. I think he's out with Frank,' she told me. I can't remember if I thanked her before hanging up."

This didn't sound good. "When was that?

"About five. I called Tom, another of the Greens. He wasn't home either. His wife also thinks he's with Frank. I don't know what's going on, and I'm scared."

Mackey kept his voice gentle, calming. "Do they go out together regularly? Where do they go?"

She sighed. "I don't know exactly. They try not to be seen together. When they meet by day, they sometimes take boats out to an island down the channel. It's after dark now, so they wouldn't be out on the water. At least they shouldn't be, they don't have boat lights."

"Any other hunches?"

"One other that makes me most worried of all. Frank's hazmat clothing is missing from the pegs near the back door, mask and all."

"Definitely not good. Could the clothing be anywhere else in the house?"

"Maybe, but I've always seen it on that hook."

"I'll go to the mill. Don't know how I'll get in, but I'll look around."

"There's an entry code. It may have been changed, but last I knew, Frank punched in a code to open the gate.

He kept it in his truck, but there may be a copy here somewhere."

She strode down the hall toward the kitchen. Mackey followed, catching up with her as she rifled through a catch-all drawer. "Nothing." Her shoulders sagged, and then she straightened. "His desk. He's been trying to write up mill stories." She hurried out of the room.

Mackey waited for her to come back. As he would have imagined, Caroline's kitchen was spotless and free of gadgets. He smelled the homey odor of chocolate, maybe cookies baking.

She walked back into the room. "Found two sets of numbers on a Grant's Mill notepad." She handed the pad to Mackey.

"Any guess which number is the newest?"

"No. They could both be used, one for the outer gate, one for the inner."

"Do you have a flashlight? I'm here without my squad car."

She nodded. "We have two super-powered floodlights, for those rare times when we're caught on the water. Take both, they have straps."

Another thought struck him. "I turned in my radio with my squad. I have no way to reach you."

"I'd come with you, but…"

"You can't. The kids. And you have to be here if Frank returns before I do."

Mackey checked his watch. 11:30 P.M. No moon. He parked his car two blocks above the mill, at an overlook of the bay, normally a pretty place. He rummaged in his car and found the battery-powered microphone he used for coaching soccer games. He hung it over his shoulder along with Caroline's high-powered lights, the three cumbersome objects clanking on their straps. He didn't plan to turn on a flash unless necessary. He patted his pocket for the gate codes before half-running toward the mill. The road was relatively smooth. The reflection of security lights cast beams while making deep pockets of shadows here and there.

Sure enough, the main gate had a code box beside it. He pulled out the notepad Caroline had given him. The spotlight over the gate shone down on the paper. He punched in the first set of numbers. Nothing happened. He tried the second, and the gate slowly swung to one side. He walked through, tiptoeing, even though the sound of machinery covered his footsteps and the clunk of the gate. He thought for a moment about punching the code to close the gate but decided to leave it open in case he had to get out in a hurry.

He walked down the steep hill to the main building on the side of the road, staying as deep in the shadows as possible. The building entrance sported a heavy steel door, corrugated so it could roll up. He needed a flashlight to read the other code, and punched it in.

The door rumbled as it rolled slowly upward into the overhang. Inside, lights blazed. Off to Mackey's right, he could hear a roar like a giant waterfall, perhaps the water hose for blasting bark off the logs. An iron stairway nearby led up. Height might help him see what was going on, so he climbed slowly, looking around him with every step. At a small platform, the stairs turned up higher. He saw no people but got a look at the layout of this part of the mill. With one more turn and rise, he could see logs traveling along different tracks, one toward the water gun, another toward the saws. A grinding noise echoed, its source somewhere straight ahead.

Nora's quotes of Gallagher's jokes about the chipper made him follow that sound. He moved cautiously on a narrow gangplank next to a track with logs rushing past him. He could feel the movement of the air as each log thrust forward. He pulled his arms tightly to his side, an automatic reflex to prevent being dragged into the machinery. He smelled acid fumes from chipped cedar, the heavy odor of machine oil, and own sweat from fear. Before long he reached a larger platform, surrounded by rails that looked like the spaghetti curves of railroad and tollway interchanges.

He continued climbing until he reached a larger platform shaped like an L with control panels full of levers and buttons. Looking down, he saw people, three in hazmat suits, their hands bound with steel bands used for tying large bundles of paper, their headgear lying on the floor. Four big men, one wielding a crowbar, formed a circle around them. Nora was nowhere to be seen.

A microphone and two large lights in a brightly lit space were not great weapons, but Mackey used what he had. He cleared his throat, turned the mic on and called out, "Hands up down there! Police."

The clank of machinery muffled the sound.

He turned the volume to high and yelled into the mic. "Police! Hands up down there!"

That got some attention. The four bruisers looked around for the source of the voice. A red-shirted fellow moved toward a post at one side.

A fatter man nearest the stairs spotted Mackey and pointed. "There! There he is. That's no policeman."

Red Shirt grabbed a rifle from behind the post. He

swung it up and sent a wild shot careening through the layers of stair grates.

Mackey ducked behind a control panel. "Where's the woman?" he yelled. "Bring her out in full view."

Red Shirt swung the rifle toward him, laughing. "We have her, all right. We asked her if she wanted to be sliced or chipped." The man aimed the rifle. "She don' get to decide, though. When she drops into the chips, she'll compost like garbage. Cook right up. Nothin' will be left for evidence but some ashes."

The gun roared in the metal-walled room. Mackey thought he felt the bullet zing past him. He crouched down, his heart thudding against his ribs.

Red Shirt nodded toward the three captives. "Now these guys will be harder. The hazmat suits are a nuisance. We'll have to strip them before sending them on their way."

Mackey looked at the banks of levers on the panel next to him. He had no idea what lever moved which machinery, but maybe pulling and pushing one right after the other could stir things up.

He let his microphone hang by its strap, grabbed the nearest lever with both hands, and pushed down as hard as he could. A log appeared on a lower trolley, moving fast. Mackey pulled the lever back up, and the log stopped.

He yanked the next lever down. A high squeal like a dentist's drill, only multi-decibels louder, penetrated the room. He pulled that lever back up as well, and the piercing scream stopped.

Red Shirt adjusted his aim and fired. Another shot zinged past Mackey, ricocheting as it hit metal rail after metal rail, the sound fading to pings as the bullet lost velocity. With each pull of the trigger, the bastard was getting closer.

He could barely reach a lever over his head. He pulled it down, and the lights went out in the next section of the mill.

Progress. Mackey reached for the next high lever, pulled down hard, and the lights went out in the room where he was. Now he was cloaked in darkness, but so were Red Shirt and his friends.

The clatter of boots on the gallery grates warned him of a thug climbing toward him. He crouched down in a corner between two panels, calculating the distance of the footsteps.

He waited. Metal clanked on metal. The man was carrying something, perhaps one of the crowbars Mackey had seen below. He waited some more. Another bang of metal on metal rang out, closer. Mackey recalled what his father had told him on his first deer hunt. *"Wait, son, wait. Biggest mistake hunters make is shooting too soon."*

Footfalls vibrated through the metal grating. Mackey waited. His attacker climbed two more steps.

Mackey took the biggest flashlight and aimed it at the sound, counted silently to three and turned it on. The beam hit the face of the brute coming after him. Blinded by 2,000 lumens flashed in his eyes, the man cried out. Mackey threw the microphone straight at him as hard as he could. It struck the man in the head. The attacker screamed in pain as he fell backwards down the steep stairway.

Mackey had slowed one, but he guessed the other three wouldn't give up so easily. His spotlight had given Red Shirt a focus. The rifle roared. The bullet hit the panel next to Mackey. A clunking noise in the distance stopped as another piece of machinery halted.

The cuffed hazmat guys had taken advantage of the darkness, rushing the brutes like footballers blocking a run. A muffled cheer hinted at victory for the good guys, but Mackey knew the odds were against them. He headed back down the stairs as quietly as he could manage, looking for things to throw. On his way up he had seen metal log hooks placed here and there along the rails. He presumed workers used these long tools for wrestling unbalanced logs. If he could remember exactly where and lay hands on one, he would have a powerful weapon.

Running his hand down the top rail, he finally felt what must be a log hook. With luck, it would have easy release clasps for quick access in emergencies. He felt up and down the hook, found a clip, pressed down and pulled the hook from its brace. Armed with this, he moved steadily down toward the assembled men below.

Lights flashed on. He was caught in the full glare, his arm raised high with the menacing hook ready to swing.

A big man surrounded by Grant's Landing police shouted at Red Shirt, "Put that gun down and raise your hands high." Next, he yelled at Mackey. "Put that hook down and raise your hands, *now*. My name is Gallagher, I run this place, and I want to know what in hell is going on in my mill."

A general hubbub followed. Gallagher recognized the fired mill workers in hazmat suits. Each man had to call out his name: Frank McDonough, Jason Graham, Tom Jameson.

Red Shirt hollered at Gallagher, "My men and I are protecting your mill. Like you and Miss Hobart hired us to do."

Gallagher ignored him and pointed at Mackey. "Who in the hell are you?"

"Constable Albert Mackey, Provisionary RCMP," Mackey replied.

Gallagher sneered. "Where's your uniform? Your badge?" He turned to the police officers. "Take him in with the others."

The police handcuffed everyone—the Greens, Red Shirt and his cronies, and Mackey. "Where's Mrs. McKeever?" Mackey demanded, screaming at Red Shirt. "You said you had her. Was that a lie?" His gaze shifted to Frank McDonough. "Did she come with you, Frank?"

"McKeever?" Gallagher said, before Frank could answer. "That news woman? What's she got to do with any of this?"

"That leaking pipe," Frank said, staring at Gallagher. "The one I warned you about. There's more to it than a leak. Nora McKeever found evidence."

Gallagher glared back. "Evidence? Of what?"

"Tankers. In the harbor, taking on dirty water from the mill and then dumping it. Tom and Jason and the rest of us already had our suspicions, even before Mrs. McKeever went out in her skiff taking pictures—"

"Ridiculous," harrumphed Gallagher. He turned to Red Shirt. "What d'you know about this?"

Red Shirt's chin jutted forward. "We ain't talking without a lawyer."

Gallagher's anger flared. "Was she here in the mill tonight?"

"Yeah, but she disappeared before that guy came in." He nodded at Mackey. "Mebbe he knows where she is."

Mackey yelled at them. "She's in danger. They've threatened to force her into the log chipper. I came here looking for her."

The police assigned three men to search the mill. The rest loaded the handcuffed prisoners into boxy transport vans. Red Shirt and the other three thugs elbowed and kneed Mackey at every opportunity until they were all belted in. He couldn't stop worrying about Nora. He would be trapped in jail when he should have been out looking for her. He was the one who persuaded her to turn herself in for protection. Fat error.

He also faced his shame, riding behind those screened windows, imagining the sneers on the faces of Sergeant Biddle and his Mountie buddies when they saw him.

The van jolted to a stop. He stumbled out of the rear, his movement made clumsy by tied hands he couldn't use for balance. After they'd been fingerprinted and given their names, addresses and birth dates, they were slammed together in a large cell, earning the goons more opportunity to kick him in the groin or bump him against the wall. He kept away from them as best he could and watched as one by one, the Greens left on bail. He wanted to apologize to Caroline when Frank left the cell, but the bailees were released in another room.

He had some satisfaction that no one came to bail out the goons. After a long while, a policeman called his name. Mackey followed the officer out into the next room to find Caroline waiting.

"Frank told me what you did at the mill," she said. "A little bail money is the least we can do in return."

"Does Frank know anything about Mrs. McKeever?"

"He's certain she followed them into the mill. He says they tried to persuade her not to come with them, but she insisted. She told them, 'I'm a reporter. You're following my tips. Right or wrong, I need to see for myself.'

"Frank thought he could out-stubborn her, but they were in a hurry to get into the mill and out before the night guard came by, so he let her follow. They lost track of her pretty quickly. He doesn't know what happened."

Chapter Sixteen

Uncertain of the flooring, Nora kept her gaze on her feet as she stepped slowly inside the mill behind Frank and the Greens. A muscular arm hooked around her, and a hand pressed a heavy cloth over her mouth. She struggled and tried to scream, but her captor's strength subdued her. She felt a jab, a sting, and then nothing, nothing, nothing.

Later, she awoke with an aching head. Had she been unconscious? Where was she? Lying down, someplace dark. Something was tied around her eyes, tight. Panic surged through her. She tried to lift her bound arms and bumped against a hard surface above. When she swung her legs, her kick caused a ripple of metal clanks and then silence. Wedged in, unable to see, at least her mouth was uncovered. She sucked in her breath and released it, feeling her chest rise and expand. With full strength, she blew her breath into a scream.

Silence. Nothing happened.

She tried puffing and releasing air to build force into a second scream. No one responded. Exhausted, tears of frustration wetting her cheeks, she counted to one hundred, an old trick for calming worries. The counting didn't help. Nevertheless, she counted again.

Bodily needs became her gauge of time, thirst, far more severe than she'd felt on her failed escape from Sedna's, dry lips, dry throat, and a caking fuzz in her mouth gagged her. The need to pee overcame her longing to drink. She gripped her groin muscles to resist the urge. She pressed her hands beneath her belly, hoping that might help and tightened her buttocks. The urge grew. As soon as she relaxed her buttocks, a warm liquid spread down her legs. She smelled her urine, sweet with an overlay of fish smell.

Relief and shame came together. Her bowels emptied next, wet, putrid acids stinging her thighs. Changing baby diapers had not revolted her, yet this did. Charlie had been a finicky baby, crying as he pulled on her skirt: "Charlie boo-boo. Charlie boo-boo," tears streaming down his cheeks. Poor Charlie. She understood his anguish now.

Time stood still. The sting of wet clothes, the putrid reek of her own waste added to her panic.

Her prison swayed, a rise up, a dip down. The motion spread the foul liquid higher on her body. Pain gripped her stomach before another bowel release exploded into her trousers.

She heard distant squawks and squeals, a clamor of noise, a familiar noise. She tamped down her fear and tried to remember. Not babies' cries, though they sounded almost like that. Too many cries at the same time. She had listened once to alley cats fighting. Some of the sounds this time were similar, but… *No, that's not right*. Animals in a zoo? Birds? Several piercing squawks rose above the others. Gull alarms, the sound when one gull stole a clam from another.

A day fishing with Joe came to her, a day she had loved on their first trip to the area years ago. It was sunny, warm. They circled Mitlenatch Island, a bird sanctuary. She had watched the little guillemots with their red paddle feet and dipping heads. Gulls dive-bombed the water from high cliffs. Cormorants sat on rocky shelves, looking like Greek urns, their long necks stretched up immobile as statues until one or another fanned its wings.

Joe had pulled their little boat into a natural harbor, the water flat and smooth. A cabin sat at the harbor's end. She had wanted to get out and explore, but it was late, and they had no food or drink. Joe promised they would come back some day. On the way out of the harbor, they watched lumbering sea lions stretching and growling on sun-drenched rocks, the biggest barely able to move its giant body until it plopped in the water to chase a smaller sea lion waving its fan-like paws in the air.

Yes, the swells up, the swells down. She was in a boat. Perhaps in Mitlenatch Harbor? She had no idea what had happened between seeing Frank McDonough's back and now, but there was a small bit of comfort in guessing where she was.

Her prison lurched. Whatever had clanked near her feet rattled and banged. As a child, she and her parents once took a boat ride on Lake Minnetonka with her uncle. Because she was small, she had been assigned to the anchor locker to check the anchor chain as her uncle winched it back into the boat. "Don't touch it," he'd said. "The chain could cut off your hand. Call out if it kinks as we rewind it into the locker."

Maybe her prison was an anchor locker. She had hated that close space then. She hated it more now.

She tried mind tricks to calm herself. She was a princess captured by a pirate ship. She would be sold. Surely, she could think up a rescue. No ideas came to mind.

She recited poetry. Her old Chaucer favorite that she had recited in front of the whole school: *When that April with its showres soote, the droughte of March hath perced to the roote...* She couldn't remember the next syllables. Her memory failure added to her panic. Had she lost her mind as she was losing her life?

Her prison bounced. Footsteps pounded over her head. Metal clattered at her feet, loud as a roar. Someone was winching in the anchor. Remembering her uncle's long-ago instructions, she moved her feet as much as possible to keep them away from the anchor chain.

The metal clanking stopped. The prison moved again, a steady rise up, down, up, down with no motor sound. Her jail stirred like the gentle rocking of a branch swaying in a breeze, or a swing pushed by a tender parent, or a cloud sliding across the sky. To calm her nerves, she pretended she was riding on an eagle's back with its pulsing wings.

The motion ceased. Had her abductor docked?

As she lay in her own filth, the smell of cooking hamburger suffused her space.

"Hungry?" asked a male voice, with the sound of water flowing. "Thirsty?" The voice paused. "Where are they?"

Nora didn't answer.

"Food and water when you tell me."

She managed to croak out a response. "Where are what?"

"The photos. You must be hungry by now. Thirsty, too. Food and water when you tell me."

"I don't know." *That's the truth.*

"I'm not stupid. Of course you know. Tell me where they are and you'll go free."

She said it out loud. "I don't know, and that's the truth."

"Why did your husband take pictures of the mill?"

Her mouth was so dry, it was hard to talk. "That was me. I wanted pictures to paint."

"Come now. You can lie better than that."

"No. Like Monet's train station, steam." Should she mention Mackey's name for her freedom? He'd promised to secure the photos. After all, what could this man do to a Mountie?

Her bowels let loose another flow. Nora clamped her teeth onto her tongue until it hurt. Letting him hear her tears, she repeated, "I don't know where they are."

He asked her two more times, then cursed and gave up.

She listened as he clumped around overhead. She heard running water and dishes banging. Then silence for a long time. Had he abandoned her and his boat? She returned to Chaucer. Useless. The familiar words wouldn't come.

Movement above. Then it stopped. Something, no, someone, jerked her body. The ropes on her ankles cut into her skin. Her hair caught as someone pulled her out of the locker. She shivered in a burst of cool air. The person yanked her over a bump and up a stair. Holding her at waist level, he lifted her and pushed her feet around and over a rail.

Fearing she was being tossed into the ocean, Nora screamed.

With a hard shove in the middle of her back, Nora's body left the rail edge, floundered briefly in space, then slammed onto a hard surface.

Silence. Her head hurt more now. She lay

motionless for a while, expecting another shove or blow, but nothing happened. With little hope, she reached her bound hands in front of her and folded her knees under her, stretched her body forward, lay flat. *Again,* she told herself. *Again.* Pushing her hands forward, bending her knees, stretching, she moved worm-like over the surface beneath her. It felt hard like concrete.

After five knee curls and thrusts, her fingers felt space. She had come to an edge. She pulled back and angled her thrusts sideways until she felt a metal surface. Her fingers explored this odd pole-like form, straight across the top, a flange. More fingering revealed a T shape, a cleat. She rested her head on the edge of it, hooking her blindfold at one end of the T. With careful jerking and yanking, the blindfold loosened. She rested. Jerk, pull, yank, pull. Her hair caught and she cried out in pain, but no one slapped her or stopped her efforts. She clamped her jaws tight for a hard snap of her head, and the blindfold dropped away.

She laid her throbbing head down on the concrete and rested, letting her tears dry. She could see the night sky with a hint of early morning light at its edges. She'd been right to be cautious. She was lying on a narrow concrete strip with boat cleats along its edge. With each minute of increasing daylight, she had a better view. The concrete strip was perhaps a city block removed from a harbor, not the harbor where she had landed with Mackey, but a different one with floating docks and a tall platform overlooking the moored boats.

If her hands and feet weren't bound, she could swim that distance with ease. She slipped her hands over the cleat and tugged, but pulling on the rope cut her wrists more deeply, and the binding did not give. She glanced across the water and saw a rim of trees at the harbor's edge.

Trees, land. Please, let me get back to the land.

John treasured the early mornings before noise and arguments assaulted his ears. Especially now, in tourist season, he made an effort to get to his observation post early. If he looked south, he could see the RCMP dock. If he stood and looked north, he could see the public dock where Grant's Landing residents moored boats. He relished the green-gold gleam of sun on water before it turned into a rosy glow, then watched the gulls dive with pink-flecked wings into the quiet surf, looking for food.

Arriving at his harbor, John took inventory. Too early for customers at the gas dock. The slack tide meant fishermen had not yet unhitched their boats. Alone like this, he felt as if he ruled all that he surveyed. To broaden his territory, he peered across the water at the public harbor. He could make out the floating docks. Yachts and sailboats filled the rental spaces for Grant's Landing residents with a line of rowboats tied up on the docks in the shallow water. Nothing stirred. Straining for a wider view, he spotted what might be another dead seal on the distant concrete dock. He went to his crate for his binoculars and trained them on the huddled mass. *No, it's not a dead seal. My God, it's a person.*

He crossed a street and stumped down the long ramp to the water's edge. He tumbled himself into one of the rowboats on the shallow side of the first floating dock, unhitched it from its mooring and began rowing toward the far dock.

He hadn't pulled an oar for years. His strokes started out unevenly, jawing his boat to starboard, then to port. He stroked around the inner floating docks toward the separate, outer concrete band. *By God, it's a woman!*

He pulled alongside the concrete slab. Its surface sat high off the water level. She'd have to drop at least two yards, possibly three, into the boat. Someone had bound her arms and legs, and she smelled bad. No time now to ask what the devil was going on. "Let me cut the rope on your wrists," he said. "I've got a knife. Hang your arms over the ledge if you can."

She was crying wildly. "Easy now, easy, lass. We got to work on this together. Twist around if you can."

His words sank in after a couple of seconds, and she inched forward to do as he'd asked. Standing in his boat, moving carefully, John reached for her wrists. He had to stretch over his head. His boat rocked, and he feared he might cut her as he pulled out his knife and began to saw away on the ropes.

"These bands are too tight. Your hands are swollen. Hold on. Hang your arms further over the edge if you can do that without falling."

He continued to slice with his knife. Nora's crying slowed down to moans. With a snap, the bindings broke.

She tried to wiggle her fingers, but they didn't respond. John patted her arm to calm her. "Now swing your feet toward me if you can."

With more squirming and twisting, she hung her feet over the edge, tilting, almost falling forward in the effort.

"Whoa, there, lass. Lean back, not toward me, while I work on these."

She did as he asked, her breath coming in hiccups from crying, but already somewhat calmed. He sliced through the rope around her ankles. "You may not feel it yet, but your feet are free. Ease into the skiff. It's a long drop. If you come down too fast, the boat might tip and we could both drown."

She nodded, drew a deep breath, inched forward off the dock and fell into the boat on top of John. The boat bounced but stayed upright. John managed to grab an oar and turn the little craft about as they floated free of the concrete slab. He paddled toward the boat launching ramp, pushing as far up the slope as he could manage. "Crawl out, ma'am, and I'll follow. Can you make it? We have to get up this steep slope to the phone."

She shivered, crawled an inch and collapsed to lie flat with her head on the ramp's stone surface.

"You're Nora McKeever, aren't you? The one everybody's looking for."

She didn't respond. The woman lay there as if dead.

John alarmed, pushed himself up the steep incline to the telephone. His heart raced from exertion and worry. He dialed for an ambulance.

Chapter Seventeen

August 14-15, 1998

Nora saw two faces, then none. Her gaze blurred. She didn't recognize the person leaning over her. Two eyes, four, two mouths, none. She moved her head for a clearer view. It ached, so she held still. Then the faces went blank.

Sometime later, Nora awoke to a gentle voice. "My name is Josephine. Call me Josie. I'm a nurse. You're in the hospital. You had us worried there for a time. You were severely dehydrated, but your pressure is coming back." Josie adjusted the tubes attached to Nora's arms and feet. Nora's head throbbed. She tried to sit up but fell back onto the bed. Confused, she stammered, "Where's Caroline?"

"Caroline sends you her best. The police won't let her visit until after you've answered their questions—something about Caroline's connection to your case."

"Can I see Joe?"

"Caroline said to tell you. Your husband opened his eyes while you were missing. Dr. Cameron checked him yesterday. The swelling has subsided. His body temperature is good, his heartbeat's steady." Josie paused to check a tube. "We'll let you go see him soon, but you must rest more."

Soon, soon, soon, echoed through Nora's head. Then

the crooning stopped. Nora focused on Josie's face. Two eyes, one mouth. A soft towel wiped her damp forehead.

Later in the afternoon, Josie got her up and eased her into a wheelchair for a visit to Joe's room. His face had gained color, and when Josie moved Nora's hand to Joe's arm, she felt his body's warmth. "He's no longer in shock," Josie said. "Dr. Cameron will be in tomorrow with a full report. Back to bed now for you."

Nora missed the sights and sounds of the sea. She wanted to see gulls swooping and smell fresh air. Her room facing the parking lot, car rooftops gleaming in the late afternoon sun gave her no encouragement. She closed her eyes and slept.

By the next morning, Nora could sit up without an aching head. Josie cranked her bed into an upright position. "How does that feel?"

"Good."

"The police are demanding interviews as soon as I give the word."

"Frank? The mill?"

"I'm not allowed to brief you, even if I knew the answers to your questions. They want your story unfiltered by the opinions of others."

Josie stalled the police until after breakfast before finally allowing them in. Two RCMP officers grilled Nora with the same questions over and over. "Why were you in the mill? What did you see there? How did you escape the hospital? Who is your accomplice? Where did you stay when you disappeared? Where were you these last three days?"

Nora repeated the same answers every time. "I was kidnapped. He wanted me to tell him about some photos I took." She tried to keep names out of her comments. "I snuck out of the hospital right under the noses of those officers. They were talking and didn't notice." That was true, though their noses had been in a different hallway.

More questions. "Tell us about the photos. Where are they? What's in them? Do they even exist?"

That last one made her sit up straighter. "I don't know where they are, but they're real," she snapped. "Why don't you believe me?"

"Why should we?" the taller officer said.

His partner shot him a look and then asked, more quietly, "Why did you take the photos?"

"I wanted to paint the steam from the mill."

"Come now. Tell us the truth."

"My kidnapper asked that same question. He didn't believe me, either."

The first officer broke in. "Why should we believe you were kidnapped?"

She gaped at him. "I was dumped on the outer harbor wall, blindfolded and with ropes around my wrists and ankles. Ask the man who rescued me."

"John Bellows says he found you. How do we know you didn't get there on your own? You might have had an accomplice tie you up to make it look right?"

That was too much. Her voice quaking, she cried out. "I want to call my children. I need help."

Josephine came in from the hall, shaking her finger at the policemen. "My patient's monitor shows high blood pressure and stress. As Mrs. McKeever's nurse, I'm closing down this interview."

"For the record, this is a first interview," the taller Mountie said. "We'll close this session for the day, but there will be more."

Nora sank back onto her pillows. She wondered if this nightmare would ever end.

Chapter Eighteen

August 16-17, 1998

The next morning, Josie ducked into Nora's room. "Caroline's taking over. The police relented after their interview. I'm assigned elsewhere now, but it's a pleasure seeing you recovering."

"Thank you, Josie. I'll tell Caroline you're a good protector."

Caroline came in as Josie was leaving. Nora sat up to give her a big embrace. "Josie said you weren't allowed to see me. Is it you or me that they're afraid of?"

Caroline smiled. "A bit of both, I guess. They accuse me of knowing too much when I really think I know nothing at all, but I'm truly, truly happy to see you looking better."

Mackey visited her a little while later, bringing a bouquet of lavender from Sedna. He told Nora about his night-time jaunt to the mill, and everything that happened there. "Gallagher saved our lives. But the mystery about who's behind the action in the mill is unsolved. The anti-Greens won't talk. They're in jail, the red-shirt guy on an illegal firearms charge, the rest for trespassing and unlawful restraint of Frank McDonough and his buddies."

"And what about you?"

He shrugged. "Frank, the other Greens, and I are still

accused of breaking and entering, but at least we're out on bail. You should know, Gallagher rehired Frank and his friends. With the goons in jail, he needs experienced hands at the mill. That's one step forward, but we need to figure out what happened to you."

Nora frowned. "I think I was in a motorless boat. I could swear the boat moved twice, maybe more, and I think it was anchored for a time in Mitlenatch Harbor. I recognized the gulls' cries. I didn't tell that to my questioners yesterday. They were fierce."

"I'll ask around, see if any local fishermen saw a sailboat in Mitlenatch Harbor recently." His voice dropped in concern. "How are you doing?"

"All right, considering." That wasn't strictly true. She'd hardly begun to sort through the mess of the past few days, let alone what happened to Joe before that, but she wasn't up to talking about it now. "I'm going to call my kids today and ask them to come help me."

"That's good. I'd been hoping you would do that. Why the change?"

She managed a smile. "Sedna taught me that stories need to be shared. Also that family can help. Plus, I need them."

"Sedna's in town today."

"She's in town? That's new. I thought she pretty much stayed in her cabin."

"We've lots to tell you. Sedna's been visiting Joe, trying to comfort him in your place. He was restless, his blood pressure fluctuating. It worried Caroline and the doctors. He calmed when Sedna sat by his bed."

"The healer at work. Please ask her to come by if she has the time. I've missed her."

After lunch, Nora squeezed in phone calls with the

kids. Their voices were filled with such tenderness and worry that she found herself sharing more and more of the horrors of the past days. "Now I'm a pincushion and they've booked me for every body-part therapy you can imagine—fingers, hands, arms, legs."

Charlie's voice rang through the line. "Mom, Nell and I've been planning. I'm coming right away. Nell will arrange with her boss to take a leave at the end of my break. We'll overlap for a day, and she'll stay on. We'll rotate like that for as long as needed. I have time before I leave for some pre-trip errands. Anything you need from here?"

"Only you, and what a grand gift that is."

She meant that. Nora sank back into her pillows. Maybe it had been a mistake not to urge them to come sooner. *It's no matter. They're coming now.* She felt tight muscles relax. *I'll sleep well tonight. And, if Joe...* But she couldn't complete that thought yet. It might jinx his fragile recovery.

The next day, hospital routines kept Nora busy. In the late morning, another two RCMP officers came by. She braced herself for more hostile questions, but all they wanted were some hairs from her head. She let them pull out a few, gritting her teeth against the pain and indignity. When the woman officer dropped the hairs into a plastic evidence bag, Nora asked why they needed them, but neither Mountie answered.

In every break from her therapy routines, Nora sat by Joe's bed. He opened his eyes, looking at her. Once he even smiled when she took his hand.

As the hospital routines calmed down in the late afternoon, Sedna and Mackey arrived. Nora was sitting up in a chair next to her bed. They both beamed at Nora, and Sedna leaned over and gave her a quick kiss on the forehead. "Albert has news. We wanted to tell you together."

"Wait, wait. I'm frantic to hear your news, but first, thank you, dear Sedna. Mackey tells me you sat by Joe's bed for hours every day, calming him and keeping his blood pressure down. He opened his eyes and smiled at me today."

"He was helping me heal, too. I thought he needed a quiet voice, so I told him about my grandfather, and my parents, all those things I'd kept to myself until you pulled the stories out of me. You and Albert," she turned to Albert with a radiant smile, "lured me out of my solitude. I think Joe listened, but I'm not sure. He may not have been helped, but sitting with him was good for me."

Nora took Sedna's hand, nodding at Albert. "I'm ready to hear this news that's making you both beam at me."

Mackey drew in a breath. "I talked to the fishermen, like I said," he began. "Several of them spotted a sailboat in Mitlenatch Harbor recently, and one guy was sure it had been there for two whole days. Mitlenatch boaters are usually day-trippers, so that stuck out to him. Then later, I met Sedna for dinner, and—" He glanced at her. "You should tell the next part."

Sedna gave Mackey a long look then turned to Nora. "Albert and I planned dinner at a restaurant to celebrate my first day of teaching classes at the Community Center. The restaurant and the Center were both firsts for me. I was seated at a table in the middle of the room while Albert parked. There was a couple in the far corner, a man and a woman. He looked a bit older than her, but lean, fit, with curly, almost-white hair. She was wearing a body-hugging dress, the kind strangers look at twice, men and women, me included. He talked to her like a lover, holding her hand, stroking it while he talked. I held up my menu high enough to watch without being caught staring.

"Bless Grandfather, lipreading can be fun—and useful. I could see the man was angry though not at her. I paid attention to what he said. He leaned across the table and told the woman, 'I threatened her. She told me a cockamamie story about taking photos so she could paint steam. Steam, for God's sake. Really.' Then he said, 'I kept her for three stinking days. Her bowels almost ruined the boat. I thought I'd never clean out the smell. God bless bleach.'"

Nora pressed a hand to her mouth. "Go on," she managed to say through her fingers.

"He said, 'I couldn't stand nagging her any longer. I thought about pitching her out somewhere deep in the Strait. I found lead weights I'd used for prawn traps to be sure she would sink to the bottom. But I thought no one would connect me to her body, so I tumped her on that emergency dock, you know, the concrete slab in the north harbor.'"

Sedna knelt by Nora's chair and touched her shoulder. "They were finishing their meal and getting ready to leave. I wasn't sure what to do, but thank goodness, Albert came in right then. I stood and grabbed his arm. Albert is intuitive. He allowed me to nudge him to the restaurant door. I whispered to Albert. 'That man who just left.... Nora's captor. Albert went outside, fast, and caught the license plate as the man's car pulled out of the parking lot."

"Who was he?" Nora asked, her voice faint. "Do you know?"

"The mill investor," Albert said. "Jeremy Foster. John pointed him out to me once, when Foster's yacht went by in the harbor. I knew we'd have a hard time proving any of this to my sergeant, so I went and found the fisherman who'd spotted the sailboat in Mitlenatch. Luckily the tide had turned, so he was willing to quit his fishing and come along to headquarters. Sergeant Biddle didn't believe our story at first, especially that Sedna knew what Foster had said. He tested her. He sat Sedna outside an evidence room with glass windows. He asked two Mounties to whisper a conversation inside the room. No one on Sedna's side could hear anything. Sedna nailed their talk word for word.

"After that, Sergeant Biddle said he'd fill out a search warrant to inspect the boat, and he sent men out early this morning. The boat was spic and span except for a few hairs caught on the stairs from the anchor locker to the deck."

"So, that's why two policemen came here asking me for hairs from my head. Maybe that's a reward for all the pain of them being yanked out." Nora leaned her head back. "I'm grateful to you both." She stared at her cramped fingers. "I guess I haven't any answers about Joe's accident, or those men at the cabin." She lifted her head and tried to smile. "At least I'm not hallucinating my capture."

"I agree. We haven't solved the case yet. Sergeant Biddle still thinks you knocked your husband out of the skiff. He also doubts that a successful man like Jeremy Foster would worry about a few mystery photos. Frank McDonough thinks they were dumping pollutants. But we don't have proof."

Caroline entered the room then with a glass of water for Nora and put it down on Nora's tray table. "I couldn't help overhearing. Frank and his friends need to find out what's going on. No one will explain what that whole crazy scene at the mill was about. They were almost killed, and they're angry.

"The police don't know the full story. They haven't figured out how Nora escaped when you returned her to the hospital. We're all implicated."

"And no one but us has seen the photos," Mackey said. "They're in my safe deposit box. Sergeant Biddle hasn't connected the dots. For all he knows, those photos are figments of Nora's imagination."

Nora sat up straighter. "Wait a minute. I'm almost as skeptical as Mackey's sergeant. We haven't connected the dots, either. Why would a man like Jeremy Foster go ballistic over a tiny bit of unreliable evidence that he's involved with dumping mill pollutants? That's pretty far-fetched."

Mackey nodded. "Nora's right. We have to start at the beginning. And we need helpers.

"Caroline, can you ask Frank and his buddies if they'll meet with us? They know the mill, the town and the problem."

Chapter Nineteen

August 18-20, 1998

At ten the next morning, Frank and two of his friends, Jason and Tom, joined Mackey and Nora in the hospital courtyard, a little garden with benches used by convalescing patients. Nora meant to open the meeting with a stimulating challenge but found herself at a loss for words. She began with a simple statement. "We need you to solve a mystery about Grant's Mill and its current investor, Jeremy Foster." She swallowed hard. "He kidnapped me from the mill the night I followed you all there. He's after some photos I took of cargo ships in the mill harbor. We were hoping you might know why he wants them so much."

A little silence fell. Then Tom spoke. "Foster bought into Grant's Mill in '92. The previous owners took a big hit after the chlorine explosion in '86, so he probably got his shares for a song. Folks had seen him around here even before he bought into the mill. He came up the coast in his yacht in the summer of '91, July I think it was, and in August the summer after. He bought his shares in the mill that September. Don't know if that helps, but…"

Nora nodded. "I remember the explosion. McKeever and McKeever did a story on it. The cause determined at the time was chlorine gas trapped in an enclosed space."

Frank's co-worker Jason spoke up. "My wife's dad likes to fish the whirlpools by Bradley Island. I take him there at least once a summer. Seen Foster up there more than once with Gallagher's assistant, the looker who's rude every time we try to make an appointment with Gallagher about plant doings. My wife's dad says Bradley Island is being ruined. Bulldozers tore a chunk of it apart to build that golf course they got now."

Nora perked up in her wheelchair. "Bradley Island? I had a weird experience there a few weeks ago." She described the two barges, one that served as a high-tech hub and the other as a helicopter landing pad. "I had an unsettling encounter with the mystery man who appeared to be in charge of things. I turned down his invitation to lunch three times before he let me go. He sent me off with a muscle man pilot in a copter with a corporate logo. EnerGy, Inc. Capital E, capital G."

Tom broke in. "After Gallagher fired me, I timbered up near Prince Rupert. There were EnerGy, Inc. copters buzzing all over the place, lots of times coming in low and slow. At first, we thought they were studying the trees, but they paid more attention to the clear cuts and river channels. When we got off on Saturday nights, we'd see some of the pilots in their EnerGy, Inc. jackets in the bars, but they kept to themselves, no poker games with grunts like us. Pity. We might've pulled some fancy money out of their pockets.

"It's real tense up there, even worse than down here. Some people are tryin' to break tribal fishin' rights. Stateside canneries are pricing out the locals. Gas docks are being closed down by 'special' regulations. Felt real peaceful to come back here to Gallagher's bullying."

Nora frowned. "What is Foster up to? If he gets

scrutiny for dumping pollutants in the harbor, what else does he think might be exposed?" She gave a faint laugh. "You know, I've never seen Jeremy Foster or his wife, but I've met Gallagher's assistant, Gloria Hobart. She's a looker, all right."

Folks with sandwiches were trickling into the garden. Their secrecy threatened, Mackey suggested ending things for the morning. He promised Nora photos of Foster. "I'll contact everyone if I can find out more about EnerGy Inc."

Mackey went to the Grant's Landing Herald office to search through the paper's morgue for news of EnerGy, Inc. He found several photos of the Fosters from last year's festival, and another without Mrs. Foster from this year, but it took him all afternoon to dig up items about EnerGy, Inc. What he did find was inconclusive. EnerGy, Inc. had purchased shares in several pulp mills up and down the mainland coast. They also bought several fishing boats way north between Bela Coola and Prince Rupert, paying exorbitant prices for old boats with commercial fishing licenses. There was one seemingly unrelated mention of Jeremy Foster supporting a political party in eastern Canada.

He copied the photos and articles and left the newspaper morgue with a sense of futility. Sedna and he had planned to meet in Nora's hospital room, so at least he could share his lackluster news with them both at the same time.

At the hospital, Nora inspected the photos and articles Mackey had collected. "For sure, Jeremy Foster is the same guy who 'hosted' me on the Bradley Island barge."

Mackey had also found a few group images that

might have included EnerGy, Inc. employees. Nora looked carefully at each of the newsprint copies. "I don't see the slippery-looking fellow who landed in the copter. I'm guessing the towel-wrapped female I saw might have been Hobart. But what does that tell us? Nothing, except that Foster is cheating on his wife."

They had hit a dead end.

The story about Foster's political support awakened Nora's news nose, but she could think of no Grant's Landing resources for researching this vague lead. Then she thought of Nell at the *News Daily* in Boston and Charlie studying at Rutgers in New Jersey. Between the *Daily* and the university, they had resources for researching the political party to which Foster had contributed. A long lead to nowhere maybe, but she felt it worth some phone calls. Besides, it gave her a thrill to bring her children into the case. She had hated keeping them at arm's length when Joe was first injured, when she'd felt so uncertain whether she was to blame. Now, maybe, they could begin to be a family again.

After Mackey and Sedna left, she called both the kids and described the trouble at Grant's Mill along with the links to EnerGy, Inc., possible EnerGy, Inc. activities north of Vancouver Island and Foster's political donations. Charlie, as usual, sounded eager to dive in. "You caught me at a good time, Ma. I have a last interview with my professor about my thesis before I join you day after tomorrow. He might be interested. He's been investigating the repression of tribal rights in British Columbia."

Nell was more hesitant. "You expect a lot from a newbie intern, Mom, but I'll poke around in the files. There's a senior reporter who pretends to like what I've done so far. I'll talk to him too."

Nora passed the day and a half before Charlie's arrival by continuing her therapy exercises. Little by little, she was beginning to make her arms and legs obey her. Her fingers could hold a pen, but her handwriting was shaky at best. When she wasn't in therapy, she sat for hours by Joe's bed, telling him all the amazing things she had been learning in the past week. She kept her voice soft and quiet. Her tellings were meant to connect with him, not to make demands or even suggest expectations of a response. Joe watched her, sometimes waving a hand when she paused for a sip of water.

She also tried to keep her eagerness to understand the mystery in the back of her mind, so she could sleep at night. Otherwise, she might start blaming this beautiful place for her worries and sorrows.

The next day, Sedna came by while Nora was undergoing another therapy session. When Nora entered Joe's room, Sedna did not look up. *Of course,* Nora thought. *She didn't hear me come in.* Joe waved at Nora, like he meant her to come close. To her astonishment, he pointed at Sedna, and spoke. "We," he said. "Stories."

His words were clear. Nora held her breath. Joe pointed at Nora and then himself. "We. Schoo."

Sedna stood and embraced Nora. "I was telling him what I'm learning about First Nation residential schools. I'm sorry. I shouldn't have been sharing such heavy stuff. Can he be telling you he wants you two to report a story?"

Nora and Sedna turned to Joe together. He nodded. "We."

A day later, Charlie walked into her hospital room with an armload of flowers. She laughed and hugged him while tears rolled down her cheeks. "Darling Charlie, I know you want to go down the hall to see your dad." To gentle his first sight of his weakened father, she continued. "He might not speak or even look at you. He's hooked up to tubes, but his face has more color, and he's breathing better. Sometimes he opens his eyes, and he's spoken a few words. The doctors are hopeful." Honesty compelled her to add, "No promises, though."

Caroline went into Joe's room with them. No one spoke when Charlie laid a hand on his dad's arm. Joe opened his eyes wide and smiled. Charlie leaned close, soaking up the smile. "Dad," he said as he lifted Joe's hand and held it to his heart. They all stood in silence, clinging to the moment. Charlie leaned down, stroking his dad's cheeks before kissing him right under the bandages on his head. Then Charlie put his other arm around Nora. "You've been through a lot, Ma. It's time to get you back into bed now." They turned toward the door, and Nora saw Charlie wipe tears from his face as they walked out of the room.

Frank and the McDonough children all came to meet Charlie and celebrate. Mackey and Sedna came too, and Nora felt a rush of gratitude for the newfound friends who filled her hospital room to meet her son.

She had arranged for Charlie to spend his first night at the Harbor Inn, then drive her to the cabin the following morning after her discharge from the hospital. She encouraged Charlie to go with Mackey and Sedna for dinner. "They know a lot about what's going on in this whole mystery. Besides, I want them to know you and you, them. You and I will have a lot of time together at the cabin tomorrow and this whole wonderful week with you here."

The group had almost left the room when Nora called out. "Ouch! Our boat must still be moored at the cabin. I'd forgotten all about that."

"Not a problem," Mackey said. "I'll take Charlie to the cabin tomorrow, and he can bring your skiff back here or take it wherever he chooses."

Supper came like clockwork at five P.M. Nora was forcing down a dry piece of chicken when her phone rang. Nell's voice came over the line, crackling with energy like the baying of a hound following a fresh scent. "Mom, EnerGy, Inc. is a big contributor to the Trans Canada Party, TCP, which owns land in the oil sands of western Canada through a bunch of shell corporations. My gut tells me there's more to this story. Meanwhile, guard your photos and yourself. This is *big*."

Nora set the rubbery chicken aside with no regrets. She filled Nell in. "Your dad opens his eyes now and has said a few words. Charlie arrived this afternoon, and saw your dad for a few minutes. I'm so grateful to the two of you for taking turns to babysit your mom. The doctors think your dad is improving, but he'll need all of us as his support team." Surprising herself, Nora burst into tears. "Sorry, darling," she said, when she could speak, wiping her eyes. "Funny how the moves toward solutions make me cry, when earlier, I don't know, I felt numb."

Nell's voice brimmed with sympathy. "No, Mom. I shouldn't have implied danger. You've already been through too much. But you're well protected now, by the Mounties and all. I'll keep you and Charlie informed about whatever I find. Finish your dinner and enjoy the trip back to the cabin. I'll see you soon. Hugs and love."

"Hugs and love," Nora murmured back.

Nell hung up. Nora put the phone down and shoved her tray aside. Protected by the Mounties. Was she really? Mackey, yes, but the others? *Protect the photos. They probably think I have them. Foster and his goons might even think the photos gave clear evidence of wrongdoing even though she, Sedna and Mackey knew they were only hints of something, no proof of anything.*

The phone rang again. Nora picked it up, expecting Nell on the other end with another bit of news.

Instead, a deep male voice sounded in her ear. "Are you alone now? Have your friends gone off to dinner? I think we need to get to the bottom of your story or put your story out of commission."

Nora slammed the phone down. Angry as well as afraid, she moved so quickly that she knocked her dinner tray to the floor. The dishes shattered, sending china shards all around one side of her bed. She swung her legs over the other side, next to the wall. Where could she go? She had no clothes here. The ones she had worn during her captivity had been stripped off and tossed. She had an extra hospital johnny that she used as a bathrobe. She grabbed it and slung it over her shoulders, then stepped with care around the broken pottery bits and eased out into the corridor, looking both ways. No one was in sight. At this hour the hospital was quiet, the nurses on release between shifts. No one sat at the central nurse's station.

Nora picked a direction and edged down the hall.

Chapter Twenty

August 21-22, 1998

She opened the door next to hers to the noise of loud snoring. A dim light around the cracks in the drawn shade showed a sleeping man, mouth open, a few teeth missing. *My protection*, Nora thought as she eased her body into the one chair near the bed.

Time passed. Doors opened and closed up and down the corridor, but Nora stayed in her hideaway. The man slept on. Growing chilly, Nora pulled a cotton blanket off the foot of her companion's bed and wrapped it around herself. Soothed by the rhythm of his snores, she began to grow sleepy as well.

Lights startled her. "What are you doing here?" an exasperated voice snapped at Nora. "We've been looking all over the hospital for you."

Nora blinked awake. Angelica stood a couple of feet away, her hands on her hips. "This job is too much. I called Caroline. I told her this crazy, overwrought lady is driving me nuts. She can deal with you."

Shortly after, Caroline came in and led Nora back to her own room. "We found the tray on the floor, and the broken dishes, and no you. What happened?"

Nora explained about the phone call. "I'm frightened, Caroline. It's probably stupid, but I'm suddenly scared, more than before." She started to shake.

"Come with me to the nurse's station," Caroline said in her professional voice. "I'll call Mackey."

No one answered at Mackey's place. Caroline kept calm, which was more than Nora could manage. "I can't call Sedna, she doesn't have a phone. I won't leave you here alone. You're being discharged tomorrow anyway. Come home with me." She went to the closet that held discarded clothing, the same closet they'd used to find clothes for Nora after the boat accident. "Put these on while I sign your checkout papers."

The trip to Caroline's house didn't take long. Frank, his Irish spirit surfacing, greeted Nora with a welcoming hug. "Almost breakfast time, I'll make an omelet while Caroline fixes a bed for you."

Caroline chimed in. "And I'll call Charlie to let him know where you are."

Later that morning, Mackey arrived. Charlie McKeever was already there. The four of them gathered in Caroline's kitchen to discuss the phone call threat while Nora napped. "Nora admitted that Nell's warning made her hypersensitive, but she also swore the phone call was real," Caroline said, looking troubled. "I asked the hospital phone operators to check. They said there were no registered calls to Nora's room after a call from Boston at 5:45 last night."

Mackey didn't want Nora to know that. "She's under enough pressure. Hallucinations would be perfectly normal, but thinking this an illusion would upset her. Is there any way to erase the record of a call, or any reason one wouldn't come through the hospital switchboard?"

Caroline sighed. "Not that I know of. I want to believe her, but…"

"There must be some explanation," Charlie said. "I don't think my mother hallucinated anything. Can we set a trap of some sort to bring out the person who threatened her? If we do nothing, she may suspect we don't believe her." He caught Caroline's eye. "May I call my sister? Maybe there was someone listening in."

That afternoon, Nora, Mackey, Caroline, Charlie, Sedna, Frank, Jason and Tom gathered in Caroline's kitchen. Mackey opened the meeting. "Let's review. First, Charlie, what did Nell say when you spoke to her?"

"She didn't know about someone on the line at the hospital. But there's something strange going on." He glanced around at the others. "My sister's an intern at the *News Daily* in Boston. She asked local reporters about several matters, including possible connections between EnerGy Inc. and Canadian political parties. This morning, a senior reporter she knows, kind of a mentor, warned her away from her research. When she asked what was up, he confessed a Toronto news friend wanted to know why an intern in Boston got assigned to a minor story about a Canadian pulp mill when nothing had happened in the mill, the town, or the area. 'Pull her off it,' the Toronto guy said. That got the *Daily* guy's hackles up, and Nell's too. I mean, why would someone in Toronto call a Boston reporter and try to squelch an intern's non-story?"

"Whatever's going on in Grant's Landing has national and international attention," Mackey said. "Even though all we've got are photos that might— *might*—provide evidence of a pollution leak. Meanwhile," he glanced at Nora, "our photographer of the possible, if improbable, proof is being threatened. What do we do to help her out?"

Nora looked around at the faces surrounding her. Mackey, whose career she'd jeopardized because he trusted her word; Sedna, who had abandoned her solitude in the woods for Nora's cause; Caroline, who had lied to protect her and also jeopardized her job and her family; Frank, who had stood bound with his buddies through gunfire, all to protect her little photos for a watercolor project; and Charlie, her beloved son, who had taken on her issues even after she'd pushed him away. Plus, Nell, who might face repercussions in her career when she'd barely gotten started.

"I have a suggestion," she said. "These photos, these inconclusive photos, have attracted interest way out of proportion to their real value. What if we call in the local press and disclose them? Show the miserable, blurry bunch of nothing. Let the public, Mackey's sergeant, and everyone else reckon with the consequences. You all won't have to protect me anymore, for I will have nothing to disclose. Albert might salvage his career, since no one but us knows he has the photos in his care."

She paused, then went on in a stronger voice. "McKeever and McKeever believed that public knowledge is the source of power and change, the necessary transparency that engages citizens in solutions. So, let's put that belief into action."

Silence fell, becoming a presence in the room.

Mackey was the first to speak. "What happens if they charge you? I'm pretty sure my sergeant will do it. He really didn't want to swear out that warrant for Foster's sailboat. Besides, you know the news business. Wouldn't the issue of illegal dumping in the harbor first create a stir, then vanish from people's minds? You know. On to the next story."

"Maybe. But so would the danger. To me and to all of you."

Frank shuffled his feet. "Your safety means a lot to me, Nora, but, well, the mill…." He let his voice fade. Sedna crossed to Nora's chair and took Nora's hand but said nothing.

True to her straightforward manner, Caroline followed Frank's thought. "My guess is people will give Nora a lot of grief. First, they'll blame her for raising concerns about the mill without evidence. Then they'll act like Nora bumped her husband into the drink and made up some nonsense about being kidnapped to cover it up. Then, who knows what will happen, but Nora is likely to take on the whole town's anguish, and the mill's issues will be ignored."

"But wouldn't a few smart people ask questions?" Mackey said. "Mabel Joiner, for instance. She's committed to protecting the environment in the water and elsewhere, and she doesn't back down. Even I could ask questions. My first would be, why would a successful man like Jeremy Foster send goons after an American tourist who took pictures of the mill harbor? Why would he follow that up by kidnapping and torturing her for photos of no consequence?"

Charlie chimed in. "Why would anyone scare a rookie reporter in Boston from researching a story about a Canadian company registered in Toronto? With some extra effort, we can find others who'll pick up the questions. But Mom, we'll have to use you in a role you won't like, the innocent ignorant tourist."

Smiling, Nora waved her hand, palm up, fingers motioning toward herself, the come-on gesture used by schoolteachers to encourage a student. Charlie followed her lead and continued. "I'll bet my professor can find some good, solid British Columbians to join in, keeping the story fresh. If we work it hard enough, Dad might even get his strength back in time to turn it into a Canadian American TV special."

Nora couldn't bring herself to dampen Charlie's hope about that, so she kept her doubts to herself.

It was decided.

Charlie called the Grant's Landing *Herald* and announced a press meeting in a conference room at the hospital. A group of reporters gathered from Grant's Landing, Campbell River, and a few other mill towns on the coast.

"My mother, the recovering victim of a kidnapping reported in yesterday's paper, has a statement," he said to the reporters who turned up. "She has asked me to release photos that are presumed to be the reason for her abduction."

Charlie laid the photos on the table. "Please, examine them as you wish. My mother believes you and the world will find little in these photos to cause the break-in at the mill or her torture by her captor. She has been confined to the hospital until her health recovers."

The *Herald's* story was rude and angry.

> Mrs. Nora McKeever, a United States national vacationing in Grant's Landing, was accused by witnesses of attempted drowning and murder of her husband, Joe McKeever on August 2.
>
> Sergeant Harold Biddle of the RCMP confirms that she vanished from her husband's bedside two days after the incident and the mounties could not

locate her until she finally turned herself in on August 10. When police permitted her a brief visit to her husband's hospital room en route to being placed in custody, she disappeared again.

On the morning of August 14, she was found by John Bellows on the auxiliary dock at Grant's Landing's North Harbor with hands and feet bound.

Mrs. McKeever subsequently alleged she had been abducted to force her to reveal the whereabouts of some photographs she had taken of tankers in the area of the harbor near Grant's Mill.

Police investigated the kidnapping claim but have found little evidence to support her story.

The photographs themselves, released for public scrutiny and obtained by the *Herald*, depict nothing incriminating or newsworthy.

Seargent Biddle of the RCMP has charged her with attempted manslaughter, compounded by public mischief in a continuing conspiracy to evade arrest, all together a Class 3 felony.

The trial date has not been set.

Chapter Twenty-One

August 23, 1998

Back in the hospital after her overnight at Caroline's, Nora had been reading quietly when a phalanx of Mounties appeared in her hospital room with two members of hospital personnel. "We have orders to take you immediately to jail," said the lead officer, a brusque woman with captain's bars on her Mountie uniform.

Overwhelmed by surprise, Nora decided quickly not to jeopardize Caroline by calling for her help. She would go quietly. "I insist that my son, visiting from the States, be notified immediately," she said to the Mountie captain. She then spoke directly to the hospital personnel, "I trust you have received official papers and will record this event for your protection as well as mine."

Two female Mounties stood by as a nurse dressed Nora. She was handcuffed to a Mountie corporal, a young woman who looked as ashamed as Nora to be in this position. The procession out of the hospital was followed by a *Herald* reporter with a camera who had been notified of this event. The reporter yelled a few questions at Nora as she shuffled out the main doorway, but Nora refused to speak or turn to look at him.

Cameras flashed as the van door opened. Nora

climbed in. She had been with a camera crew at several incarcerations of prisoners. These events had always transfixed her with pity rather than anger. She had witnessed shame, sorrow, often tears from the presumed guilty. Nora looked up to see Angelica raising her fist at her with a broad grin. This gesture of triumph over her demise stiffened Nora's courage. "Goodbye, Angelica," she called out. "Thank you for your good care." She hoped her sarcasm was not lost on Angelica.

She thought of her momentary defiance all through the tiresome paperwork routine of assigning her to a cell. Remembering her response to that fist-raising nurse gave her little jolts of pleasure. *You're a fool, Nora McKeever, but you're not going to let them—what was on those t-shirts?—grind you down.*

The noon meal served after her arrival was as bad as, but no worse than, the hospital food. She had no visitors, not even Charlie, but she reminded herself that he had been scheduled to go with Caroline to the RCMP station. Perhaps he had not returned from there and still didn't know what had happened. She had brought the novel she had been reading when the phalanx marched into her hospital room. She opened it to begin where she had left off, but her eyes danced down the page without following the plot. *Can I convince myself that this jailing is just a temporary blip.* "All will be well as soon as Charlie and friends find out what had happened," she said out loud to the empty cell. *Something's wrong with me. My fight, my spirit, has crumbled. I'm becoming my mom. I can hear her say "What will be, will be."*

Before supper was served, she heard angry voices in the cell block. The clamor came closer, and she recognized Charlie's voice. "You have no right to keep me from speaking to my mother." Then, silence again.

Her calm disappeared. Her actions, even her non-actions, were wounding her darling son. Her spirit returned to make her pace her small cell and bang her fist on the bars, both useless gestures of rage. The lights went out in the cell block even before the summer sun set. Slight pink shone in the high cell window. Subdued, stiff and somber, Nora stared at the ceiling above her until black night descended.

Mackey learned that Nora had been dragged out of the hospital to jail. Knowing he was unlikely to get permission to see her, he stopped by to see John who, after his rescue, had developed a sense of ownership of Nora's well-being. John, he hoped, might be able to get a message to Nora that friends were with her.

As he had imagined, John stirred off his crate with new purpose. "Of course, I'll go to the jail. I'll do one better. I'll take Mabel, a force for good."

Next morning, handcuffed again, Nora was led out to a special room with a glass partition between the jailees and visitors. To her surprise, John Bellows sat waiting with the vegetable-selling environmental activist, whom Nora had watched during her exploration of Grant's Landing. John began introductions when Mabel interrupted. "Never mind, John, I've sold her vegetables. We're friends."

Nora nodded and looked for a mic to speak.

Mabel spoke again. "Albert Mackey heard you were here and sent us with messages. Your son is calling lawyers in Vancouver. Albert is interviewing suspects. You probably feel all alone, but we've come to let you know that the 'cavalry is coming.' Isn't that what the Stateside westerns say? But we really mean your friends are gathering, and it's these bands, not the cavalry, that will win this one."

Nora looked at both of these almost-strangers, their sun-creased faces furrowed with genuine concern.

"Are they treating you good?" asked John.

"Tell everyone that except for my pride, I'm okay, and I'm ever so grateful for this wonderful cavalry of family and friends. But I'm desperate to know what's going on."

"We'd tell you, if we knew, but we're only the messengers," Mabel responded. "Is there anything we can do for you while you wait?"

"I could certainly use one or two of Mabel's peaches and maybe a tomato or two."

"That's the spirit," John said. "You get out of here real fast, and Mabel'll feed you plus march you along with her brigade."

While John was speaking, Mabel leaned over to a sack she had sitting by her feet. "They didn't want me to bring this in, but one of the guards is the son of a customer, and I showed him that I only brought a few of my peaches. I gave him one to try. You have here a few peaches minus one, but no tomatoes."

The guard came to tell John and Mabel that time was up. Nora blew a few kisses to her messengers and waved goodbye.

The despair of yesterday's dark night had been toned down by hearing about this developing brigade. She walked back to her cell thinking of names for her band: flocks of friends, sympathizing sisters, or maybe swarms of sisters, broods of brothers, the caring cavalry, hordes of helpers.

Buoyed, Nora started thinking about prison. True,

the food was awful. But she'd never lived by dreams of food. What were her desires, her dreams. What was missing here?

She had had a passion for stories since childhood, reading, imagining and telling them. Certainly she could find stories in here, even guards probably had stories. Yes, but she ached with missing the things she had learned with Joe, the passion of building a story together and his touch on her skin. She missed mist on her face as she walked in the early mornings, a sense of freedom with each footstep and the fun of holding those tiny hands of first Nell, then Charlie, as they walked to school. Even before sitting alone in a jail cell, she often looked back with longing for those years of their childhood, the trust shared with the clasp of those plump palms. Then, here in a British Columbia jail, she longed for the sound of the soft sighing of the sea as it lapped on the shore, the silky sliding of the ocean across her skin on her swims, the squawk of gulls, the plaintive call of the loon pulling her into her hunger to be part of an ancient lore, to be one with a natural order.

Nora admonished herself: *Careful foolish woman. Soon you'll be waxing sentimental about the nightly invasion of mosquitoes on the cabin deck after the sun goes down.*

She had no sooner reached her cell, than another guard came to take her back to the visitor's room. There was Charlie looking frantic.

After John and Mabel's visit, Nora knew the jail-room system. She reached for the mic immediately. "Darling Charlie, I'm so happy, so very, very happy to see you. But I hate to see you looking stressed. Is your dad okay? Tell me what's going on."

"We're all worried about you, and here you are turning those worries around. Yes, Dad's maybe a bit stronger. He asked about you. I didn't tell him you're in jail. It seemed too complicated to explain. Besides, it might have set his health back. Now, first before I say anything more, how are you?"

"John Bellows, my rescuer, and his friend, Mabel Joiner, came to visit this morning. Imagine. I hardly know them. They said Mackey is at work looking for new evidence. I feel a community of support is building. Tell me more."

"When I'm not sitting with Dad, I've been on the phone. The calls were worth it. My professor has environmental lawyer friends in Vancouver who have been investigating EnerGy Inc. activities. A team will come up tomorrow. They have agreed to take your case. My guess is they'll have you out on bail in rapid time. The policeman isn't going to give me long here, so I'll hurry up my news. Sedna plans to come to see Dad every day. And Mackey and she have told me about you at Sedna's cabin. They are special.

"The policeman's approaching. I'll really pack in the news. Frank's working at the mill again, along with his other pals in the mill that night. Caroline is angry with the hospital and some of the nurses, so angry she may quit her job."

"Oh, Charlie, please, don't let her do that. She's a gifted nurse. You? Nell? How are you? Where are you sleeping?"

"I'm going to the cabin at night. Albert showed me the way. He said you swim every day. Zounds! How do you do that? It's cold."

They saw the policeman pointing at his watch.

"The loons and I, Charlie, we're tough old birds. You should hold your breath and try it. You and Nell both swam near here when you were young. Be a tough old bird like me."

She held her arms out to him with the best mock embrace she could manage in handcuffs. He did the same.

"Thank you," she called after him as he turned to leave, hoping he did not see the tears on her cheeks.

Chapter Twenty-Two

August 23, 1998

When Mackey went to the hospital, Nora's room was empty.

Seated behind the nurses' station, Angelica greeted Mackey with a smug, know-it-all smile. "Well, your favorite is in a mess now. They've taken her off to jail, charges of manslaughter. Serves her right. After the supposed fishing accident, Caroline told me not to leave her alone with her husband, and now I know why."

Mackey gripped his elbows to help him control his temper. "Where's Caroline?"

"She called me in to replace her so she could go off with that murderer's son. Attempted murderer, I guess I should say. I don't know where they are. That Stateside woman has been nothing but trouble. 'Check his movement,' she'd say to me every minute. I think she was trying to figure out if she needed to bop him again. Those Statesiders think they can boss everyone around."

Mackey turned on his heel and marched out of the hospital before he could yell at the young nurse. How could she be so certain of Nora's guilt? *We're back at square one, like on the day of the accident.*

He walked down to the harbor. John wasn't sitting on his crate. Disappointed, Albert turned to walk back along the main street. In the distance he spied the drunk,

Butch, swigging a beer with another fellow, both of them wearing *Don't Let the Bastards Grind You Down* t-shirts. Albert turned a corner. He didn't want to hear Butch spouting anger, but it set him thinking again about Butch's statement the day the jerk got into it with John at the dock. "Quota guy, First Nation designated." Did his fellow officers think that too, and shun him? He wouldn't believe it of them. He liked his buddies. They had spent numerous off hours talking together about everything and nothing. Some had taken assignments for him so he could explore the area. He'd returned the favors with pleasure.

Yet, he had been thinking of resigning from the RCMP ever since meeting Sedna. Following her lead, he had begun to long for a sense of attachment to the land. He also knew he didn't like chasing people, questioning motives. He didn't want to leave the Mounties because of the guys. Most of them had become pals. He just knew he wanted something more. He'd begun to think how his life could change by living in Sedna's woods.

Mackey walked until his anger ebbed from a slow boil to a simmer. Where was Nora by now? She must have been moved from pre-trial custody in the hospital to the jail. He wanted to go there and even started toward his parked car when common sense made him halt. *They won't let me see her. Biddle will make sure I'm kept away from her.*

Sergeant Biddle, an old-timer, was different from his other Mountie pals. One of the guys had told Mackey that Biddle had been a rising star before coming to Grant's Landing, but he'd changed. The scuttlebutt was money troubles with the wife. But why would that make Biddle go after Nora as he was now doing? He tried to put these questions out of his mind, but what should he do now?

He thought about heading to the McKeevers' cabin in case Charlie was there, then recalled Angelica's angry comment about Caroline and Charlie going off someplace. Charlie was as likely to end up back at the hospital as anywhere else.

Mackey returned to the hospital and found Caroline at the nurses' station, sitting with her head in her hands. She didn't even look up when Mackey walked to the counter. When he spoke her name quietly, she lifted her head, rested her chin on her crossed hands and opened her mouth, but no sound came out. She looked back down at the countertop. Finally, she raised her head. "The RCMP has dragged Nora off to jail with the hospital personnel officiating. I don't know what to believe. Nora sat by her husband like she was as wounded as he. Charlie and I went to Sergeant Biddle this morning to ask questions. Instead, he questioned us.

"He was rough on Charlie. 'What do *you* know, boy? Were you there? Tell me about the arguments between your mother and father. Do you know your mother pushed your father out of the boat?' Charlie couldn't answer, of course, but he kept his cool. I was impressed."

She shook her head. "I didn't keep my cool when Sergeant Biddle turned on me. 'That woman escaped from the hospital room when you were on duty. How did you let her out of your sight? Where did she go? I hear your husband broke into the mill the same night that woman claims she was abducted. Why would he do that? She followed him and his buddies in. How did he connect with that woman without your help?' I stood there like a lump, but I could feel my face heat, and I wanted to scream.

"Then the sergeant marched out from behind his desk and stood right in front of me. He accused me of aiding and abetting a criminal. 'That woman wants us to believe she was kidnapped by one of this town's leading benefactors. She and that rookie constable want to put my head in a noose, and I am not, you hear me, am *not,* going to let them get away with it.' That's what he said, word for word.

"I was shaking like a leaf. No, like a whole tree in a hurricane." She met Mackey's gaze, her expression troubled. "What do we really know about Nora McKeever? Is she just a tourist whose husband had a boating accident?"

Mackey tamped down his irritation. None of this was Caroline's fault. "Biddle's right, I am a rookie constable, but I believe he's wrong about Nora. I think I have to follow the trail. I'll start digging again. Where's Charlie?"

"He's off making phone calls. He and his sister are trying to hire a lawyer. In the meantime, 'that woman'—don't you hate the expression—can't have any visitors if she comes back here for therapy, and she can't see her husband. The hospital is understaffed, and my nurses are taking sides, which doesn't help."

Mackey decided there was no point in going back to the fishermen for more details of Joe McKeever's accident. The finger pointers would be even more convinced of Nora's guilt after reading the *Herald* article. He ran over all the players he knew and decided to interview Gallagher next. What had the mill manager really known about the water pipe leak? He had seemed bewildered and unknowing when he barged into the gunfight that night at the mill.

Mackey went straight to the mill, not bothering to make an appointment. If Gloria Hobart was Jeremy Foster's girlfriend as well as Gallagher's assistant, she might be deeply involved in this whole mess. A substitute filled Hobart's role at the mill. Mackey asked for an appointment with Gallagher.

The manager greeted him with a sardonic comment. "I'm curious about how a rookie constable, as you called yourself that night, got mixed up with two fighting mill factions, the locals and the new hires."

Mackey entered the inner office and found it exactly as Nora had described. There was nothing on Gallagher's desk. He saw the giant table made from an ancient tree and the shining view of the Strait with sailors tacking into the wind. "What about those factions? I know some of the locals. Tell me about the new hires," Mackey said.

Gallagher scowled. "Hobart hired them. We needed replacements, and I had other things to take care of. Managing a pulp mill is a big job."

"Replacements for guys like Frank McDonough?" Mackey kept his tone friendly, but Gallagher clearly didn't like the question. Mackey pressed on. "What happened with that leak he reported to you? Did anyone follow up and take care of it?"

"I never heard anything about leaks. Hobart took care of sending workers to check on any trouble, and she got the reports. When she came and told me that Frank McDonough had gone to the safety inspector, I admit I blew my top. His report could have affected the life of the mill. Hell, it could change the life of the entire town. If the government shut us down, everyone in Grant's

Landing would suffer." He sighed. "Maybe I was wrong. I don't know. All I know for sure is, it's my job to keep this mill running, so the men can put food in their kids' mouths and keep roofs over their heads." He waved his damaged hand at Mackey. "You want details about a leak, go talk to Hobart, if you can find her. She hasn't come in to work for days."

Chapter Twenty-Three

August 23-31, 1998

Mackey went to the jail in search of Red Shirt and the other thugs from the mill. Now that he knew they had been hired by Hobart, he had reason to believe that they might have important stories to tell.

He tried to swallow his personal feelings about them. For sure, they'd taken their anger out on him, but with no one else to bother, they might be beating up on each other. Who knew?

The sergeant in charge gave Mackey an interview room where he could talk with them one-on-one. Apparently, word hadn't filtered down to block him from interviews in the jail. Remembering his failed interview on his inquiry with Nora, he requested a detective to sit in the room with him as he cross-examined each man. All four of the bruisers were new hires, not local men, and admitted that Hobart recruited them. None had been asked for credentials, and all had prison records in other Canadian provinces.

The first man he spoke with started to talk. "That bitch abandoned us. She promised me forty thousand quid in U.S. dollars. I dunno what she promised the others. Mitch was the leader. Maybe he got more." Mackey kept control, not letting his excitement show on his face. He asked more questions, but the goon looked around fearfully and clammed up.

Mackey interviewed the next two flunkies, saving the leader, Mitch, for last. Each told about being promised money for jobs outside the mill without giving details. All three were angry about being in jail, placing much of their ire on their leader.

Next, he interviewed Mitch. He used the other conversations as a starting place. "I hear Hobart paid you guys for special jobs, jobs outside the Mill. Tell me about the McKeevers' cabin."

Mitch, Red Shirt, clenched his fists. "I never got a dime for my work."

"What work? Do you admit to trashing that cabin?"

Mitch lowered his head, sitting silent.

"Why did you go to the mill the night we were all hauled off to jail?"

Mitch stared at the floor, saying nothing.

Mackey thought he should try another angle. "You know your pals are angry with you. They think you've been paid more than they. They feel as if they've been double-crossed. If the others testify and you do not, you may be left out in the cold. It's possible they could get off with minor offenses, leaving you in the slammer long-term, taking the rap. They all call you their leader."

"Yeah. And, if I do talk, what'll I get out of that?"

Mackey thought for a minute. "I'm not in a position to make any promises, but my guess is it might soften your charges."

Mackey went straight to Joe's hospital room, where he found Charlie sitting by his dad's bed.

"Can you step out of the room for a minute?"

"Sure." They went into the hallway. Before Mackey could speak, Charlie exploded. "Have you heard about

Mom? They've dragged her off to jail. It's a good thing the Vancouver lawyers have accepted Mom's case."

"Good work. She needs good lawyers, and I've a suggestion for them when they come. I just finished talking to the thugs who accosted Frank and his buddies in the mill. They are pissed. Lawyers may be able to get confessions for trashing the cabin. That's a small part of the incidents, but it would give a boost to your mom's story. They wouldn't promise me anything, but it sounds as if Hobart, Gallagher's assistant, offered them money for something and never paid."

Events unfolded rapidly over the next several days. Three lawyers arrived in Grant's Landing the next morning, armed with files, tape recorders, and solid knowledge of court procedures. The next day, the lawyers won the right to speak with their client. By the end of the third day, Nora was released on bond and given the right to visit her husband and children.

The RCMP insisted on a protective detail standing by in Joe McKeever's room. Nora decided that wasn't worth fighting. She had no proof that she would be proven innocent. Mackey's description of his conversations with the thugs reminded her about her image of the men in yellow slickers pulling away from the accident scene. Could there be something in that? Maybe. The doubt lingered. If so, would the thugs talk? Would Sergeant Biddle and the reporters accept the fisherman's testimony about seeing a sailboat in Mitlenatch harbor? Would anyone believe a deaf woman's story of eavesdropping?

Thrusting her doubts aside, Nora ran straight to Joe's bedside and brought his hand up to her face, forgetting she had an audience. The room was full of the team, Charlie, Caroline, Mackie, and one of the lawyers who accompanied her from the prison. She ignored the Mountie standing by the door.

She looked at her husband and realized his eyes were open. Not just open, but alert and focused in a way they hadn't been, not even on the day Sedna told him about Indian Boarding Schools.

"Nora," Joe said and squeezed her hand. "Nora."

"Mom," Charlie said from somewhere far away, but all Nora could do was say Joe's name. She leaned over his arms, still connected to tubes, and kissed him right on his mouth before she remembered they were not alone. She pulled back hastily and looked immediately at Caroline who gave her a broad smile and a thumbs-up.

In a celebratory mood, Charlie and Nora joined Mackey and Sedna at a restaurant for dinner. Sedna and Mackey were both glowing. Nora had the feeling there was more to celebrate than her release and Joe's latest step toward recovery.

"Sedna and I wanted to tell you. I asked her to marry me." He laughed. "We were at her cabin. She was silent after my proposal for what felt like an eon. I was frantic, sure she would turn me down. Then she asked me if I would be willing to live in the woods with her. I was so overwhelmed I could hardly speak."

Sedna took up the tale. "The silence was terrible. I thought expecting Albert to accept my simple life was asking too much. I turned my back on him and started for the garden. He grabbed my arm and turned me to face him, and…"

"I couldn't let her walk away." Mackey glanced shyly at the tabletop, then back at Sedna. "We haven't made all the plans yet, but I'm moving to Sedna's this week."

Nora got up from her chair and hugged them both. "How did this happen? Tell me everything," she said, taking her seat at the table again.

"Grandfather had been dead for a year," Sedna began. "I'd stayed quiet in his house, hiding from the world. Albert came often, trying to build my confidence. Then he brought you. On a quiet day after you left, he asked if I could meet with his soccer team, the boys he coaches in his off hours. He wanted them to learn about the forest and its gifts. He brought a few boys to meet me near that cow skull on the cliff edge. We walked through the woods for two hours. The boys were curious and mischievous. We laughed and had a good time. I took a picnic of boiled sea gull eggs, salmon berries, crab claws. They asked dozens of questions. They listened. It was wonderful. Almost like talking to you and Albert."

She smiled. "That was encouragement. I've signed up to teach a course about healing plants and folklore at the local community center. I could never have done that without Albert's interest, and the talks I had with you. It was a few days later when he came and asked me."

Mackey took Sedna's hand. "Things are changing around here, some for the better.

When I spent more time in Sedna's woods, I found a new peace, working with her collecting herbs and leaves for potions. Digging in the soft forest turf helped me connect with my memories of my father reading me passages from books about compost and soil improvement. I'd been thinking about resigning from the RCMP. So, I finally did it. I've signed up for forestry classes at the University. They have some professors there who believe in replacing clear-cutting with selective tree management.

"Sedna and I have dreams of supporting new ways. Big foresting companies think clear-cutting is cheap and efficient. But those giant bulldozers pack down the soil. With no trees for protection, the soft forest undergrowth gets washed or blown away by storms. The companies replant, but the little seedlings have no support. Making big corporations change is a big leap. Who knows how far we can take the idea, but it's a hope we can help build and grow."

In efforts to hold onto the positive vibes, the conversation changed to Charlie's plans. They skirted the worrying subjects of Nora's upcoming trial and the long-term issues of Joe's prognosis for recovery.

Nell arrived in Grant's Landing a day later, having stopped over in Ottawa for some on-the-ground snooping. Nora, Nell and Charlie sat in the hospital community room, drinking tea. "It's no fun to sit in front of microfiche rolls," Nell told them. "You have to lean into the viewer box; the light is dim; the angle gnaws at your back muscles; if your hand bumps the button that rolls the wheels faster, the print blurs to gibberish. Even with all that, a name or a location can pop out."

Nell leaned forward and spread a pile of printouts she'd collected across a table. "I studied these by night in my motel room. Three politicians in the Trans Canada Party, the group Jeremy Foster gave money to, received regular donations from companies located in northwestern British Columbia. One of the donors purchased a fishing fleet. Another invested in a cannery that closed a year later. Two other canneries had closed down not long before that, so I investigated all three, and found overlapping investments from people in Toronto and politicians in Ottawa." She sat back and sipped her tea. "So, I vetted names with some ace reporters recommended by my mentor, and it turns out two of the investors worked for EnerGy, Inc. for a year or two before moving out of Canada." She pushed the topmost printout toward Nora. "This article has a good photo of one of them. Harold Bennett. He not only worked for EnerGy, Inc., he's a major investor in it as well."

Nora picked up the printout and studied it. Her eyes narrowed. "I recognize him. Foster called him 'Harry.' Harold Bennett is the man who helicoptered onto Jeremy Foster's barge off Bradley Island."

"So can we put those ace reporters in touch with Mom's lawyers?" Charlie asked.

Nell raised her tea mug with a satisfied grin.

Two days later, Mackey found Nell, Charlie and Nora visiting Joe at the hospital. Before he could say more than hello, Charlie gave him the latest. "The lawyers tell us they'll be in the courts for years, dealing with all this stuff. It'll be a long haul, but at least your efforts slowed down a few get-rich conspiracies. It's a start."

"I've news for you as well, more local than Charlie's." Mackey leaned against the wall, arms folded across his chest. "The investigators from Vancouver followed the money, including Sergeant Biddle's bank records, and those of the Grant's Landing Festival for the past few years. The Civic Festival Society paid, as agreed, for all the RCMP personnel assigned, only the money ended up in Biddle's private account along with contributions from Jeremy Foster, Gloria Hobart, and a guy named Harry Bennett, all doled out in small increments. Biddle acted surprised when the data exposed him. He resigned one step ahead of a criminal inquiry."

After more tests, the doctors advised that Joe should relocate from the hospital to a rehab center, where he could continue therapy by day and live at home at night. Charlie, Nell and Nora found a small rental home near the center, and Charlie offered to move their things from the cabin at Grace Point to the new house in Grant's Landing.

"I'll help load the boat, and maybe scoop up a few oysters from the beach at the same time," Nell added.

Nora protested. "I hate to have you both trundling back and forth over that long reach." She paused. "Long Reach is an old sailor's term. That's what Dr. Cameron called the big stretch of open water between Grace Point and Grant's on the first morning in the hospital so many weeks ago. Now that I think about it, this whole experience has been a long reach, in more ways than any of us could have guessed."

For the hospital farewell, the reunited McKeever family pushed Joe's wheelchair down the corridor, with nurses, doctors and orderlies waving as the team moved slowly by.

With the family settled, Charlie made reservations for his return to college. Nora urged Nell to go back to the *News Daily, to* pick up her job where she'd left off. They arranged to return on alternate visits throughout Joe's rehab process.

Chapter Twenty-Four

September 1-15, 1998

Nora read to Joe every evening after his rehab sessions. She started with books Joe had loved as a child: *Wild Animals I Have Known* and Mark Twain short stories. All plots she hoped he could follow. She loved the quiet reading times as much as Joe did.

On one of her visits, Sedna brought strands of fibers. "Joe, you've not been to my cabin," she said, smiling at him. "When you come, you'll see that my fences and many other areas are held together by handmade ropes. I thought you could help me braid strands for places that need repair."

The rope-braiding was as good as the rehab center exercises for helping Joe loosen his finger movements. More important, the job needed doing. Real work brought Joe dignity, which was sorely tried by frustrations and occasional setbacks. Visit after visit, he and Sedna talked and braided, and Sedna told stories about what happened to her parents. Gradually, Joe began to ask questions. The newsman was coming back, along with the ability to speak more fluently.

Sedna let the tale unfurl about her parents' escape from the residential school. Deep into the topic, she shared more details with Joe about their torture, happenings she hadn't had the strength to describe to

Nora. "Grandfather told me that my dad had deep scars and seeping wounds on his back from whippings, and my mother had been tied to a chair wound with wires attached to batteries that sent shock waves through her body at the turn of a switch, a make-do electric chair."

Joe, alarmed and angry, stood abruptly, tumping the piles of fibers from his lap. He grabbed the back of his wheelchair and pushed it around the room, his face contorted with rage. Sedna, equally alarmed, called for Nora. "I'm so sorry. I shouldn't have told him those stories."

Joe turned to Sedna with tears in his eyes. "No, Sedna, I need to know. World needs to know. More. More. Nora, you and I need go work."

From then on, Nora brought harder books to read to him. Reading through John Milloy's newly published *A National Crime* gave a lot of facts to digest about the history of residential schools. Joe asked Nora to take notes of particular points, including the continuing refrain in government documents: "Kill the Indian in the child…"

"Yes," responded Joe. "And kill child." His face reflected his fury.

When they came upon strong points, Joe would signal Nora to make a note. Sometimes she would suggest a phrase for the script. In the past, they had taken different tasks. She, the outreach and research. He, the interviews and the telling. They now shared both. He reached for her hand to affirm an agreement on an important point or paused to smile at her and nod. She loved this connecting with Joe. He seemed equally invested in seeking out the details of the full story as she absorbed his visceral attachment to the expressions of telling.

At Joe's urging, Nora found photos of the abandoned school that had abused Sedna's mother and father. With all this stimulation, Joe's thoughts and words became more and more clear. After a few weeks, he and Nora had a script.

They showed it to Sedna, who approved. "It is good, and important. You and Nora can make it public."

"No." Joe pounded his fist on the table. His sudden fury startled Sedna, Nora and maybe Joe as well. Joe maintained his loud tone. "It's your story. You tell."

Sedna abruptly rose to go, grabbing her basket with shaking hands. She walked out of their small house without a word, leaving the script behind.

Nora did her best to mend things. "We've gone too far too fast for her, that's all. We'll have to forget this story. No, not forget it, set it aside. Sedna will find her way."

Joe didn't sleep well that night. In the ensuing days at rehab, he lost his temper over minor mistakes. Determined to keep him from losing ground, Nora sought fresh topics to engage him.

She read local books aloud, including *Once Upon a Stump,* the book of early settlers' recollections she'd found on her solo trip to Grant's Landing before Joe's accident. Joe paid little attention.

She invited Mabel Joiner and John Bellows for visits, both good storytellers. Joe listened to them as if distracted, not fully there in the same room. Nora feared that his recuperation was going backwards.

One day, late in the afternoon, Sedna came by with a basket of lavender. She didn't sit. "You're right, Joe. I've been asking questions," she told them. "The young ones at the community center don't understand the silence of their parents and grandparents about the residential schools, so I talked to the Center's Tribal Council. It has been decided." She glanced at Nora. "You remember I told you about Grandfather's work helping us relearn our languages, songs and dances? The Council is forming a group to do that. We'll travel from tribe to tribe, listening for their stories, including the hidden stories about the schools."

"That's wonderful," Nora said. Joe eyes never left Sedna's face.

Sedna went on, smiling broadly now. "Albert will be part of it, too. His RCMP savings will be down payment on a boat. In the summer between classes, he'll work at forest preservation at each village and join us in the storytelling and singing at night. We'll be gathering our stories our way, the traditional way."

They talked the rest of the afternoon about Albert's and Sedna's plans. Nora asked, "Can you collect the stories for future records?"

Joe looked at Nora, eyebrows raised. "Nora, what do you think? We could buy—" he said slowly. He floundered for a moment, searching for the right words, then his anxious look smoothed out. "—tele-cam to take on their travels?" Nora nodded with enthusiasm. "Nora will teach you and Albert to use it," he went on, still speaking slowly, but every word precise. "She trained our best cam men," the word camera half stated.

"And camera women," Nora added.

"For sure." Joe grinned. "Sedna and Albert. A team. Like McKeever and McKeever."

Chapter Twenty-Five

September 16—October 10, 1998

Calmed by Sedna's response and the plans for action, Joe's agitation eased. He began sleeping through the night. Nora continued gathering friends, Sedna, Mackey, Caroline, Frank, Tom, Jason, Mabel and John to share their love and concern for the beauties of the Georgia Strait; the joys of pulling crab pots in the last light of day; of watching a solitary heron standing statue still, stalking its next dinner; of shucking oysters with friends, beers and laughter. She even included Gallagher, who seemed more concerned about pollution than anyone could have expected.

After working together on the residential schools, she and Joe found a new role for their work. Using the tools they knew best—research, interviews, listening with cameras—they could record or cause to be recorded the issues that most mattered to people working to conserve a community's life and future.

Nora and Joe's breakfast and dinner conversations attacked subjects that had often been at the back of their work, but never topics for discussion. Why do people change their minds? What information does the public need to know? How are laws changed?

With his words surfacing slowly, Nora knew that Joe could not take on an anchor's role for a good long time. Joe liked working on a new business plan, so she suspected he wanted new job descriptions.

Joe's word facilities were better some days than others. Nora spoke to his therapists about this, and they nodded with sympathy. "That happens. It takes patience from him and you. Our best advice is to listen carefully, responding without correcting him when you can."

In these discussions about purpose and process, Nora was determined to introduce the problems that had arisen in her dismissal from McKeever and McKeever. She wanted to spark understanding. One afternoon, sitting on a bench in their small patio with breezes of fall ruffling leaves in a nearby maple tree, Nora spoke directly. "We lost our way for a time, Joe. You may have been hurt and angry about my ways. I know I was hurt about your ignoring my help. We forgot our old warning code, 'Walking math book.' "

To her relief, Joe laughed. "As I lay in the hospital bed, I heard. I couldn't speak. No words. Terr-terr-terrifying. Frus-mad. Still is."

Nora took his hand without saying anything, to give him time.

"I lie there. Think of past. I planned story, more story. You looked for details, more details. You speak stories with details. Listen, speak. Good." He stopped as if exhausted.

Nora moved close to Joe on the bench and laid her head on his shoulder. "You understand. Thank you."

Nora and Joe worried together on rules for partnerships and collaboration. "Maybe we can find hints, or prompts that help people listen, then respond," Nora said.

"Not rules," Joe offered.

"Attitudes," Nora suggested, "that give space and time."

"Path," Joe said.

If they had a disagreement, Joe would ask, "Is this a path issue?"

They began plotting new roles for their work. They could teach tools they knew best—research, interviews, listening with cameras. They could demonstrate ways to record or cause to be recorded the work of caring humans striving to conserve a community's life and future. They made outlines of probable ways to find the people who would want to build understanding through listening and storytelling.

With endless long-distance calls, they brought Jordan and Bridget into the discussions of an evolving business. Together they began to compare the issues of Grant's Landing to the world they had explored through McKeever and McKeever before Joe's accident. They admitted with sorrow that pollution, residential schools, neglected communities were as prevalent stateside as in British Columbia, perhaps more so. The need for community conservation and people's engagement was pressing everywhere.

Nora regularly gathered friends—Sedna and Albert, Caroline and Frank, Tom, Jason, Mabel and John. Gradually, the brigade, as Mabel liked to call them, joined in with discussions about projects, along with good food. Sometimes, the arguments were fierce.

"It's hopeless," Tom yelled one night. "Don't even bother trying for changed laws. Just go out and catch fish while you still can."

Jason piped in. "I agree, do-gooders force a new law about dumping, and before the print is dry, a mill owner gets the ear of the government, and the law slides away."

Mabel, red in the face, stood on a foot stool and waved her arms. "So, you lazy bums, drink your beer, jeer to your heart's content. But don't forget. Gallagher is on our team now. Took a lot of mess, almost a life, but the mill's installing a closed water system. Plus, he's talking to other mill managers about making changes."

"Yeah. Just wait," Jason rejoined. "When your back is turned, that water will be pumped right back into the Strait."

Eager to put the ideas in motion, Joe and Nora welcomed the arrival of the new camera, a lighter version than those Joe and Nora had first used. Mackey and Sedna came for practice sessions, which Mackey shared with John Bellows. John, thinking of Mabel's brigade of sludge busters, told her about the training, so the teachings grew.

As Joe grew stronger, Mabel led road trips for Joe and Nora to backwoods and secret beaches where she could point out good farming techniques, the benefits of individual forest harvesting with seedling trees planted close enough to their elders to receive the elder trees' nurturing. "I've talked myself hoarse over all this," Mabel said. "Don't tell Tom and Jason that I get discouraged. I can't lecture change. People need to feel the need. It's slow, so, so slow." But then, true to form, she made herself sound optimistic. "We've a new recruit in Mackey's forest work. My motto: Keep on plugging, one, by one, by one."

The trainings included a few of the sludge busters, even Jacob's wife joining in along with Albert, Sedna and Mabel. Joe and Nora began to make lists of helpful suggestions about changing camera angles to focus in on special testimony; providing "B rolls," footage for scene-setting to use before, during or after the main topic discussions; and useful hints for involving local news stations.

Sedna suggested that young people at meetings needed action roles to encourage their participation.

"Right on, Sedna. Why not give them small cameras, you know those cheap ones you can buy at drugstores, to record the crowds who gather, or other things they find interesting. It will add to the records."

"Yes." Mabel boomed. "If you don't have a job that needs doing, invent one. Better yet, invent two and more."

After one session, Joe, weary but smiling, turned to Nora. "I begin to feel useful again."

Chapter Twenty-Six

October 10-13, 1998

At long last, Nora's trial date rolled around. Charlie took a leave from college to attend. Nell, who had been given a staff position after her Canadian research, couldn't come. She had been assigned to a voter fraud issue in Alabama, a welcome promotion.

Charlie navigated Joe to the courtroom in his wheelchair. They sat with Mackey, Sedna, John, Mabel, right behind Nora and Robert Redburn, the lead Vancouver lawyer. Caroline and Frank couldn't leave work, but Joe and Nora knew they were there with their thoughts. Charlie promised to call Nell and Caroline with the verdict as soon as it came down.

The lawyers for the State called William Martin to the stand. Mackey sucked in his breath, knowing this was the angriest of the fishermen witnesses he had interviewed. Martin placed all of the blame on Nora as Mackey feared. "The man was clinging to the side of the boat when it started going in circles. The boat came back around, and he was gone. She had pushed him into the drink. That murderess waved an oar to keep us from rescuing her wounded husband."

"Objection," called out Redburn.

"Objection denied," said the judge.

Next, the prosecutor called Jacob. Jacob looked over

at Nora and Mackey shaking his head. "To tell you the truth, I don't know what to think. Her boat was going in circles. The wife says she wouldn't know what to do if she were in her shoes."

The prosecutor interrupted. "Was your wife a witness?"

"No, sir. She don' go out with me, 'cept on special occasions."

The prosecutor droned, "Judge, please ask the jury to overlook the wife's comment as immaterial to the case."

Jacob reported that he had seen the victim hanging on to the side of the boat.

The trial plunged on. Nora twisted a handkerchief in her hand, and occasionally wiped her face with it. Her doubts of her innocence had been stirred by the testimony. She was consumed by the memories of the accident and the agonizing days after it.

Nora was called to the stand.

She raised her hand to swear to tell the whole truth. When the prosecutor asked her to tell the jury exactly what had happened, Nora whispered, "To be honest, I don't know what happened. I was beating a fierce dogfish on my line, when I heard a groan, I looked up and my husband was gone."

The prosecutor demanded, "Was he hanging on the gunnels until you beat him off?" Redburn rose. "Objection. The prosecutor is leading the witness."

"Objection denied." The judge responded. "That statement was sworn by a witness."

The prosecutor repeated the question. "Was your husband hanging on the gunnels until you beat him off?"

Nora was fighting back her fears of doubt. "I don't

know. I did try to pull him in, but the boat almost rolled over with both of us on the same side. Then I crawled to the stern to press off the motor."

Prosecutor: "Did you wave an oar at boats coming to rescue your husband."

Nora: "I pulled the oar out from the gunnels to try to paddle the boat toward Joe who was all bloody in the water."

Prosecutor: "I'll ask you again. Did you wave that oar at rescuers? Did you yell at them to stay away."

Nora: "I thought I could use the oar to lift Joe out of the water, but he was too heavy. I screamed and screamed at them to watch out. I was afraid they would run over my husband."

When Nora was released from the stand, she stumbled toward her chair, certain that her testimony had lost the case.

The rest of the morning crept by. Nora remained too numb with the return of her original confusion to absorb the rest of the prosecutor's case.

Nora was unable to eat during the lunch break. Redburn and her caring cavalry tried to console her, but she hung her head in certain defeat.

The Defense was called in the afternoon.

Redburn first called Gallagher to the stand, who explained that he was passing the mill when he spotted the open gate and door. "All Hell was breaking out in the mill. Rumors of a leak, which I knew nothing about, gunshots, new hires holding well-known mill hands captive, a kidnapping. None of it made any sense to me."

By mid-afternoon, Redburn leaned over to Nora. "Please, don't be alarmed. I'll call another witness and then ask you to come to the stand to tell about your kidnapping. Gather your strength. This could be the turning point."

"I call to the stand Michael Stafford, who has been arrested for breaking into Grant's Landing Pulp and Paper Mill and illegal possession of a gun."

A big man, no longer in his red shirt, took the stand and swore to tell the truth.

Mackey tapped Sedna's hand, showing his fingers crossed.

Redburn opened his questions. "Please, tell the jury, were you hired to work at the Grant's Landing Pulp and Paper Mill?"

Stafford answered, "Yes, me and my buddies."

Redmond: "Please, tell the jury what you were hired to do."

Stafford hunched his shoulders up to his ears and let them down again. He wiped his hands on his knees. "We did odd jobs around the mill, moving things, hauling boxes, you know, stuff."

Redmond: "Were you hired for jobs outside the mill?"

Stafford responded. "You bet we were. Always one thing after another. We were expected to work days and nights. The demands kept piling up. Do this, do that. We never got any thanks or money for the extra work."

Redburn: "Is it true that you were at the mill on the night of August 10, 1998?"

Stafford: "I don't know no date. I was arrested in the mill at night."

Redburn: "Please, tell the jury what caused you to be in Grant's Landing mill on the night of your arrest?"

Stafford: "We, my buddies and I, were new hires at the mill and were attacked by these guys, supposedly at the suggestion of a crazy lady who we never saw that night."

Redburn: "And why were you in the mill that night?"

Stafford looked down at his hands. His face registered no emotion, but he wiped his hands on his shirt and then, again, on his knees. "My buddies and I had been hired to drain a tank in the mill and pipe the stuff to a ship in the harbor. It was no big deal, though it puzzled us as to why it had to be done at night."

Redburn: "Please, tell the jury, were you given work outside the mill?"

Stafford bent his elbows and tightened both hands into fists, then loosened them and opened them to the ceiling in an exaggerated shrug. "Yeah. I'll tell you." He pounded one balled fist on one knee. "We've been royally cheated. Before that night at the mill, we had been promised 40,000 American dollars to bump someone in a white hat with a scarf hanging down the back out of his fishing boat. We'd seen the same guy sitting in his boat outside the mill the day before. Knocking him out of his boat wasn't hard. He was standing with his fishing rod in one hand and guiding his little skiff with the other. We didn't hang around to see what happened. We just pulled away after bashing him. Next thing we knew, we were told we'd be paid to trash his cabin looking for photos. We never found nothin' and weren't paid a dime for that neither. A crazy lady came in a boat all be herself to try and stop us. We thought we scared her off real good, but she's sitting right there." He pointed at Nora.

Laughter rang through the courtroom. The judge banged his gavel.

Stafford, ignoring the laughter, raised his voice. "We only followed orders. We can't be accused of murder because nobody is dead. Me and my buddies want out of jail."

Redburn: "I call Nora McKeever to the stand. "Please, tell the jury what you remember of your kidnapping."

Nora, relieved of her morning's doubt and first memories of the accident, had an easy time answering this and all his questions.

A fisherman testified about seeing the sailboat in Mitlenatch Harbor.

Redburn did not call Sedna to the stand. He had decided that her lip-reading might raise a discussion of hearsay, adding an unnecessary complication to the case. He planned to save that issue for Foster's trial a few weeks hence.

Redburn summed up the testimony and closed his defense statement.

The jury retired to deliberate.

"I think that clears me," Nora whispered to Charlie when he joined her on the way out of the courtroom during the jury's deliberation.

He gave her a startled look. "What, Mom? You didn't really think anyone was blaming you, did you?"

Nora burst out laughing. Abruptly, her laughter turned to sorrow. "All this time I've been blaming myself, worrying that I might have tried to kill your father over some lousy personal pique. Years and years of good work together, and he puts me out to pasture. I let myself go loony with self-doubt."

"I was at college when you retired. That Sergeant Biddle asked me about the fights between you and Dad."

He lowered his voice. "Mom, I'd never seen you two argue."

She looked at this handsome boy with pain spread across his face. "Our fights were recent, and they were more silences than fights. I guess pressures can build. Life can get in the way. Long marriages can lose their focus, but I never thought it could happen to us. It's taken a lot of reflection and the peace of Sedna's care to help me see the whole story. Funny, this accident, incident—I never knew which to call it—helped me remember how much your dad and I shared and will continue to share. I've confronted my own efforts for control. Both of us had lost our gifts for listening to each other. Seems silly. Here we are, old marrieds, learning how to talk openly about our needs."

She paused, searching for words. To underscore her meaning, she thought it important to tell her son how it had been with her and Joe, their commitment to the news business and each other, the slow growth of their ambitions along with their personal bond, lovemaking and all. Was he too young to know about passion?

She flapped her hands. "From the beginning, we wanted so much. We were caught up in 1968. Riots, deaths, Martin Luther King and then Bobby Kennedy. We worked together through long days and nights, exploring, telling the stories as best we could. After the terrible riots at the Democratic convention, your dad moved into my miserable apartment, but it didn't seem miserable to us. We were too busy forging our passion for the news into our passion for each other. We lived together for a year before we married, and two years before we dared start McKeever and McKeever Independent News. It was…"

She trailed off. Charlie was blushing now.

She made herself plunge on. "I want the same someday for you and for Nell. Good, strong, passionate sex with someone you deeply respect."

Charlie slid an arm around her shoulders and gave her a quick hug. "It's okay, Mom. Wait until I tell my buddies Mom says sex is good," he teased. "But seriously, I hope I'll have a bit of what you and Dad shared." He grinned down at her, the blush fading from his cheeks. "Now, let's go join the others while we wait for your verdict."

The jury's deliberation was swift. Nora was cleared on all counts.

Outside the courtroom, the lawyers assured the assembled brigade of friends that first there would be a trial of Jeremy Foster for kidnapping plus illegal financial conspiracies. The lawyers also committed to continuing trials exposing the theft of fishing rights of First Nation tribes, trials pushing against land grabs to increase mining, trials against expanding a northern harbor and building oil pipelines, all activities to ensure that already-rich men would keep money rolling in.

The golds and reds of autumn peeked through the pines and cedars. With the trial completed and Nora cleared, they were free to go home. The doctors confirmed that Joe should continue therapy, perhaps for years, but he was strong enough for the long journey. They advised traveling with Joe's wheelchair, as airport distances and the hours waiting for flight connections could be troublesome. Much to Nora's relief and gratitude, Charlie stayed for the few days necessary to pack up the little house, settle all accounts and to help navigate the trip home.

All packed and ready for departure, Joe, Nora and Charlie waited for Albert who had offered to drive them to the airport. Tears flowed down Nora's cheeks.

Joe put his arms around her. "Don't cry, Nora. This is our special place. We'll come back often."

Albert arrived with a small bunch of Sedna's lavender surrounded by sprigs of the ever-prevalent salal to take with them. "Sedna said you should put these in your suitcase to remind you of her garden and British Columbia."

Nora looked at Mackey, Joe, Charlie, their familiar faces now changed for her by the past months. She knew the next days, weeks, perhaps years, held serious challenges. *Yes, I need to hold onto all that I learned here from the special caring friends, the nurturing tides, the water's changing waves, the loons' lonely calls.* She gave Mackey a goodbye hug and turned to follow Charlie pushing Joe's wheelchair toward the airplane.

Acknowledgements

My thanks to Diane Piron-Gelman, a skilled developmental and word editor, who helped me clarify the three months of action sequences in *Long Reach,* allowing me to braid in Nora's and Albert's memories.

Wendy Littlefield was *Long Reach's* first reader. She asked probing questions about Nora's goals, important in Nora's development. Wendy was a constant nudge for me to rescue *Long Reach* from years of neglect when time and circumstances left it hostage on my computer.

To Pat Wilder and Judith Stockdale, two dear friends who took time to read and comment on the novel's slow evolution, encouraging me to take it out of hiding.

Chris Neher's careful reading caught several critical errors of fact, plus gave me hope that the family might survive the embarrassment of a publishing parent/parent-in-law.

A word about the author...

Nancy Stevenson holds a Masters degree in American History from American University and a MFA in Writing for Children from Vermont College, now Vermont College of Fine Arts.

She, her husband and family enjoyed a cabin on a beautiful heart shaped island in the Georgia Strait, British Columbia, Canada for over 20 years. They explored the waters and lands of the Strait at every opportunity.

Afterword:

Long Reach evolved over many years. It began with curiosity about clear cutting before climate change became a public cry of the heart and constant source of news, before heat waves penetrated the Strait of Georgia, before the bodies of First Nation children were found in boarding school graveyards in Canada and the United States. The research and the daily news confirm that this story is evidence of my own ignorance and insensitivity, but an effort, nevertheless, to probe a real world of people and places.

When I worry about what right I have to imagine myself into the lives of my characters, I understand that even my memories are fictions of a sort. The Preface of the 1999 Edition of A National Crime: The Canadian Government and the Residential School System:1879 - 1986, includes these paragraphs about residential boarding schools for First Nations children: "The system is not someone else's history, nor is it just a footnote or a paragraph, a preface or a chapter, in Canadian history.

It is our history, our shaping of the "new world"; it is our swallowing of the land and the First Nations people and spitting them out as cities and farms and hydroelectric projects and as strangers in their own land and communities.

"As such, it is critical that non-Aboriginal people study and write about schools, for not to do so on the premise that it is not our story, too, is to marginalize it as we did Aboriginal people themselves, to reserve it for them as a site of suffering and grievance and to refuse to make it a site of introspection, discovery and extirpation—a site of self-knowledge from which we can understand not only who we have been as Canadians but who we must become if we are to deal justly with the Aboriginal people of this land."

It is my hope that this statement serves as a partial justification for my imaginings of lives unknown to me, lives in other places, times and circumstances.

I have smelled the heavy orange streak of sulfur fumes in weather inversions. I have seen with my own eyes the hard surfaces of clear-cut land with bulldozed hard pan, and the limited borders of First Nation reservations. I have seen helicopters dropping water on forest fires, a rare sight in the 1990s, commonplace in 2021. And I've had the great good fortune to spend treasured time in this region of miraculous bounty, beauty and benevolent people who appreciate this precious corner of the world.

In the hope that readers may be interested in pursuing the wonders of British Columbia's history, pioneering spirit, spectacular abundance, and unfolding science of forestry and oceanography, a few great reads are listed below.

Sources for Long Reach

Benedict, Ruth. Patterns of Culture. Boston. Houghton Mifflin, 1934.

Bierhorst, John. The Mythology of North America. New York. Morrow, 1985.

Bringhurst, Robert. A Story as Sharp as a Knife: The Classical Mythtellers and their World. Vancouver. Douglas &McIntyre, 1999.

Boas Cannings, Sydney; Nelson, Joanne; Cannings, Richard. Geology of British Columbia: A Journey through Time. Vancouver. Greystone Books, 2011.

Boas, Franz. Indian Myths and Legends from the North Pacific Coast of America: a Translation of Franz Boas 1895 edition of Indianische Sagen von der Nord Pacifischen. Vancouver. Talon, 2002.

Carson, Rachel. Silent Spring. New York. Fawcett Crest, 1964.

Duff, Wilson. The Indian History of British Columbia: The Impact of the White Man. New Edition.Victoria. Royal British Columbia Museum, 1997.

Ford, Clellan S. Smoke From Their Fires: The Life of a Kwakiutl Chief. New Haven. Yale University Dept. of Anthropology, 1941.

Hoagland, Edward. Notes from the Century Before: A Journal from British Columbia. New York. Random House, 1969.

Holm, Bill. Spirit and Ancestor: a Century of Northwest Coast Indian Art at the Burke Museum. Victoria. Douglas & McIntyre, 1988.

Lillard, Charles. Seven Shillings a Year: The History of Vancouver Island. Ganges, B.C. Horsdal and

Schubert, 1986.

Milloy, John S. and Mary Jane Logan McCallum. A National Crime: The Canadian Government and the Residential School System: 1879 – 1986. (Critical Studies in Native History).Winnipeg. University of Montana, 1999.

Modzelewski, Michael. Inside Passage: Living with Killer Whales, Bald Eagles, and Kwakiutl Indians. New York. Harper Collins, 1991.

Proctor, Bill and Yvonne Maximchuk. Tide Rips & Back Eddies: Bill Proctor's Tales of Blackfish Sound. Madeira, B.C. Harbour Publishing, 2015.

Raban, Jonathan. Passage to Juneau: A Sea and Its Meaning. New York. Vintage Partners, 2000.

Royal B.C. Museum. First Nations Research Guide, B.C. Archives, a helpful guide to sources.

Suttles, Wayne. Coast Salish Essays. Vancouver. Talon, 1987.

Spradley, James P. Guests Never leave Hungry: The Autobiography of James Sewid, a Kwakiutl Indian. New Haven. Yale, 1969.

Stewart, Hilary. Cedar: Tree of Life to Northwest Coast Indians. Seattle. Univ of Washington Press, 2003.

_____. Indian Fishing: Early Methods of the Northwest Coast. Vancouver. Douglas &
McIntyre, 1977.

_____. Stone, Bone, Antler and Shells: Artifacts of the Northwest Coast. Vancouver. Douglas
& McIntyre, 1996.

_____. Totem Poles. Vancouver. Douglas & McIntyre, 1990.

Swan Luke and David W. Ellis. Teachings of the Tides. Pentiction, B.C. Thetis, 1981.

Thompson, Bill. Boats, Bucksaws and Blisters: Pioneer Tales of the Powell River Area. Powell River. Powell River Research Association, 1990

———. Once upon a Stump: Times and Tales of Powell River Pioneers. Powell River. Powell River Research Association, 1993.

Wallace, James. Kwakiutl Legends. Surrey, B.C. Hancock House, 1989.

Valiant, John. The Golden Spruce: A True Story of Myth, Madness and Greed. New York. W.W. Norton, 2005.

Plants and Animals

Hutchins, Alma R. Indian Herbology of North America. Shambhala. New Haven. Yale, 1969.

Moore, Michael. Medicinal Plants of the Pacific West. Santa Fe. Red Crane Books, 1993.

Paine, Stefani Hewlett. Beachwalker: Sealife of the West Coast. Victoria. Douglas & Mcintyre, 1992.

Simard, Suzanne. Finding the Mother Tree: Discovering the Wisdom of the Forest. New York. Alfred A Knopf, 2021.

Turner, Nancy J. Plants in British Columbia Technology. Victoria. Royal British Columbia Museum, 1998.

Technology

Bircher, Nancy. Fifth International Conference on Environmental Compliance and Enforcement

Environmental Law Research Foundation Newsletter, Vol. 15:3, January 21, 1991; Vol 15:5, February 12, 1991; Vol 15:6, March 14, 1991; and many other volumes of this informative newsletter.

Reach for Unbleached: www.rfu.org/cacw/production.html2/1 2000

No Margin of Safety

Pulp and Paper Mill Effluent—Environmental trends in British Columbia, 2002.

www.env.gov.bc.ca/soerpt/994txic/halide.html

Reference has been made to several poems:

Epigraph. Allison, Alexander W., Barrows, Herbert, Blake, Caesar R., Carr, Arthur J, Eastman, Arthur M, English, Jr, Hubert M, eds. The Norton Anthology of Poetry, Third Edition. T.S. Eliot. From Four Quartets, The Dry Salvages. New York, Norton, 1983, p.1013.

Chaucer, Geoffrey. The Canterbury Tales.

Thank you for purchasing
this publication of The Wild Rose Press, Inc.

For questions or more information
contact us at
info@thewildrosepress.com.

The Wild Rose Press, Inc.
www.thewildrosepress.com